Sticks and Stones

by

VALERIE KNUPP

OTHER BOOKS BY VALERIE KNUPP

In the Twilight of Dawn

The quiet moment between night and day, the moment while the world slumbers and the heart captures the essence of peace.

In the twilight of Dawn, the beauty of the sunrise reveals itself over the still waters of the lake, and the wind quietly awakens the rose with its kiss, so loving and free the way life was meant to be.

~Anonymous

This is a work of fiction. Names, characters, places, and incidents either are the product of the author's imagination or are used fictitiously, and any resemblance to actual persons, living or dead, events or locales is entirely coincidental.

ISBN 10: 0989902943
ISBN 13: 978-0989902946

Printed in the United States of America

Prologue

The wind pushed and slapped.

It makes my face sting. I don't like it.

Keep walking, just keep walking.

The car is close by. I can't wait to get inside. Heat, I need heat.

Even under the thick trench coat goose bumps covered every inch of skin. Prickly skin matched prickly nerves.

Don't let it set you off. You don't have to feel it.

How do I stop from feeling it? For God sakes, it's so cold it hurts. It REALLY hurts.

I know, damn it. I know. Stop arguing and just get to the car.

Another gust of wind slapped, thunder clapped, and the icy rain came down harder. The street was absent of any people now, and the street lamps cast eerie shadows on the frozen sidewalk. The car was just ahead, a sanctuary from the elements and the people that no longer existed.

You could have done it, you know? Why didn't you do it?

Shut up. I will do it, but when the time is right.

Really? That's what you always say. You always put up with it all. Always have, always will.

No, I won't. I have a plan. I know what I'm doing.

The car sat under a street lamp parked parallel on the one-way street.

Put the key in already. What are you waiting on? You're the one that was complaining about being cold.

I am. Can you just be patient?

1

Get in; it's cold. Well, come on. Shut the door already and start it up so we can get warm!

The car's engine groaned against the low temperatures and high wind, and then caught. Impatience demanded that the heater fan be turned to high, blasting the car's interior with cold air.

Pulling away from the curb, images of the evening pushed their way in with the same angry force of the wind outside. The windshield wipers dug into the icy rain and caused frosty smears across the glass, making it difficult to see.

Need to get home. Have some wine. Calm down.

No! Need to do it. Do it tonight. Not too late yet.

It is too late.

But, late is better. Dark, no one will see. Need to do it now! Do it right NOW!

Who? Where? Who?

You know who, him. You know. Do it now!

Chapter One

Detective Colton Drake reached for the screaming cell phone on the night stand next to the bed. His fingers curled around the device as he struggled to sit up in bed. His throat rasped out a gruff hello through the lingering whiskey and smoke. He listened on the other end, and even with his head still swirling from the alcohol he got the necessary details.

Glancing at the clock next to the half empty bottle of Jack Daniels, he paused for a moment considering the amber glow of 2:06, and responded with "ten minutes," then hung up and tossed the cell phone on the covers next to him.

He rose from the bed and pushed his feet into his boots, then swung open the door to the bathroom and hit the light switch, causing him to squint under the glare. Stooping over the sink, he turned on the water and splashed the cold liquid over his face, scrubbing away the sleep and fog that he'd finally succumbed to two hours earlier. He scrubbed at his teeth next, followed by a quick swirl of mouthwash. He looked at his face in the mirror and finger-combed his tossed hair. His eyes were red. Nothing he could do about that. He briefly considered his rumpled clothes; this would have to do.

After grabbing his gun and badge from the dresser just outside the bathroom door, he reached for his coat and thrust his arms inside. He swept the cell phone off the bed and fisted his keys into the coat pocket as he headed down the short hallway and through the sparsely decorated living room. The coffee table was littered with newspapers.

Stepping out into the night, he was immediately brought to full alert, the cold wet air stinging his tired eyes. With hands buried deeply in his pockets he walked briskly to his truck. The old Ford was his trusty friend, his only friend. It matched him—rugged, cranky, and strong despite its flaws.

He climbed in the cab, closing the cold wind out behind him, and shoved the key in the ignition. The truck grumbled but fired. Shoving the gearshift into first, he jumped the four-wheel drive away from the curb and barreled down the street as he navigated his way through the city streets. Drawing on his memory and years of homicide work, he didn't have to work hard to decide the fastest route to the scene.

He pulled up on two patrol cars, the coroner's bus, and another unmarked car.

Flipping open the glove box, he retrieved a bottle of Pepto-Bismol and shoved two of the pink chewable tablets in his mouth, hoping the chalky pills would quickly go to work on his sour stomach. He stepped out of the truck, slammed the door, and flipped the collar of his coat up high on his neck.

Approaching the site, he ducked under the yellow crime scene tape that was secured to the guardrails protruding from the bridge. He was careful to not slip on the rain-soaked trail that wound down the hillside. Flood lights shined into the opening of the drain that carried the rain water out into the lake. By now the rain had converted to sleet. The tiny ice chips pinged at Drake's face with a bitter sting.

Stepping down into the opening, his feet immediately felt the chill of the water that seeped through his boots. He resisted cursing out loud as fellow detective Kacey James approached splashing through the water seeming to not notice the impending frost bite that Drake was certain they would have before this was over.

"You look like crap, Drake." Kacey popped off with first, and then backed down when she saw the look on his face. "You okay?"

Drake gave her a sideways glance and without acknowledging either of her comments responded, "What have we got?"

"Squatter found a floater. Well, the water's not deep enough to float, but definitely in the water." Kacey nodded her head over her shoulder as she turned and started to lead Drake towards the area where the lights were shining brightly.

Drake avoided looking at the body, first studying the surroundings and not quite ready to lay his eyes on the body. He'd been doing this for nearly twenty years and had seen a lot in his time. Even as a young beat cop he'd seen his share of violence and death.

Both he and Kacey had moved up through the ranks quickly. She was a good cop and even better detective, and together they could clear a lot of cases. They had shared a few personal moments too.

At one time, maybe before things happened, they might have even had a chance, but that was a lifetime ago. Now they were co-workers and sometimes friends. Kacey was tough and to the point. Drake drank way too much. Both had isolated over the years and didn't let anyone get too close.

Drake looked down the drainage passage. "Where's the squatter?"

Kacey nodded to the cruiser back up the hill, "Enjoying some coffee and a warm car."

"What's the story?"

"He was going to sleep in the drain tonight, knew he could have cover and sleep up towards the top far enough from the cold water. When he entered he saw something shiny, thought it might be something of value so he went over to it and found the body wrapped in plastic."

"Any ID?"

Kacey shook her head. "Not yet. Body is clean. No clothes. Doc got here quick and set up," she said, referring to Coroner Warren Patterson.

Patterson had been around longer than either Drake or Kacey and everyone just called him Doc. He was a skilled pathologist and they'd built a solid working relationship with him over the years. He was an unusual character, standing no more than five foot six, but seemed much shorter because he tended to stoop forward when he walked. He wore glasses that always appeared just ready to slip off his nose. Drake always had this itch to push up the glasses he didn't even wear whenever he was around

Patterson. Doc didn't seem to mind the nickname and even had it printed on his lab jackets.

Returning his thoughts to the scene, Drake finally allowed his eyes to drift to the body. Doc had cut away the plastic and had it captured in an evidence bag. The supine male body lay on a yellow tarp. The lights were shining brightly, giving the body an even more blue color than it actually was.

Doc looked up as he saw Kacey and Drake approach. "Hey, glad you could join us for swim lessons."

Drake shook his head. He didn't think he'd ever get used to Doc's dark humor. He just assumed it came with the role of constantly dealing with dead bodies. Doc had seen it all, that was for sure. Drake responded, "No one told me to bring my inflatable arms."

Doc chuckled then stood with a liver thermometer in his hand. "I won't be able to get a good time of death. The temps are low and with the water…," he trailed off and shook his head. "Best I can say, at least twenty-four hours."

Drake knelt down next to the body and studied it. He snapped on rubber gloves that Doc handed him before reaching out and touching what appeared to be a burn in the shape of a plus sign on the man's left pectoral.

Kacey knelt near the man's head and asked, "Any other marks like that on him anywhere else?"

"None that I've seen. I'll know more when I get him back to the lab and clean him up."

"Is this the scene?" Drake asked, referring to the scene where the death had occurred.

"Not sure about that yet either. As soon as I can empty his lungs we'll know if he was alive when he went into the drain."

"How soon?"

"You cops are always in a hurry," Doc complained. "Couple of hours. Come see me around eight. I'll let you know what I know then."

Drake studied the body a bit longer as crime scene analysts had just arrived and were splashing through the tunnel looking for any possible trace evidence or clues that may have been left behind.

Standing up he nodded at Kacey and spoke, "Meet you in twenty to talk to our homeless guy. Maybe he'll come up with something."

Kacey nodded and stood to leave. Drake followed as he tried not to notice the way her wet uniform pants hugged her near perfect curves. He could still remember the times they'd spent together. He was freezing cold, and her warm body sounded like a good idea right now. He noticed that she was hugging her coat tightly around her body as she made her way back up the embankment and to the car she had parked near the guardrail. He almost smiled thinking how tough she always tried to play, but she was freezing cold too.

Realizing his thoughts were useless, he pulled himself up the embankment and over to his truck. He shook his head as he saw a news crew pulling up next to a Mercedes Benz that sat parked at the side of the road. A body could barely get cold in this town before those vultures showed up to stir the pot, causing city wide fear all in an effort to make money.

Just as he crawled into the comfort of the cab he saw news reporter Jillian Sperry standing in front of the guardrail. Cameras were already rolling. Even without any information on the victim, he could only imagine what God awful storyline she would spin.

Chapter Two

Drake leaned back against the straight back chair at the station and glanced over at Kacey and shook his head. The squatter was not able to provide any more information. After thirty minutes of asking questions it was clear that all he truly knew was that he found the body.

Drake thought of the irony. Most people would think finding a dead body one of the low points in life, but for this guy he was getting warm food, shelter, and hot coffee. For the moment he was having one of the best days he'd likely had in a very long time.

Kacey nodded back at Drake and both stood as they thanked the squatter, who they now knew was named Marvin Spratt, but was well known on the streets by just his last name. Before closing the door behind them they promised Spratt that a patrol car would take him to a shelter for what little was left of the night.

Drake turned to Kacey outside the door. "Go home. Get a couple hours of sleep. I'll meet you at Doc's at eight."

Kacey looked up at his tired face. "You gonna get some rest?"

"Yeah, I'll try."

She laughed knowing it wasn't likely. "Okay, see you at eight."

Drake saw her look back over her shoulder as she walked down the drab grey corridor. She seemed to be the only light in the hallway. Her hair swayed with the same confidence she seemed to hold in her body. Kacey had always been a strong woman. Drake knew she had a rough childhood. He wasn't sure of all the details,

9

but he was sure that life as little Kacey had been hell and no one could pull any shit on her as an adult.

He didn't know many details of her past except that her father died when she was really small, then her mother and brother died when she was young, and after that she was raised by her drunken stepfather. He suspected she'd gone through some things no little kid should.

Knowing from the time they'd spent together outside of work, she was a wildcat. She never quite let him in, and despite some really good times she always left after the sex, never letting it become more than just good sex. And it was good sex. He would have liked the relationship to have meant more, but he wasn't any better at opening up than she was. He had his own reasons for that and had some regrets for not sharing more with her.

Then they worked a case together that neither of them seemed to be able to shake. It'd been almost two years now and after that case the sex stopped, and then they somehow just settled into being really great cops working together to solve some of the toughest crimes the city faced. They each welcomed the middle of the night calls and despite their groaning about it they both had nothing else to do. They'd become the job.

The old Ford fired up, and Drake turned onto the street towards a nearby café going the opposite direction of his apartment. It was a place called Freddy's where most of the local cops and firefighters frequented. He needed some hot coffee and only wished his socks inside his boots would dry out.

Pulling into Freddy's parking lot, he saw a couple of squad cars and then almost laughed out loud when he saw Kacey's car. She wasn't getting any sleep either.

As he entered the café his eyes scanned the room, and he saw Kacey in a booth with a couple of beat cops. He nodded to the table but moved towards the counter and slid onto an empty stool.

The waitress, a sixty-something woman named Judy, approached and poured a cup of coffee without even asking. He'd been here dozens of times, and she knew what he would want.

"Good morning, Detective. You look like the rain got the best of you."

"Well, good morning to you too, Judy," Drake said rubbing off the teasing she tossed at him.

"You want some breakfast this morning? Biscuits and gravy, maybe? Biscuits are fresh – just came out of the oven."

Drake considered his stomach and decided food was probably a good idea. It was more than likely going to be a long day. "Sure, that sounds good, Judy, and a couple of eggs too."

"You got it, Detective."

Drake lifted his cup, and just as he was about to take a sip, Kacey slid onto the stool next to him. "I thought you were going to get some sleep."

"I thought you were too."

Kacey shrugged. "Was too wet and too cold to go home, I guess. Needed some of Judy's food and coffee. I figured you'd be over here too, and we could hit up Doc afterwards to see if he has anything for us yet on our vic."

The two beat cops Kacey had been sitting with stepped up to the counter to pay. The tall one, whom Drake knew as Craig Dermot, was a young buck and totally full of himself. After paying he leaned over to Kacey and whispered something in her ear.

Kacey punched him in the shoulder. "Piss off, Dermot."

Drake lifted his cup to hide his smile.

"Aw, come on, Kacey. You know you love me," Dermot responded, though his red face said he knew otherwise.

His partner laughed out loud. "Give it up, man. You're not her type."

The two left as the door let cold air in, followed by a few chuckles from others who had seen the exchange. Kacey shook her head. "Dermot is an ass."

"Ya, think?" Drake responded just as Judy was setting their plates down in front of each of them.

"I assumed you wanted yours here," she told Kacey.

Kacey nodded, already digging into her own plate of biscuits and gravy.

They ate in silence then sat sipping on their coffee refills. Kacey finally spoke up, "It's only six. You think Doc has anything yet?"

"I don't know, but let's head over there anyway. Worse thing that happens is he gives us grief for the next two hours."

11

Kacey laughed. "That's an understatement."

"Want to ride along? I can drop you off here on the way back to the station."

Kacey gave him a sideways glance before answering, "Sure."

The ride over to the coroner's office was quiet. Drake searched for something to say, but it seemed like nothing would come.

Kacey finally broke the silence, "What do you make of our victim?"

Drake thought for a moment. "Not sure yet. No one reported missing that I'm aware of. Could be homeless someone dumped. Can't really even be sure it's a homicide yet."

"What about that burn on the chest?"

Drake glanced over at her as he pulled the old truck into the lot of the medical building that housed the coroner's facilities. "I don't know, but I think we are about to find out."

He pushed open the vehicle door and followed Kacey across the paved parking lot. The rain had finally stopped, and now it was just cold. Drake pulled the facility door open and waited for Kacey to enter as they were greeted by a waft of warm air.

The walls in the building wore a single color of grey. Drab and dreary like the things that went on inside the rooms within. It was dreary like the death, decay, and trauma.

Drake hated this place. He'd seen the unimaginable here. He glanced at Kacey, noticing a stall in her pace. She'd witnessed the same horrors that he had. Both of their lives had changed forever within these walls.

It was two winters earlier. They'd been called out to a domestic dispute that had gone bad. When they arrived at the scene a father, Robert Fields had already killed his wife and two of his children. He was holding a third child hostage, an eleven-year-old girl and the oldest of the children. While they'd tried to talk him into releasing the child and coming out, convinced that he would let her go, the bastard had made them listen to all of it on a telephone for nearly six hours. He'd done everything from raping the girl, to torturing her in a variety of ways, including beating and burning her with her own curling iron. The girl's body had hundreds of burns. The child died from the trauma, and they had come here after taking the man into custody.

Doc had covered each detail with them, explaining the things she'd endured. The bastard had laughed at them as they stormed in after finally realizing the girl was going to die no matter what they did. He stood covered in her blood, naked and laughing. He continued to laugh during the entire trip into custody.

Neither detective had spoken of it once the court proceedings had ended. The father had been found not guilty by reason of insanity. It was quite possible that he would get released one day, a thought that could bring Drake to dry heaves. One he tried to keep pushed as far back in his mind as possible. Kacey used humor to get through her days, acting like everything was fine, and Drake used alcohol, knowing nothing would ever be the same again. The alcohol didn't change anything but somehow it seemed to make it better.

The case left them both devastated. Whatever relationship they had ended that night. Maybe being together was just too much of a reminder. Maybe finding comfort in each other was the real issue. How could they find solace in each other when a girl had died because of their inability to help her?

They both had seen a lot of death, but it was different coming up on someone dead–already dead. Listening to the slow and brutal torture of a young girl was just too much to be able to face each other afterwards. Each had isolated in their own ways and that was how it had remained.

They stopped outside of Doc's pathology lab. Drake looked at Kacey, and for a brief moment their eyes locked. "Ready?"

She nodded but didn't say anything.

He wondered what she felt each time they came here. He wondered if it took everything in her being to walk through those doors, if she shook on the inside in the same way he did when filled with despair and guilt from the past and fear that they'd be forced to face the same kind of horror every time they entered that room. He knew in some ways they did face those horrors every time they entered that room because every time they walked through those doors it was to face another dead body. Another murdered victim, another senseless death.

Drake pushed the door in and followed Kacey through. Doc was inside leaning over a body on the shining stainless steel table. As expected his glasses were perched too far down on his nose. Bright lights shined down on the bloated body. A hole gaped down the center of the man's chest, typical of the autopsy incision, allowing visibility to all the vital organs and stomach contents.

Doc looked up at the two detectives then glanced at the large clock on the wall. Standing as straight as he ever did, he made his typical sarcastic remark, "It's not even close to eight yet, detectives."

"Yeah, well we couldn't sleep so we decided to come on down. Besides we know how good you are and figured you'd be way ahead of the game." Drake decided to throw in an ego booster in an effort to butter the doc up.

"Nice try, Drake, but I know what you are trying to do." Doc sighed shaking his head. Despite his objections he immediately started explaining what he had found so far.

"Estimated time of death is between twenty and twenty-eight hours ago. That's taking into consideration the cold and the temperature of the water he was floating in. He wasn't a homeless man, in my opinion. He was well groomed, nice clean nails, a fresh haircut and freshly shaved before death. Last meal included steak and baked potato and asparagus. He's had extensive dental work, including some very expense crowns. We'll be able to make a positive ID if we can get dental records to match them to."

"So basically, other than searching missing person's reports we've got nothing."

"Not so fast. I was starting to get to the interesting part just as you arrived."

"And that was?"

"Two things, first the burn on the chest was made in a fairly crude manner, made from something pointed with a smooth tip on the end."

"Like a fire poker?"

Doc nodded. "Could be. I would say it was definitely metal. There's no trace evidence in the wound, so it was definitely not wooden, plastic, or glass. Each of those would have left some residue. The symbol appears to be some sort of a plus sign."

"We can run it through tattoo databases to see if anything matches up," Kacey said.

Doc nodded, "Here is what had my attention." He moved to the top of the body and stared down at the face. "There is something in his right eye. I was just about to extract it to see what we have."

Drake and Kacey surrounded the body on opposite sides of Doc. Doc moved in closer. He had a camera projection on a TV screen above the table that he angled over the man, oblivious to the odor of death that permeated from the body. The open cavity had released gases that left a foul odor in the room that some cops could never stand up to. Drake and Kacey had unfortunately faced it too many times.

The eye was now filling the entire TV screen, and there was obviously something stuck deep into the center of the iris. Doc took a thick tweezer-like tool from the instrument tray and pulled on the item. It was lodged deeply and didn't budge. Next he took a scalpel and made an incision in the eye then pulled again with the tweezers. A thin, long metal object slid from the organ. Dropping the item onto the metal tray and rinsing it off quickly, Doc lifted it with his gloved hand.

Kacey asked, "A needle?"

"Standard sewing needle, it would appear," Doc replied.

"What the hell?" Drake spouted.

"Shit." Kacey stood with her hands on her hips.

"Any chance a print might be on that small of an item?"

"Doubtful, but I'll try. It's so thin it's highly unlikely I can get enough of a print to get a match."

Drake and Kacey looked at each other both knowing there was no way it would be that easy.

Drake asked, "What about the other eye? Anything in there?"

"No, that was the first thing I checked when I first realized there was something in the right eye. Nothing in the mouth, ears, or any other orifices."

"Is there anything else, Doc?" Kacey asked obviously wanting to get out of the room.

Before the doctor could answer Drake added, "Cause of death?"

15

"No COD yet, toxicology hasn't come back. I ran that first. It's up at the lab. Hopefully, I'll have that back by eight," he raised his eyebrows and placed emphasis on the time.

Drake raised both hands palms facing the doctor in surrender. "Got it. Can you call when you get the results?"

"You know me. Ole' reliable," Doc grumped at them then went back to exploring the gaping hole in the eye.

"Thanks, Doc," Kacey said as they both turned to leave the room.

Outside the cold air actually felt good. Drake breathed in deeply, allowing the wet wind to fill his entire chest and then purging the putrid smell that would likely linger for the next few hours. He always felt like the smell of death permeated his clothing and would love to go home and shower but knew there was no time. They needed to get to work.

As soon as they were in the truck Kacey spoke up, "Want me to take tattoos, missing persons, or repeaters?" She wasn't asking for Drake to give her the assignment; they just usually worked in this fashion. Drake had seniority over her, but that never played a factor in how they worked together. Other detectives sometimes gave them a hard time, teasing them about their working style and frequent bantering, but they'd gotten used to it and Kacey was certainly capable of holding her own against any of them, just like she'd handled that asshole Craig Dermot.

Drake knew she was referring to possible other cases where a needle may have been driven into a victim's eye. That one could be a long shot. Searching national databases was time consuming and time was a commodity they didn't have much of. He also knew if something like that had happened locally they would have heard about it. At least if it had happened recently.

"I'll take repeats. You take tattoos. I'll call Scott Jackson over at missing persons to liaison with us. He's a good guy and won't give us any lip. I'm thinking someone has got to be missing our John Doe. Clean cut guy, probably a family man."

Kacey just shrugged. The rest of the ride back to her car was quiet as they both processed what they'd just seen. Before Kacey got out of the old Ford she made a chilling statement, "Drake, we may have a serial on our hands. Call it gut instinct, but this doesn't feel right."

He watched her walk away after shutting the passenger door and a shiver passed over him. He knew her instincts were often spot on. It was only a matter of time before they would find another body. Unless…they could figure out who was doing this before the killer had time to kill again.

Chapter Three

Drake and Kacey sat at desks facing each other. They'd been working for a couple of hours when Drake's phone rang. Answering he said, "Homicide, Detective Drake."

"Drake, it's Doc, I got the tox screen back from the lab. A couple of interesting facts, our vic had two drugs in his system, first, a paralytic and second, a tranquilizer."

"Does that give us cause of death?"

"The tranquilizer was fatal. Nearly four times the expected dosage."

"Anything unusual about the drug that would help us track down the killer?"

Drake heard Doc click his tongue before he responded, "Not really, it's a pretty common tranquilizer, used by vets, doctors, street drugs. Both drugs you could even get mail ordered from Mexico or Canada. It will be like a needle in a haystack to try to find who killed our John Doe from the drug alone."

"Thanks, Doc," Drake said sighing before hanging up the phone.

"Nothing?" Kacey asked.

"Commonly used tranquilizer. The vic also had a paralytic in his system. Probably how he was immobilized. We've got nothing."

Before Kacey could say anything, the phone rang again. Drake locked eyes with hers as he picked up the phone. "Drake," he said answering the phone.

"Hey, I forgot one thing," Doc puffed through the line. "Our John Doe was alive when the needle went into his eye. Based on the absorption of the drugs in his system, the killer paralyzed him them left him awake to experience the burns and the stabbing of his eye before administering the tranquilizer that killed him. Sorry, I forgot that part. Oh, and there are no prints on the needle, not enough of a surface to get anything from."

"Thanks, Doc," Drake hung up the phone again.

"John Doe was awake during the burning and stabbing of the eye. And we are out of luck on the prints on the needle."

"Sadistic."

"The analysts are still going through the stuff found at the scene. I talked to one of them earlier, and he said most of what they gathered is likely just junk left by the homeless community."

"Sadistic, organized, smart," Kacey said. "He'll kill again."

"I agree."

"You find anything in the database for similar crimes?"

Drake shook his head. "Nothing. There have been eye injuries but nothing quite the like this. What have you got on the tattoos?"

"Nothing and too many. There are hundreds of symbols that are similar but nothing that matches quite right. Either the shape is off or the placement on the body is wrong."

"Scott sent me a couple of photos for recent missing persons, and so far they're not a match. He'll send any new ones that come up. It's only been a couple of days and it's Saturday. It may be Monday before we hear anything when the guy fails to show up for work."

Drake pushed back and laced his fingers behind his head, his elbows spread wide. "Let's give the chief an update and then go get some sleep. My gut tells me we're going to get real busy soon."

Standing up, they both took a deep breath as they left their desks and approached the chief's office. The Chief of Police Fred Dalton was a gruff Viking-looking kind of man. He stood a good six inches taller than Drake's six foot two frame, and his shoulders were about a half a foot broader. But it wasn't his exterior posture that was so daunting; it was the piercing stare and deep bark he would command when unhappy with the results on a case. They both knew he was going to be unhappy with this case.

Drake rapped on the door and waited for what sounded like a deep grunt, which he knew was permission to enter based on past experience. He'd often watched in amusement as a rookie waited at the door afraid to enter, which only further exasperated the experience.

Drake opened the door and stepped in first, letting Kacey follow him into the room. "Chief, we just wanted to give you a quick update before we go get some shut eye."

"Whatta' ya' have?" The chief raised his eyes but not his head, a pen sat poised in his hand, his deep blue eyes seemingly capable of cutting glass.

"Not much, I'm afraid. No trace, COD was via tranquilizer, common drug, could get it almost anywhere. The killer tortured the victim. We've got no missing persons that are a match at this point."

Kacey jumped in, "We may have a serial on our hands."

Dalton's head raised at that comment. He laid the pen down on the desk pad. "A serial? Why do you think that?"

Drake and Kacey exchanged a glance before Kacey continued. "He's organized, sadistic, it was well planned out, the dump site is not where the murder took place, probably knows the city well, knew there would be water in the drain pipe, and our perp is smart. He probably won't wait long to do this again, and he may escalate."

Dalton looked at Drake as if confirming her assessment, then returned his gaze to her. "Well, then you better get some sleep so you are ready when the next victim comes in."

"Yes, we planned to."

"Oh, and, Drake, lay off the sauce. You look like shit. You two are the best I've got, and I need you keen."

Drake nodded, but didn't answer. They turned and left without saying another word.

Outside the room with the door safely closed behind them Drake said, "I'll see you later. Get some rest Kacey." He walked away, grabbed a file from his desk that he'd begun compiling, and snagged his coat. He left Kacey at her desk pulling on her own coat.

Chapter Four

Stretching out in the bed, long muscular legs ached from the rest and the rigor of the chase. Even though it had been a day and a half since the kill, adrenaline still pumped, sleep was restless and dream filled.

I'm still tired. I need more sleep.

No time to sleep. It felt good, really good. Need to do it again.

Can't do it again so soon. We have to be careful.

It was easy. You were brilliant.

Even if I was, we still have to be careful. Need to see what happens now.

You can fix it. You know how to hide the evidence.

Don't get too arrogant. That is how we'll get caught.

Rolling over in the bed with arms hugging the pillow, the bed felt great but more sleep was desperately needed. For whatever reason sleep seemed to be the thing that would never completely come.

Close your eyes if you want to sleep.

Can't sleep. Just have to get up. Have to be at work again soon.

All work and no play.

Yeah, well you do like to eat and to have things like this warm bed, right? Have to work to pay the bills.

You're right. Always right, so smart.

The sheets fell away as feet hit the floor. Slipping on a sweatshirt and pants, there was a chill in the room that seemed to reach deep into bones and caused a soreness that added to the ache from lack of proper rest.

Check the paper. See what they're saying about him.

Good idea.

Walking down the hall of the small apartment towards the living room, cold feet padded against the hardwood floors. Opening the front door and crossing the breezeway to the bank of mailboxes caused a cold blast of air to rush into the apartment and push the chill even deeper.

Shit, it's cold!

Hurry up, get the paper and close the door!

In one swift move, the newspaper was snapped out of the newspaper holder that hung just under the mailbox and the door was swiftly closed. Another shiver ripped through causing a shudder.

Quickly pulling away the wet plastic protective bag, fingers unrolled the bundle and eyes scanned the front page. A large photo covered the page. Crime scene tape was tied in front of an embankment, and police cars stood in the foreground at odd angles. The caption read, *Man's body found in drainage ditch, police have no leads.*

Good. No leads.

I told you how smart you were. Do it again. When can we do it again?

Calm down. When the time is right, but not before.

Now, now, now!

Shhh, I need to read this. Now hush.

Eyes scoured every word. Then re-read it all again, devouring every detail, searching for any indication that mistakes had been made, searching for details—any details—guesses and speculations.

Nothing, they've got nothing.

People will pay. Oh, yes, make them pay.

I'm going to make them pay.

Iz is gonna make them pay.

Shut up, I need to think and get something to eat.

Sorry.

It's okay.

A pot boiled on the stove with noodles swirling around in the bubbles. Iz took a fork and tested the pasta's texture then clicked the gas burner off. A small sauce pan sat on the next burner. The smell of garlic, tomatoes, and onions filled the room. Pouring the noodles into a colander, Iz rinsed them then dumped them into the tomato-based sauce and stirred the mixture together then moved the burner flame down to low before reaching into the oven and removing a small loaf of garlic bread.

Inside the oven the red and blue flames created a glow, a mesmerizing glow. Staring into the flames, memories began to flood in of the constant taunts, name calling, and angry words, children in a circle hurling hateful names. Even as an adult hateful people are everywhere.

"SHUT UP!"

Calm down, it's okay.

"It's not okay."

Then do something about it. Do it now.

After turning the oven off and fishing a plate out of the cupboard, Iz spooned the spaghetti out of the pan then selected two buttery slices of bread before moving over to sit at the small kitchen table.

The room was mostly dark with only a small lamp in the living room to light the apartment. The curtains were always drawn tight– privacy an absolute must. Spooning the food, heart racing and filled with anger, Iz took a napkin from the small plastic holder on the table and mopped at a wet brow.

With each mouthful of food, Iz began to calm down. Remembering the taunts was only a sign of what needed to be done to set the record straight. Another person would pay.

Tonight? Iz, you gonna make them pay tonight?

Shhh! I need to think now. Be quiet so I can plan.

Okay, quiet now.

It was nearly midnight when Iz became restless enough to decide to go out for a cup of coffee. Leaving the apartment in dark clothing, a hoodie and gloves, Iz got in the car and drove to an all-night café.

The windows seemed to stare at the car. Taking a deep breath Iz got out of the car and pulled the hoodie up tight before going inside. The door chimes rang in what seemed like a loud clatter, causing the other patrons to turn and stare. Iz quickly sat at the counter and ordered a coffee to go. Coming here was a bad idea.

Glancing around, three women sat in a booth in the corner. Based on their clothing they were hookers. Iz hated hookers. Taking the cup of coffee and dropping a couple of dollars on the counter, Iz turned to leave. Laughter rang out in tune with the door chimes.

Back inside the car, sweat covered Iz's brow despite the cold temperature. "Fucking bitches!"

Kill them. Kill them. Don't let them laugh at you like that!

Iz backed the car out of the space and watched the hookers through the window. They were still laughing, their ugly red lipstick outlining their ugly, drug-addicted teeth.

Back at the apartment Iz retrieved a package from the freezer then grabbed a neoprene ski mask from the closet. Neoprene was smarter than the sweater kind. Everyone knew those would leave behind fibers, have to be careful.

Driving the car down the city streets, Iz headed for the west side.

Iz, where are we going?

You'll see. Just wait.

Why can't you just tell me? I don't like waiting.

You can't get hurt if you don't know. Now stop brooding. You'll see soon enough.

A man walked down the street a few blocks from a night club. There were few cars parked along the curb.

What about him? Get him. Get him!

No, he's not right.

Why not? Why not?! He looks good.

Because he's not. Slow down, I know what I'm doing.

The streets grew darker as the city lights thinned out. Soon the car was crawling down a narrow street well known for prostitution. Iz watched out the window and was thankful for the clear night. A woman stood on the sidewalk near the corner. Her skirt was far too short, resting just below her butt, and her top showing off her bare belly despite the cold temperatures.

Iz watched studying the woman, thought for a moment and determined that the hooker must be really high to be able to stand the weather. After carefully watching her mannerisms once sure this was the right woman Iz pulled next to the corner and rolled down the passenger window.

The cold, half-clothed young woman walked up and leaned in. Iz looked her over remembering and realizing she wasn't any prettier than the last time they'd met. In fact, she might even look worse, the streets taking a toll on her. Iz knew she was a runaway, and after about a minute of negotiating, she slid inside the car, shuttering as she settled into the seat. She appeared obviously grateful for the warmth of the vehicle and the possibility to make some money tonight.

Smiling and thinking how easy it was, Iz pulled away from the curb with the girl in the car.

Good one! Make her pay! Make them all pay!

Chapter Five

Kacey's phone rattled on the night stand. She reached over dragging her body across the bed scooping up the phone. Her eyes squinted at the screen with Drake's name on the display.

"Drake? Do you know what time it is?"

Without answering her question he said, "We have another body."

She cleared her throat and tried to sit up. "Well that was fast."

"The old salvage yard on 4th and Dupont. Want me to pick you up?"

"No, I'm on my way," she replied rolling off the bed and tugging on the jeans she had dropped next to the bed earlier when she finally gave her body permission to try and sleep. She felt her way in the dark to the bathroom to flip on the light, quickly brush her teeth, and rip a brush through her thick black mane before sliding on a sweater and snapping her Glock and badge off the nightstand that was next to the bed. She slid another small gun into a clip on the inside of her boot, pulled on her coat, and headed out the door, locking the deadbolt behind her.

Kasey saw that Drake was already at the scene. His old Ford sat outside the chain link fence. Two women who looked like working girls were standing next to a patrol car, and animal control was loading a couple of pit bulls into a paddy wagon.

Drake approached as she pulled up next to his truck. "What's with the pros?" she asked.

"Not sure if this is our boy. Might be just a psycho pissed off at the hookers." He nodded his head towards the prostitutes.

"Great, so now we have two killers on our hands? Shit."

"Maybe, Doc just got here. He's setting up. This one is fresh. The dogs went crazy, and the neighbor called the junk yard owner after getting tired of the noise. Owner came down here to check it out, found the dogs and the body. I guess it's not all that uncommon for the dogs to bark, but when they didn't calm down and the neighbors couldn't sleep they finally got pissed and called to complain." Drake started walking towards the middle of the salvage yard.

The property was probably only about an acre. It was filled with mostly old car parts and junked cars where people could come looking for an old alternator or bumper. Most of the cars were circa nineteen eighties and were the wannabe drug dealer model favorites. It didn't look like much but Drake guessed that in this area business was pretty good.

Doc had lights set up, and two patrol officers were standing around looking like they wanted to puke. The body was on the ground, and Drake kept his eyes away as he scanned the rest of the area first. It was hard to know if anything else was out of place. Everything looked out of place. The salvage yard had the kind of inventory control that only the owner would understand. Crime scene analysts arrived and began the search of the surrounding grounds.

Finally allowing his eyes to land on the victim, Drake shook his head in disbelief. The woman's body was sprawled out. One shoe lay a few feet away next to a purse. A wig lay on the other side of her body, and her head rolled awkwardly to one side. Most of her face was missing. Her left shoulder appeared to be disconnected, almost ripped free of the body, and there was something wrapped around her neck.

Doc looked at the two detectives. "Not quite seen anything like this before. She was strangled with a piece of barbed wire, but there is something around her neck besides the wire. I think it is some kind of meat. Not much left of it. The dogs had their fill of it and some of her, I'm afraid."

Drake signaled to one of the CSI team members to collect some bits of white paper that were lying on the ground next to the body. "Looks like butcher wrap to me. Bag it and get it analyzed right away. See if there are any letters, words, anything that might indicate where it was purchased."

Doc had another analyst take photos of the ligature marks on the victim's throat, and then more photos of her hands, legs, and exposed torso. Obvious bite marks and tears covered the body.

Kacey stepped forward and kneeled down to take a closer look at what was left of the victim's face and shoulder. "This is just a girl. She's probably not more than seventeen." Looking even closer at the wire wrapped around her neck, the barbs dug deep into the skin. Kacey could see a few scraps of meat hanging loose on the twisted wire. "What the hell?"

Drake leaned in to take a closer look at her feet and hands. There didn't appear to be any defensive wounds, but it was hard to say out here in the dark. Even with the flood lights there was a lot that would have to be told by Doc back at the lab. Drake imagined walking in and seeing this young girl on that table and swallowed hard, his Adam's apple bobbing in his throat.

Doc looked at them as Kacey reached over with a gloved hand and lifted the purse. A small, silver glitter-covered wallet was inside, and when she flipped it open she found a photo ID inside. The name on it was Candice Jackson, age seventeen.

Kacey jotted down the name and address from the card then handed the purse to the analyst who dropped it into an evidence bag. "What's with the two working girls out by the patrol cars?"

One of the patrol officer's spoke up, "They heard the squad cars pull up and came over from a couple of blocks away. They were asking if it was Candy, said she'd gone off with a trick and should have been back by now."

Drake stood up. "We'll talk with them. Maybe they saw who picked her up. Can you take them to the station? We should be there within fifteen to twenty minutes."

Kacey asked, "Do you have time of death?"

"Yes, based on liver temp, factoring in the outside temperatures and blood coagulation, she died between four and five hours ago. The dogs did a good amount of damage, and based on the blood loss, she bled out from the wounds."

Looking at his watch Drake muttered, "Between 12 and 1am?"

"Give or take an hour."

"Thanks, we'll come see you later on. If you find anything important, call." Drake turned to Kacey and nodded his head to the exit. "Let's go talk to the girls and then we can try to track down Candice's next of kin."

Kacey followed Drake as he walked to his Ford. "I've got this bad feeling this day is going to suck worse than it already has," she said.

Forty minutes later both Drake and Kacey were each sitting across from prostitutes in two rooms having decided they needed to talk to them separately. It was possible one or the other had seen something and they were more likely to talk separately.

"Ginger," Drake said, intentionally keeping his voice low and unintimidating. "I know you're upset about Candy, and I'm sorry about that. I just need to know if you saw the trick she left with."

Ginger sat across the table with her arms folded in an obvious effort to shut Drake down. "I ain't seen nothin'."

"Look, I'm not trying to roll you, Ginger. I'm not interested in your tricks or what you were doing out there on that street in the middle of the night. I'm only interested in trying to find out who did that to Candy."

Ginger settled a little in her chair. She crossed her legs the opposite way, and her face relaxed some, but she refused to talk, still definitely resistant to cooperate.

Drake kept pressing, "I also need to make sure you and the rest of the girls are safe. The kind of person that did this to Candy is not likely to stop hurting girls."

He could see that had her attention. Her shoulders dropped and the defiant look on her face softened. "Candy left around midnight with a trick. I barely saw the ride. I was down the street quite a way. It was dark, and the car wasn't in the light, but was a white man's car, newer."

"A white man's car? Like a sedan?"

"Yeah, something like that."

"What color was it?"

"Brother, it was dark. I don't know."

"What time should Candy have been back from her trick?"

"You know that depends."

32

"Okay, what would be the longest she would have been gone?"

"Most times the men pay for thirty minutes. It don't take much for most of them," Ginger laughed at her comment. "Could be an hour, not many go longer than that."

"So you girls look out for one another?"

"Yeah."

"Does Candy have a pimp?"

"We all work for John John."

"Would John John have any reason to be pissed at Candy?"

"She was new. Only been around for a month or so. John John likes her real good. You know, he's still trying to break her in."

Drake nodded. He knew what it meant. John John was having his own fun with Candy in between turning her out on the streets. "Where can I find John John?"

"Oh, no. I ain't telling you nothin' 'bout John John."

"Fine. We can find him if we need to. Had anyone been hassling Candy?"

"No. Girl was new. Ain't nobody got any issues with her yet."

"Okay, is there anything else you can think of that would help us understand who might have done this to Candy?"

"I told you, I didn't see nothin'."

"Here's my card if you think of anything else. Please call me. We'll have the patrol officer take you back...home," Drake offered sliding his business card across the marred table.

"Well, can you hurry up? I ain't gonna make no money tonight, and John John is gonna be pissed."

"One more thing, did Candy say where she was from?"

"Jersey, said she took a bus here. Took her a full day to get here. Something about an aunt, but then when she got here her aunt was gonna make her go back, so she hit the streets."

Kacey was having a very similar conversation with the prostitute who called herself Cinnamon.

"I was with a trick when Candy went out, and then caught up with Ginger when I got back. Then the cops come, and we went over to see what the commotion was all about."

Kasey was a little more successful in finding out where John John could be found. He had a flop house on 3rd and Washington about two blocks from where Candy was found. They would track him down later, a few hours after daylight when he was likely sleeping. These people were like roaches coming out only after dark and sleeping all day.

Meeting back at their desks, Drake and Kacey compared notes. The girls hadn't been much help. They'd gotten a sedan out of the conversation, a sedan with no color. Not a lot to go on.

"You think John John could have done this?"

Kacey thought for a second. "Maybe, if she wasn't bringing in enough dough, but fresh on the street usually does better than the two used up hookers who are constantly needing a fix."

"Maybe she wanted out."

Kacey nodded. "Could be."

Drake's phone rang, and he lifted the receiver. "Homicide, Drake."

"It's Doc. Got prints back on our John Doe. We got a match in the system. He was registered."

"Who is he?"

"You aren't going to like this Drake."

Drake held the receiver tightly. "Who is it, Doc?"

"It's Frank Parker, as in the uncle of the…"

"Shit!"

Kacey stared at Drake. "What is it?"

"Doc, I gotta go," he said before slamming down the phone. "We need to see the chief."

"Drake, what the hell is going on?"

"The John Doe was Frank Parker."

"Shit!"

"Exactly, let's go."

Walking to the chief's office Drake didn't even hesitate to knock, but found the door locked. He realized it was only six in the morning. Reaching in his pocket, he pulled out his cell phone and selected the chief's name from the contact list.

The phone connected on the second ring, "Chief Dalton."

"Chief, it's Drake. Sorry to call so early. We have a problem in the John Doe case."

"Drake, it's six in the morning. This can't be good. What kind of problem?" The chief's words were gruff and impatient.

34

"The vic is Frank Parker from the Fields case. He was the uncle that…"

"I know who Frank Parker is. Damn it, how is it that neither you nor Kacey couldn't recognize him?"

"He was bloated from the water and cold. It's been two years, sir."

There was silence on the line before a grunt and a gruff. "See me at seven, my office."

Before Drake could respond the line went dead.

"Well, that went really good," Kacey said sarcastically. "Why the hell would someone kill Parker?"

"I don't know, but he made wild threats to both of us before leaving the court room."

"He blamed us for the death of his niece. Hell, even we blamed us," Kacey admitted.

"So what is this, someone getting him back for blaming us, a coincidence, or some other vendetta from someone else?"

"Who would want to do that? It's been two years."

"What is the date?"

"January 12th, why?"

Drake opened his desk drawer and thumbed through several file folders. Finding the one he was looking for, he pulled it out and flipped through several pages until he came to the page he was in search of.

"January 9th. The jury verdict was January 9th. He was killed on the anniversary of that day in court when the verdict came in and Robert Fields was found not guilty by reason of insanity. Frank Parker went crazy in the court room, shouting accusations at you, Kacey and Fields shouted crazy heckling comments at us both."

"So what are you saying? Based on time of death, he was killed on the anniversary of the jury verdict?"

Drake nodded. "It would seem that's exactly what happened."

"That's no coincidence."

Drake picked up the phone and dialed the missing person's office and within a few minutes had asked his contact Scott to check and see if Parker had been reported missing by anyone. So far nothing had been reported.

"I don't think there were many other relatives. Robert Fields killed Frank Parker's sister and the kids. I don't believe he was married, so there may not be anyone to call it in."

The chief arrived a few minutes before seven and jerked his head towards his office as he passed their desks. Other officers were starting to populate some of the surrounding area, and they got some raised eyebrows at the bristled request.

Rising from their desks, they shared a glance before following the chief to his office and closing the door. The chief hung his coat on the coat rack in the corner before dropping into the oversized chair suitable for his oversized body.

Drake and Kacey waited for him to settle, knowing a barrage of questions was imminent, and they weren't disappointed.

"Now, what the hell is this that the John Doe is Frank Parker? I still can't understand how neither of you recognized him at the site. Do we know anything about where he was the day of his death or, better yet, who he was with last?" The press is going to cream us on this, and the mayor will be so far up my ass I won't be able to swallow."

Drake took the first stab at answering the questions before more could flow. "The body had been in the water for a while and as a result was fairly bloated, making him unrecognizable. It also has been two years since we've seen him. As for his last days, no, we don't have any information. To our knowledge he has no known relatives except for his brother-in-law who is still upstate in the looney bin. We checked missing person's again specifically looking to see if Parker had been reported missing, and there is no report, at least not yet. We'll go over to his last known address first thing to start searching and get our hands on contacts he has had as well as any appointments he may have had on the day of the murder."

"What about the press?" the chief barked.

"We can anticipate the minute they get wind of this, they will immediately start playing the video from the courtroom," Kacey stated.

"Yeah, and immediately they will point the finger at our department. They'll say someone from the inside killed him. Jesus Christ!" Dalton tossed a pen across the desk that he'd been

36

twirling in his giant fingers ever since he sat down. "I'm going to have to come up with something soon. What about the hooker? Please tell me there is no way those two cases are related."

"We don't have any reason to think so, sir, but we have little information yet. We need to contact next of kin and see what the family can tell us. We know the girl was new to the area, only been in town for about a month. So unless Parker hooked up with her, there really doesn't seem to be any connection."

"Look for every angle. We need to be ahead of this before the press is." With that he waved his hand at them to leave his office as he reached for the phone. They knew it would be a call to the mayor, better to call first than let him read it in the paper or see it on Channel 8 news with Jillian Sperry adding her two cents to the story.

After walking out of the office, Kacey turned to Drake. "What do you make of this? Is it possible Fields could have done this from his padded cell?"

Drake considered the idea before answering, "Hell, anything is possible with that bastard."

"How do you want to play this?" Kacey asked before continuing with options. "We could split up, one of us works on notification of next of kin for the girl while the other goes to Parker's place and searches."

"No, let's stick together. We can have Janet track down the girl's address while we go out to Parker's. Then we can request a patrol from New Jersey to go out to the residence. We don't have time to leave now to do any personal notification. Besides, it seems like Parker is our priority at the moment."

Drake's grimace at that last statement told Kacey how he was feeling about another young girl being dead. Any murdered young girl was always going to be a painful reminder of the Fields case and young Sophie. She nodded in agreement at his plan and followed him up to Janet's desk on the second floor.

Janet looked up as they approached. She was the best data analyst the department had and a stunning beauty. Her looks had always made Kacey feel a little jealous around Drake. Not that Drake really seemed to notice her flirtatious comments or batting of the eyes, and even though Kacey was a knock out herself Janet was the one girl in the office that always made Kacey think about what could have been with Drake…if not for the Fields case.

"Well, Detectives Drake and James, what brings the two of you up my way today?" Janet talked to both of them but her brilliant blue eyes were only on Drake.

Kacey jumped in drawing Janet's eyes in her direction, "Hey, Janet, need some quick help. We have a vic that we need last known address on and anything you can find on living relatives, history, etcetera."

Janet smiled at Drake before turning her attention to Kacey, "Okay what'd ya' got for me, and I'll see what I can find."

"Candice Jackson, seventeen, or at least that is what her ID shows. We believe she's from New Jersey, don't have a city though."

Drake added. "Oh, and once you have something, can you add to the info the contact for the local PD for next of kin. We'll need to have someone do the notification."

Janet looked back at Drake, her eyes taking in his thick arms and broad chest. "You got it. Anything else?"

"I think that's all for now," Drake finished before looking at Kacey for confirmation.

"Okay, I'm on it. I'll call you as soon as I have something," Janet said specifically to Drake.

"We're going to be in the middle of another search. Can you text over the info?" Drake asked.

Looking a little dejected, Janet merely nodded in agreement.

Kacey thanked her, never wanting her or Drake to know how she felt.

The two headed back to their desks on the first floor to get Parker's address and to call for a warrant. Drake made a quick call to a friend in the DA's office and specifically asked to keep the warrant on the down low, hoping to keep things quiet until they at least had an opportunity to search the house. Before leaving the building they checked out a plain cruiser from the motor pool.

Entering the parking garage, Kacey offered to drive while Drake navigated to the address that he already punched into his cell phone GPS. Within a few minutes they were out on the expressway and after a short ride across town were parked in front of an expansive home with well-manicured lawns and a sweeping circular drive.

"Looks like Parker was doing pretty well," Kacey said as they looked at the house in front of them.

Drake looked over at her and caught her big, doe eyes in his for a brief moment before pulling on the door handle and exiting the car. After calling his contact back Drake received confirmation that they were free to enter the home; all areas, garages, and automobiles were included in the search.

They walked up on the porch, and just as Drake was about to ring the bell, Kacey stopped him. "Hey, we need CSI here just to cover our tails. If the chief is right and someone is trying to pin this on the PD we don't want to be the only ones inside."

Drake stood for a moment looking at her then scanned the driveway. He knew she was right, but wanted to kick in that door really badly, and knew the more people they got involved the more likely Jillian Sperry would run with a sick spin on the story. Weighing the risks of both, he turned back to her and said, "Okay, call it in."

Returning to the warmth of the cruiser while they waited, Drake turned sideways to face Kacey. "Do you think this is pointed at us?"

"It sure seems like it, but it could be a coincidence, I guess. Maybe Parker made a bad business deal and pissed off someone."

"We have to figure out the significance of the needle and the burns. Fields had burned..." His voice faded out before speaking the name. He hadn't said Sophie Fields's name in over two years.

"I know. I thought of that too. Doc said the burns had a rounded tip and was probably metal. We thought fireplace poker, but..." Kacey stopped and punched a few buttons on her phone that she quickly pulled from her coat pocket.

Drake sat and watched as he waited to see who she was calling.

"Doc. Hey, it's Kacey. On Parker, the burns, is it possible they were made from a curling iron?" Without any more words Kacey looked at Drake and nodded.

Drake leaned back into his seat and rubbed his big hands over the tense muscles in his face.

Before either could say anything else, a CSI van pulled up next to them and two techs climbed out to join the detectives on the driveway. Drake and Kacey gave them the search criteria, and then asked them to pay close attention, to photograph anything that looked disturbed, and to try to find anything that had any names, contacts, or addresses on it.

One of the techs used picking tools to open the door, removing the need to kick in the door. Drake couldn't help feeling disappointed that he wouldn't be able to smash something right now. Reeling in his frustration, he stopped the techs before entering and explained the sensitivity of the case and cautioned them that the PD was going to be under fire on this case, along with having the mayor's attention. "Cross every T and dot every I in here, you hear me?"

With that, they walked inside and began their search. It didn't take long to get to the master bedroom, which was the obvious murder site. There had been a struggle in the bed. The sheets had been pulled off the bed and used to drag the body to the garage where they were found wadded in the trash outside the rollup door. They came across a window that was broken on the side of the house and a pair of men's underwear and t-shirt in the bathroom trash can.

Everything was bagged and tagged for the CSI team to search for trace evidence and prints. Kacey went on a search for a curling iron or sewing kit and found neither, but in the office an address book and the man's cell phone were retrieved. The phone was password protected, and they were unable to access it.

Kacey offered to place a call to Janet, stopping Drake just before he was about to, though she really wasn't sure why she cared. After all, things had been cooled with her and Drake for over two years. Briefly considering her motives as she waited for the line to connect, she was pulled out of her thoughts when Janet's sultry voice came on the line. She asked Janet to run a history trace on Parker's cell phone to see who he'd last been in contact with via text or call. Janet explained that it would take a bit, but she would make that her priority and would call back as soon as she had information.

The CSI team bagged the fire place poker and another tool in the garage that could be possible matches for the burn marks, though instincts told both Drake and Kacey that a curling iron was the tool they were looking for. Even so, the lab would compare the items to the wounds, if nothing else, to rule them out.

Drake searched the car that was inside the garage, and after spending a few minutes looking for the keys, he powered on the vehicle to look at the GPS to see the last place where Parker had been. After punching around on the buttons, he finally retrieved the history and found Parker had been downtown. He remembered that was where Parker's office was located.

Using his cell phone, he verified the location found on the GPS to be that of Parker's accounting firm. They'd need to interview the people he worked with. Hopefully they could identify the last person to see Parker alive at the office, and then they could work forward from there. Drake hoped that someone at Parker's office had a beef with the guy, but his gut told him that finding Parker's killer wasn't going to be as easy as that.

Drake's cell phone rang as he slid back out of the car. Looking at the display he saw it was Janet from the precinct that was calling him. "Good, hopefully she will have some information on Parker's phone and text history". Pressing the phone icon with his thumb, he answered, "Hey, Janet. Whatcha' got?"

"Hey Drake, I got in to the phone and text history, but unfortunately, there isn't a lot to speak about. Typical messages from friends. Cell history seems mostly client related. Email account is on the phone too. I've quickly skimmed through the past two weeks, and I don't see anything out of the ordinary. I'll do a complete dump though in case you want to go back through it farther."

"Okay, thanks."

Drake was about to hang up when Janet continued, "Hold on, big guy. I got the information on the dead prostitute. I'm sending it over to your email now."

"Okay, great. Local police information included?"

"Yes, it's all there. I even included a couple of photos from a recent arrest. She got popped about a month ago. Must have been right when she got in town."

"Okay, I'll look it over as soon as we wrap up here. Thanks, Janet."

"Any time, Drake, any time."

Drake ignored Janet's flirtatious tone. All he could think about was Parker and how they were going to find his killer before the press ran some crazy story on it. Oh, it wasn't that Janet didn't drip with sexiness, but she was too obvious. Drake had always been attracted to women that were mysterious and challenging, someone more like Kacey. It had been a long time since he'd allowed himself to show interest in anyone. He'd not been involved with anyone since Fields had murdered Sophie and the whole world changed.

When he walked back inside the house he found Kacey talking with one of the analysts about the items that had thus far been collected. "Hey, Janet called. Nothing unusual on Parker's phone, text, or emails."

Kacey struggled to not show her frustration with Janet calling Drake back when it had been her that had made the request, but not wanting him to see her reaction she turned to study the room with her back towards him. "Okay, you find anything on the car?"

"Yeah, he goes to work every day."

Kacey turned back to him. "Great, that's a load of help."

"I know." When he smiled the corner of his eyes crinkled with fine lines of middle age, a woeful sadness, and wisdom that was ruggedly handsome.

"She also sent over information on Candy. We can wrap up here and then connect with the Jersey PD."

"It's going to be a long day. We have a lot of interviews to make, between John John and Parker's connections."

"I know. Let's make one last sweep here and then head out," Drake offered already heading towards the back of the house.

Leaving the Parker house, Drake recommended they go see Doc, hoping he would have some information about Candy's body by now. Whatever he had they could provide to the Jersey police, offering everything they had thus far for the notification to her family. Kacey reluctantly agreed. Drake knew it was not because she disagreed with his recommendation, but rather a natural resistance to that specific building. The same reflex he had about going inside that building, each time having to force himself to do his job and overcoming his desire to never go there again.

On the way to see Doc they discussed the items recovered from the Parker house and, more importantly, the lack of evidence. They spent time speculating as to whether someone had cleverly covered up any useful evidence.

"The killer is smart and organized. Cleans up the scene, takes the items used during the crime, and it appears he leaves no trace evidence."

Kacey added, "My bet is there won't be a single print on the doors or window. He entered quickly and quietly, wore gloves, took his time, enjoyed himself, and then quietly slipped away into the night."

"What's the connection?" Drake dared to ask the million dollar question.

"Better yet, is there a connection?" Kacey added.

"In the eyes of the press there certainly will be."

Moments later they pulled into the parking lot and silence settled over them as if impending doom was about to cast its evil net.

Drake powered off the vehicle and turned to Kacey. "Shall we?"

Kacey caught his eyes, and for a brief moment they were back to before Robert Fields had tortured and killed his daughter.

Kacey pulled on the door handle and broke their gaze. They each exited the vehicle and made the walk across the parking lot to the drab building.

Doc looked up over his glasses as they walked in through the swinging doors. "Well, I wasn't sure I'd see you yet given the… other discovery made," he said referring to the identification of Parker as the John Doe.

"Yeah, well we thought we could at least get the details on this so when we called the Jersey PD we would have as much information as possible. The chief has Parker as our priority. This one will take a back burner, but we didn't want the notification to wait."

"Got anything exciting to tell us?" Kacey asked jumping right to business.

Drake glanced over at her and could tell she was itchy to get the information they'd come for and get out of here. She looked tired, dark circles under her eyes. The back to back murders and long schedule was obviously wearing on her. She was tough though; he knew that for fact. She was the toughest partner he'd ever had, a great cop, skilled, excellent instincts, and a sharp shooter to boot. All the attributes that had attracted him to her in the first place were still there just under the surface—the surface of pain, caused by a difficult childhood and the Fields case.

Turning back to Doc, he waited for the answer to Kacey's question.

Chapter Six

That was the best time we've ever had! Fun, fun, fun!

Hush, I need to think.

I'm sorry, but did you see her face? Priceless.

Iz paced the apartment for a long while before taking a hot shower, scrubbing until red skin sizzled under the spray. The scrubbing barely scratched the surface of rinsing away the filth, stench, and hate. Iz hated the dirty little prostitute, hated them all. Hated their evil words and the way they stared, the rude comments.

It was late. Iz prayed for some sleep. Prayed the nightmares would leave them alone just for one night, just long enough to rest, feel better, get stronger, and maintain control. Strength was important now; there was so much more work to do.

Not work. Fun. Loads of fun. The dogs chewed and chomped. Did you see it?

I said hush! I'm so tired. I need to sleep.

Too excited to sleep. Want to do it again. Over and over again!

Iz ignored the prodding and dropped onto the bed and pulled the covers up tight. Eyes pressed tight, so tight they hurt. Tortured dreams finally came. Iz could see the room as if floating and watching from overhead.

There were children everywhere. Lunch trays clamored, and the room buzzed with voices. Boys and girls voices chattered about anything and nothing. Loud voices made Iz's head hurt.

Under the covers hands slammed over ears in an effort to trap the noise outside. The effort failed. The noises still came. The voices changed from chatter to chants, words flew through the air—ugly, hate-filled words.

45

Iz's body twisted and turned in the sheets, trying to push away from the horrible children and their terrible ways. Suddenly, there was a new sound–closer, not quite so loud–pulling Iz away.

Eye lids flew open. A phone buzzing on the night stand, sweat covered Iz's body, reaching for the phone the display showed a familiar number–work. Damn, getting called into work again. No sleep tonight.

Chapter Seven

Doc began breaking down what he had on the body lying on his stainless steel table. The first parts of what he covered were obvious from simply looking at the body. Bite marks covered the body and face.

"She bled out from these wounds right here," Doc said pointing to bite marks across the woman's neck. "These punctures hit a main artery, and the blood loss was immense."

"So the wire around her neck wasn't used to strangle her?" Drake asked sounding a bit surprised.

"No, it wasn't. That was my first thought too, but the wire was used for something else. Something a whole lot stranger. In fact, I've never seen anything like it before."

Drake took a quick glance at Kacey and saw her biting her lip. "Okay…"

"Well, remember at the crime scene I told you there appeared to be meat in the wire. There are, in fact, remnants of meat still attached to the wire. I tested it and got swine."

Kacey blurted out, "Swine, as in pig?"

Doc nodded. "Yes." Walking across the room to another smaller table, Doc motioned with his head for them to follow, then stopped when they had joined him on the opposite side. "This was recovered by the analysts," he said lifting a bone off of a tray.

As Doc held up the bone, both Drake and Kacey looked it over. The bone was about four to five inches in length and slender with a slight T shape at one end.

"Does that belong to the victim?" Drake asked.

"No. It appears to belong to the pig. I believe it was from a pork chop."

"There was paper at the scene that looked like the kind of paper a butcher wraps meat in," Drake stated, remembering the paper he'd seen on the ground near the body.

"Yes," Doc said pointing to another tray where the paper scraps lay. "I've tested it and it matches the meat in the wire."

"So, you're telling us that the killer picks up the hooker, ties a pork chop around her neck with barbed wire, and then feeds her to the dogs, which ultimately kills her while trying to get the meat from around her neck?" Kacey asked, shaking her head.

Doc looked from one detective to the other. "I'm afraid that is exactly what I am saying."

Drake took a step back and rubbed his strong hands down his tired face and muttered under his breath, "Holy shit."

"Anything else," Kacey asked still shaking her head.

"Not so far, other than I have confirmed that she matches the identification found at the scene. She was in the system, got picked up about a month ago, so it was easy to get a fingerprint match."

Drake looked at Kacey. "Let's go notify the Jersey PD to make the notification. Then we can get back to figuring out what the hell is going on with Parker before the chief hands our asses to us."

"You drive," Drake said to Kacey as they walked across the parking lot, and he tossed her the keys. Inside the car Drake opened the email Janet had sent him and scanned through it looking for the phone number for the Jersey precinct.

As Kacey navigated her way down the city streets back towards police headquarters, Drake made contact with the New Jersey police department and after several minutes had explained the situation with the death of Candy. He obtained an email address and forwarded the entire email Janet had sent.

Settling back into his seat he sighed heavily. "Well, that's done. Let's just hope we can get this Parker thing closed out quickly so we can try to figure out what happened to that girl."

Kacey nodded then added, "In another hour or so we ought to be able to get a couple of patrol cops to go over and scope out

John John. Maybe he's a sick son of a bitch that does crazy shit to his girls if they don't deliver."

Drake looked at his watch. "Yeah, let me get that set up." He scrolled through his cell phone, and as they entered the parking lot for the motor pool cars he hung up. "They'll sweep his place about noon, should be perfect."

As they were re-entering the building, Drake said, "We'd better give the chief an update before he starts demanding one."

"Next steps? Interviews with co-workers and... Fields?" Kacey hesitantly suggested as they approached their desks.

Drake stopped and stared at the marbled floor before answering, "Yes. I suppose we have to talk to Fields to try and find out if there is any way he had someone do something to Parker from his strait jacket."

"Let's get it arranged before going into the chief's office. That way we have something."

Drake shrugged his shoulders, certain it wouldn't matter what they had unless it was a signed confession. Either way they were, no doubt, going to get badgered about not moving fast enough.

Kacey sat down at her desk and reached for the phone to ring Janet's office. She asked for the number for the mental institute where Fields had been committed and would hopefully remain a permanent resident. After waiting a few moments, she scribbled a name and a number onto a notepad that sat next to her and disconnected the call. "It'll take us an hour to get there."

"I say we go to Parker's office first before it closes. The nut house is open twenty-four seven. We'll cover more ground that way."

Agreeing with him, Kacey stood and led the way to the chief's office.

Drake knocked on the door and glanced at Kacey before twisting the knob as Chief Dalton's barked an invitation to enter. Once inside Kacey started first. "We delivered several items for forensics from the Parker house. We didn't recover any syringes, so the weapon that delivered the lethal dose has not yet been recovered."

"We focused on recovering the items that were possibly matches to the burns on Parker's chest." Drake swallowed hard, his mouth suddenly feeling dry. "We don't think any of them will match."

The chief's eyes narrowed in on him. "Why is that?"

"We believe the burns were caused by a curling iron."

"That's pretty specific. What makes you think that?" Dalton challenged, his eyes fixed on Drake's.

Drake hesitated before answering, "Fields burned his daughter with a curling iron. The burns are consistent. We've seen them before." Drake swallowed hard. .

Kacey continued before Dalton could say anything, "We are heading out to try and talk to Fields after we interview Parker's co-workers. His GPS indicated the last place he'd been was work. We want to clear those folks before the office closes for the day. By morning we will have retraced Parker's last hours and talked with Fields."

"Do you think that sick son of a bitch had Parker killed from a mental institution?"

Resisting a sideways glance at Kacey, Drake reluctantly answered, "It's possible."

"You said this was a serial. So, Fields is our serial?" Dalton asked, referring to the serial killer reference Drake and Kacey had made when they first caught the case before they even knew the dead man was Parker.

"Let us conduct the interviews first. We'll know more then."

The phone on the chief's desk rang, and he quickly snapped up the receiver while holding his index finger up on his other hand indicating for them not to leave yet. "Chief Dalton."

The look on his face told Drake and Kacey all they needed to know. The moment they'd been dreading was here; the caller was either the mayor or Jillian Sperry who had gotten wind of Parker's murder.

Dalton sat back in the chair, his broad shoulders soaking up the entire leather surface. "Mr. Mayor, sir. Yes, that is correct. We are still gathering details. I understand. Should we pro-actively release a statement?" The chief waited, a penetrating glare cast at the two detectives. "I will, sir. Four o'clock, I'll be there."

The chief slammed the phone back on the cradle. "Well, shit just hit the fan. The mayor wants to hold a press conference at four. Get in front of this before Jillian Sperry makes a damn mess of this."

"We can have the interviews at his offices conducted before four o'clock. Maybe we'll have something by then."

"Go, and get me anything you can before four o'clock."

Wasting no more time, Drake and Kacey turned and left the office and headed back out to the motor pool to pick up the car. Twenty minutes later they were walking into the building where Parker had been an accountant for over five years.

At the desk in the lobby they flashed their badges, and Drake asked to speak with Parker's administrative assistant and boss, as he figured those two would have the most information about Parker's schedule and recent meetings.

They were directed to take the elevator to the third floor where they were greeted by a fifties-something, plump woman with a bobbed hair cut that was graying along the crown. Drake caught a subtle smile from Kacey and assumed she was amused by the obvious need for a dye job.

After being presented with badges the woman began wringing her hands before introducing herself, "I'm Patrice Franklin. Please follow me."

They followed her down a corridor to a small conference room with a table in the middle that seats six. "Mr. Novak will be in shortly."

"Mr. Novak. He's the owner of the firm?"

Patrice nodded. "Yes, along with Mr. Baxter, but he's a silent partner. He retired two years ago."

As she was explaining, the conference room door opened and an older man entered the room. He was tall and trim and wore an obviously expensive suit. "Alex Novak," said in a rich Russian accent, offering his hand to each of them before taking a seat and waving his hand for them to sit as well.

Drake flashed his badge then introduced both himself and Kacey. "Mr. Novak, we're here with some bad news about one of your employees, Frank Parker. He was found dead recently.."

"Dead? Was there some sort of an accident?" Novak questioned with genuine shock on his face.

"I'm afraid Mr. Parker was murdered," Kacey stated quietly.

"Murdered?" Patrice gasped, and her hand fluttered to her chest.

"Yes, I'm afraid so. What can you tell us about Frank's schedule and behavior lately?" Drake questioned.

"Frank was an excellent accountant. He has … had three clients, all very large corporations that he supported. Patrice, go print out his appointment log and contact lists as well as phone logs," Novak instructed, then turned to face Drake and Kacey. "We charge by the quarter hour for all time spent on any account. The phone logs will account for all of Frank's time."

"Were there any issues with any of the clients?" Kacey asked.

"Or any coworkers?" Drake added.

Novak shook his head. "None that I am aware of. Frank was very professional. He had good working relationships and was good at assisting the clients through large purchases, refranchising, public trades, basically ensuring stockholders were well paid, and the company honored all accounting regulations."

"Were there any recent issues or contact from his brother-in-law Robert Fields?"

Novak stopped, laying his hands flat on the table. "Frank had put that behind him. It took him a while to get over the loss of his family at the hands of that madman. He tried to sue the police. When that failed he merely buried himself in his work."

Patrice re-entered the room with two manila folders. As she handed them to Kacey she explained, "The first one contains a log of all his billable hours. It will have all the time spent on accounts and every phone call made. The second one has a copy of his appointment calendar. Those should match to the billable hours."

Kacey flipped through the pages quickly. "Thank you. We'll have an analyst go through them."

"Patrice, did you over hear or see anything unusual in Frank's behavior or schedule lately?"

Patrice looked to Novak before answering. "No, nothing that I can think of. Frank worked long hours, but he always has."

"What about personal relationships? Was Frank involved with anyone?"

Patrice wrung her hands together on top of the table. "Paul divorced years ago, and after he lost his sister and the kids he isolated, and all he did was work. I haven't heard of him dating anyone, and there were no signs of a relationship. No phone calls or long lunches."

"What about his mood? Did it change lately?"

"He's been sullen, quiet ever since the murders. That never changed." She added, "It didn't get worse either."

"Is there anyone in the office he's particularly close to?" Kacey asked, realizing they were coming up empty.

Novak and Patrice exchanged a glance simultaneously shaking their heads. Novak ultimately spoke, "Frank was a loner. Always was but after the trial and his unsuccessful claim against the city, it got worse. He barely spoke to anyone about anything other than business."

Drake rose and drew two business cards from his inside coat pocket. His service weapon became exposed when he did so, causing Patrice to suck in a deep breath. "This has my office and cell phone number on it. You can reach either of us any time. If you remember anything or can think of details you may have not thought of, please call us right away."

The rest stood up and shook hands around the table before Patrice walked them back to the elevator. "I'm sorry we couldn't be more helpful. Frank was a nice man. I can't believe...," her voice trailed off as she fought back tears.

"I'm sorry for your loss," Kacey offered, squeezing the plump woman's right elbow.

Patrice simply nodded as the elevator doors opened.

They rode the elevator down in silence while accompanied by two other people who appeared to be employees from somewhere within the building. The doors opened on the ground floor, and they exited.

Outside the afternoon air was cold, but for the first time in a long time the sun was shining. To Drake it seemed ironic as he slid behind the wheel of the black sedan. Kacey slid in next to him as he paused before turning on the engine.

"Hey, it's cold outside, ya' know? How about some heat?" she ribbed him jolting him from his thoughts.

"Oh, sorry," he replied firing the engine. "Did you notice the way the secretary wrung her hands the whole time? Think there is anything to that?"

"Secretary, um what century do you live in?"

"Okay, Christ, administrative assistant," he said making little quotation marks with his fingers.

"Better. Yeah, I saw her. I was wondering if she was just rattled by being questioned by the cops or if she had something to hide, but she seemed willing to offer information even when Novak was out of the room."

"I thought that too. If she was hiding something then she would have said she needed to wait for him to join them."

"Let's drop these files off to Janet and have her start going through them while we drive up to see Fields."

Drake nodded as he drove back towards the precinct.

Just as they were pulling into a space, Drake's cell phone rang. Fishing the phone from his pocket, he slid his thumb over the glass and answered, "Detective Drake."

Kacey whispered that she would take the files up to Janet and be right back. Drake nodded as he listened on his phone, removing the pen from the mounted notepad on the dash.

While Kacey was inside, Drake took notes about the pimp John John from his not-so-favorite patrol cop Craig Dermot–the same guy that gave Kacey a hard time at the diner. Even though Drake hated the cocky bastard, the fact that he was cocky made him a good cop. He had to live up to that reputation and to do so meant being thorough.

Kacey swung the door open as Drake ended the call. "Who was that?'

"Your buddy Dermot."

"What'd that asshole want?"

Drake laughed. He always liked Kacey's blunt remarks. "Tell me how you really feel."

Kacey gave him a look, her head cocked sideways and jet black hair falling to one side, eyebrows raised. "And…what did he have to say?"

"Well, they found John John at home as expected. But the bad news is John John has a solid alibi, and Dermot has already confirmed it. Seems he got popped for speeding across town and because he had outstanding warrants he got dragged downtown. Didn't get released until morning."

"Great, so we could have two crazies out there killing people."

"It would seem so," Drake said as he watched Kacey settle into her seat and plug in her seatbelt. I say we get out of the city and then get something to eat. Sound good to you?"

"Sounds great," Kacey replied uncertain of when the last time was that she'd eaten and suddenly realized she was very hungry.

Drake navigated the car out onto the street and then into the highway traffic, following the signs north of the city. "Hey, did Janet say how long it would take her to go through those files?"

Kacey looked over at him trying to read his face as he spoke about Janet. Seeing no emotion at all she resisted a smile and explained, "She told me it might take her a couple of hours, would have rather had the electronic version. She'll scan the files then manipulate the data to match it up. I'm sure she will call you when she's finished."

Drake glanced her way. He knew Kacey didn't like Janet, Respected her, yes, but didn't like her much. He could only assume that she was jealous of Janet, which he really couldn't understand. Kacey had so much more to offer. Sure, Janet was voluptuous and obviously sexy, but Kacey was bold, tall, muscular, and stunningly beautiful with her olive skin, high cheek bones, black hair, and dark eyes.

For Drake it was always the bold part that had excited him. Kacey possessed an exciting independence that drove men to chase her—men like Craig Dermot. His knuckles wrapped tighter around the wheel at the thought of Kacey wrapped around Dermot.

If only Fields had never killed his family. If only he and Kacey could be together without that very long day, standing right there raw in front of them, in between them.

Kacey's voice broke through his thoughts. "Hey, there's that cool little restaurant off the highway near exit 43. You remember the place? They have great pasta and steaks."

Drake glanced at her. "I remember." They'd gone to that restaurant on more than one occasion back when they'd been spending time together. They'd often go outside the city limits to be sure they weren't spotted by anyone from the PD. Occasionally, they'd be spotted somewhere and play it off like they were working a case. They'd managed to have an affair for over two years without it ever becoming an issue or focus. Of course that was all before the Fields case. They hadn't been to the restaurant since.

Drake took the exit Kacey referred to and wound to the right off the ramp, and about a half mile down the road pulled into the parking lot of the familiar rustic cabin looking building. Lights twinkled in the windows and smoke poured from two chimneys on either side of the roof.

Killing the engine and headlights, Drake turned to Kacey. "Ready? I'm starving," he said trying to ease into going inside. The reality was this place held memories that were both pleasant and painful, and he wondered if Kacey felt the same way.

"I'm starving. I think I've eaten everything on this menu and there's not one thing I don't like. Come on, Colton," she said using his first name, something she hadn't done in a long time. "Let's go. This might get expensive."

Drake smiled remembering Kacey's healthy appetite. She wasn't like most women, always trying to hide their need to eat. She enjoyed her food, shared it freely, and had an amazing way of licking her fingers in a way that was sexy as hell.

"Yeah, you called it though, so this one is on you," Drake teased back as they exited the car and walked across the frozen parking lot, avoiding small frozen puddles that shone sparkling reflection from the lights.

Kacey reached in her back pocket and pulled out a credit card. "No problem," she laughed a hearty laugh that he hadn't seen in a long time.

The restaurant's interior was warm and cozy. They were quickly seated next to the fireplace at a small intimate table for two and fifteen minutes later they had bruschetta placed between them and were both nibbling on the savory and crunchy bread.

Across the room a couple sat cozy next to each other on the same side of a booth, tenderly kissing and oblivious to everyone around them. Both Drake and Kacey's eyes glanced at them periodically, each smiling and dropping bashful eyes away.

"Do you remember?" Kacey asked breaking the silence.

"Remember?" Drake responded coyly.

Looking shy, Kacey brushed her hair away from her face. "Never mind."

Drake's eyes stayed focused on the food, and he responded quietly, "Yes, Kacey, I remember."

She let out a low breath and nodded. The corner of her mouth turned up slightly before she popped another bite of the delicious bread in her mouth.

The server showed up and broke the awkward moment, delivering their entrees and warm bread. The aroma was amazing, and they tore into the food, sharing the combination of steak and eggplant parmesan. They'd resisted ordering a bottle of wine which would have perfectly complimented the amazing meal, but wouldn't have been good for the interview with Fields—a topic neither had raised during the meal.

The ambiance was nice, and as they ate they had mild conversation about past cases, recent events, and thoughts on the interviews today with Parker's boss and secretary. On occasion they stole frequent, subtle glances over the flicker of the short, red candle that sat at the edge of the table. After finishing the meal, Kacey paid the bill sticking to their deal, they left the restaurant and returned to the car.

Drake fired the engine, backed out of the space, and pulled the car out of the parking lot, heading to the highway and further north towards the institution that Fields called home.

"Are you ready for this?" Drake asked taking a sideways glance towards Kacey.

Kacey shrugged her shoulders. "I guess."

"We need to decide how we want to handle this interview before we get there. We can't let Fields have the upper hand."

"You mean like last time?"

Drake's hands instinctively gripped the wheel, which would have shown white had there been any light other than the overhead highway lights that flew by flashing a brief glow into the car for two or three seconds at a time. "Yes, like last time."

"I'm sorry, you're right. We need to be ready, so how do you want to play it?"

"He's going to try to rattle us. He'll talk about... that day, the things he did. We need to expect that he will go into detail. He'll

57

know that talking about that day will get to us, and he's crazy. He'll try to set us off."

"Sophie," Kacey said, then squeezed her eyes tight.

Drake waited a few moments. The name, unspoken for so long, bounced inside his head like a pinball off of the rubber bumpers inside the machine. Finally, he spoke slowly, "Sophie."

Drake's head suddenly hurt. "He'll talk all about her, Kacey. He'll say all the things he did to her. Keeping him focused on his brother-in-law is our only goal. Watching him when we first tell him of Parker's death may be all we need. I know for sure if he gets to us that sick son of a bitch wins again."

"I wish I could say that I'll be able to keep my cool, but Drake I'm afraid I might just lose it. I want to beat that bastard with everything I have. I want to put a bullet through his head and then spit in his face as he dies," Kacey said rubbing her gloved hands over her arms.

Drake reached forward and turned up the heater fan, even though he knew the chill she so desperately wanted to rub away was less about the cold than the emotional chill she felt.

"Okay, what do you think about this? We go in, you lead the questions, but when you feel like you might be losing it I take over. The minute that bastard turns the interview details about Sophie we threaten to leave. If he pleads with us to stay, but fails to provide any details about Parker, that's our tell."

Kacey considered Drake's plan. "So you think if he knows anything he won't be able to resist sharing?" She continued before Drake could answer, "It makes sense. He shared every detail before. He has absolutely nothing to lose and is way too crazy to hold back information as leverage."

"Right, he uses information as leverage. If he knows anything he will taunt us with small details."

"Okay." Kacey looked over at Drake. "What if you want to feed the bastard his ass."

"Well, then we are screwed." Drake forced a smile and glanced her way then returned his eyes back to the road. "We'll be okay. He can't hurt us or anyone else. He's locked up. He doesn't have a young girl in his grip. That means we can walk any time we want to."

Kacey's eyes watched as a highway sign passed. "Next exit."

Chapter Eight

Drake and Kacey entered the sanitarium through the main doors and were soon escorted down a long, narrow hallway. Their heels clicked on the marble tiles in the sterile lighting. There were howls from one of the rooms far at the end of the hall. A strange looking, little man stood hunched over in one of the doorways. He wore a hospital gown backwards that gaped wide open in the front. He laughed and fondled himself as they passed by.

"Lester, go back in your room and close your gown," the nurse barked.

Lester went back in his room. Laughter followed them as they continued on down the hall.

"Fields is lightly sedated. We put him in a strait jacket for your visit. He tends to become a bit aggressive and doesn't respond well to the psychiatric visits with the doctor."

"Will he talk to us?" Kacey asked.

The nurse shrugged. "He's smart, likes to play mind games, rambling one moment then completely cognitive seconds later. The doctors aren't sure if he's acting or truly that delusional."

The nurse stopped in front of a door near the end of the hall. There was a six by ten inch double paned window with cross hatched lines in it. The nurse peered through the door before taking a key ring from the right pocket of her medical smock. She turned towards the detectives, "Ready?"

Drake and Kacey glanced at each other as they both nodded. "Yes, we're ready," Drake responded.

"I have been instructed to ask you to leave if he gets too riled up."

"We understand. We just have a few questions. This shouldn't take long."

"Okay, I'll be right outside here and security is just around the corner. If you need anything, just holler or tap on the door." Sliding the key in the lock, she turned the knob and opened the door to allow them both access to the room.

Drake stepped through the door first with Kacey right behind him. The door clicked. Fields sat in a chair in the middle of the room his arms wrapped tightly in the strait jacket, his eyes on the floor.

"Robert Fields," Kacey started, "do you remember us? Detectives Kacey James and Colton Drake. We need to ask you some questions about your brother-in-law, Frank Parker."

Fields raised his eyes to Kacey, his chin still dipped low against his chest. Slowly he spoke, "I remember." There was something chilling in the way he spoke the words.

"Good. We need to ask you some questions about your brother-in-law, Frank Parker."

Raising his eyes a little farther, Fields looked at Kacey then Drake, who remained idle and quiet so far. "Do you remember, Detectives?" An evil grin sprawled across his twisted face, exposing crooked, yellowing teeth.

Kacey pushed on, "Frank Parker, your brother-in-law?"

Drake watched Fields's body language. He didn't respond at all to Parker's name.

"My brother-in-law? Perhaps you've forgotten, I'm no longer married. Maybe you don't remember." Fields laughed.

"Your ex-brother-in-law," Kacey revised her statement, trying hard not to show her frustration.

"Oh, him, Frankie. He's an asshole, big crybaby."

"Cry baby?" Kacey asked.

"Cried all the way through the trial. Blah, blah, bah-whoo the whole freakin' time. He has no clue what it's like to be a real man."

"A *real* man?" Kacey was about to lose it.

Drake could sense Kacey was about to unleash on the guy and stepped in. "When was the last time you spoke with or saw Frank?"

Fields started rocking back and forth then let out a hearty laugh. His rocking increased in pace, and Drake stepped forward, not sure what he was about to do.

Fields started talking in an almost heckling voice, "You killed my sister and her kids, you sick bastard! What you did to Sophie, you sick son of a bitch!" He sat back and allowed another loud laugh to escape.

"So the last time you saw or spoke with Frank Parker was at the hearing?" Drake pressed trying to get a confirmation of what Fields's rambling meant.

Fields's eyes rested on Drake. "Sophie was so good. Her skin burned so sweet." The rocking began again and Fields laughed then started muttering about fire and sex under his breath.

Kacey stepped forward, and Drake moved sideways enough to stop her from getting close to Fields. "Let's go, he doesn't know anything." He took her by the arm, escorting her from the room.

"You don't think so?" Fields taunted still rocking in his chair.

Turning back to face him, Drake asked, "Really, Fields, what does a crazy shit like you think you know?"

"I did it just like I did it before." Fields was nearly manic in his chair now, rocking wildly his mouth twisting, his body rocking hard. He even banged his chest into the table as he rocked.

"How, how, did you do it from in here?"

"I have ways." A sick grin lined his face as he continued.

"Fields, how did you kill Frank Parker?"

"I told you," Fields said turning his attention to Kacey with a sneer on his face. "I have my ways."

"Okay, if you want us to believe you, tell us how he was killed or where he was found."

"I have options. It could have been any number of ways." Fields laughed loudly as the rocking increased.

"Tell us? Enlighten me?" Kacey kept prodding while Drake stood glaring at Fields.

"Shot, stabbed or even burned." Fields grinned wildly. His feet tapped the floor in rapid stomps, and then he began bouncing in his seat.

61

"Let's get out of here. This isn't getting us anywhere."

"You liked it too didn't you, Detective Drake?"

"What?" Drake's head snapped up to meet the crazy man's eyes.

Fields taunts increased, "As you listened? As Sophie cried, her moans of ecstasy. Did you get hard detective?"

"You son of a bitch!"

Drake nearly flew across the table. Kacey pulled him back. "Drake, stop! He's not worth it! He's just a piece of crazy shit!"

Drake pulled his arm away from Kacey in a swift jerk as Kacey shoved him out the door.

As they walked back down the corridor they could hear Fields screaming Sophie's name and "you liked it" over and over again.

It was all either detective could do to keep from putting their hands over their ears. The nurse that had escorted them to the room followed them back to the front desk.

"Has Fields had any visitors lately? Drake managed to ask forcing himself to ignore the shrill heckling still following them from the end of the corridor.

"Let me check the logs, hold on one moment." The nurse positioned herself back behind the large desk and logged onto a computer that sat in the middle. After a minute or two she reached behind her and retrieved a piece of paper that was freshly printed. Handing it to Drake she said, "There have been no visitors nor has he received any phone calls."

Drake looked over the paper and then handed it to Kacey before making a final request. "If he says anything after we leave or over the next few days about Frank Parker, please contact me right away," Drake said handing her a business card.

The wind hit their faces as they pushed open the door. It was late now, and they still had a long drive home. Once back in the car Drake started the engine and pulled away, leaving the looming walls of the stone institution behind. It wasn't until they were several miles away that he felt like he could finally breathe.

"You okay?" He asked trying to release the grip of the evil that seemed to have wrapped itself around them.

"I could use some coffee, or some whiskey." Kacey looked at him taking in his rugged good looks. "Or hard sex," she managed a smile.

"Coffee shop just ahead," Drake replied ignoring the last comment.

"You always were easy." She laughed out loud.

Drake glanced at her and laughed too.

The laughing came to a stop as they pulled into the parking lot of a small diner. Drake's stomach hurt. He couldn't remember the last time he'd laughed, and though he knew the laughter was a moment of stress relief, it still felt good. Damn good!

Kacey nodded her head towards the diner. "Coffee?"

"Yeah, coffee," Drake answered pulling on the door handle.

They were both quiet at first as they sat in the café silently sipping on the warm liquid. In a booth in the far corner a young couple sat cuddled up on one side of the table kissing, apparently oblivious to everything around them. Drake looked at Kacey and smiled.

Drake's eyes moved to a man sitting at the counter talking to himself. Based on his disheveled appearance, it appeared he was homeless. Drake knew there was a homeless community within less than a half a mile of the location near the river bottom. He assumed the man had wandered down here to get warm before heading out into the cold for what would be a long night.

Kacey's eyes followed Drake's, then returned to staring into her cup before glancing back at the couple. She finally spoke. "I miss that," she said tilting her head towards the couple.

"That was out of the blue," Drake said then met her eyes and saw the sadness. He wished he'd said something a little more comforting. He shook his head. "That's not what I meant. It's just…," his voice trailed off.

"I know it's been a long time. I think tonight, seeing Fields again was…good…cathartic," Kacey shrugged her shoulders.

Drake nodded, but struggled to come up with any words.

"Let's face it, we both have shoved this down, ignoring it for a very long time. Tonight we were forced to face it."

"I wanted to kill that bastard. Still do."

"Me too, but we can't. Besides I don't think he knew anything about Parker. He had nothing to offer. If he had details he would have teased us with some tidbit to tell us he knew, but without incriminating himself, especially since he would have pulled it off from the inside of the sanitarium."

"Major accomplishment. He would have been compelled to brag. I agree. So if it wasn't Fields, then who the hell was it?" Drake said throwing a few dollars on the table as he tossed back the last of the coffee in his cup.

Kacey stood, and as they walked out the door, the homeless man began chanting to himself.

Drake drove them back to the city, and as the lights grew closer Kacey reached over and placed her hand on his knee.

"Can I stay with you tonight? Don't feel like being alone."

Drake's eyes dropped to her hand, then met her gaze briefly before turning back to the road. He remembered the first time they'd ended up at his place. It had been on a day like today where the leads were weak and the frustration high. Only that time he'd made the move. Rather than answering her question he just drove towards his apartment.

***

Walking into Drake's apartment Kacey's eyes wandered over the familiar surroundings. Things hadn't changed much, except it was obvious Drake had closed in even more. He had always been a mysterious, tall, dark, and ruggedly handsome man, keeping closed to the world. Even when they'd dated and spent many intimate nights together Kacey had learned very little about him. She'd once heard him talking on the phone to his mother and remembered thinking that it was strange that he had a mother. Of course he had a mother, but she never knew anything else about his family.

"I see you are keeping the place up," she teased looking at the pile of newspapers and magazines lying on the coffee table.

Drake smiled before taking her by the hand and leading her down the dark hallway. "Sheets are fresh," he offered as he leaned her back onto the bed.

Kacey's eyes slowly watched as his big hands slid up her thighs. It felt good to have his hands on her. She missed the closeness. She'd had plenty of offers for sex, but remained shut down. Tonight facing the loss of Sophie unlocked something deep within.

She slid her hands over his and wrapped her arms around his waist, then lightly scraped her nails across his broad shoulders and down his muscular back. Under his shirt she could feel the scar on his left shoulder—a bullet wound earned during a raid on a drug house nearly a decade earlier.

His hands slid up her back and cupped her head in his hands. As their eyes locked, the passion rose and their breathing matched pace. Kacey's hands moved over the front of his chest and her fingers slowly unbuttoned his shirt, then popped the button on his pants and worked his zipper down. She palmed the front of his jeans and teased his excitement, causing a groan to escape his mouth.

Sliding her hand inside, she pulled his shaft out and wrapped her long, slender legs around his back, and pulled him into her.

His hands slid her sweater over her head in a swift motion and with expert precision released her bra, freeing her firm breasts and exposing her plump nipples.

Unable to resist any longer she sought out his mouth and pulled his head into hers. His lips crushed down on hers, their tongues swimming together as they sucked in the passion so desperately needed and long lost. Within moments Drake had pulled away just long enough to slip her jeans over her perfectly curved hips. He laid his hand on her flat stomach just above the soft mound of wetness while he stepped out of his boots and freed his legs from his pants.

With their bodies now free of clothes, Drake slid her up the bed, placing her head on the pillows. He straddled her, his thick shaft bobbing, and then he pressed her against his chest, brushing against her nipples. Finding her mouth, he teased her tongue with his while his fingers swirled around her nipples then slid down and dipped inside.

She arched her back, pushing hard against him. A moan slipped out of her mouth, and she bit at his lips, nipping just hard enough to increase his arousal to the point of demand. He reached below her and lifted her back up and pressed into her, driving inside and pushing his hips deep into her.

Their bodies worked in unison with perfection that came only from familiarity until they released together. Sweat covered their bodies with a light sheen. Kacey clung to him tightly until finally they relaxed and fell into a deep sleep, arms and legs wound together.

***

Drake woke reaching across the bed, only to be greeted with rumpled sheets. Opening his eyes he glanced over at the night stand and saw that it was just after six o'clock in the morning. His eyes drifted to the pillow next to him, and for a brief moment he wondered if he'd dreamed the whole encounter with Kacey. He slid out of the bed, stepping over the wad of clothes dropped on the floor, and walked out to the living room. His eyes scanned the room then drifted to the counter in the kitchen. A small piece of paper lay next to the coffee maker.

Walking over and shuddering off a chill from his naked body, he lifted the paper. In Kacey's feminine penmanship it simply read, "Thanks for last night." A small heart sat under the words– the signature she often used when they were seeing each other before. It was all too familiar. Kacey never stayed all night; she always slipped out before Drake would awaken. He never really understood why, but had gotten used to the routine. Except at this particular moment he felt a little disappointed as he put on a pot of coffee before making his way back down the hallway for a hot shower.

Chapter Nine

Iz got home later than desired. The wind had kicked back up outside and snow seemed to be certain to come before daylight. Dropping the bundled newspaper that had been tossed outside the door onto the end table that sat next to the leather couch, Iz shook out of the heavy coat and stomped off the wet boots. The warmth of the apartment was inviting. It was already nearly morning.

Might as well take a shower before doing anything else.

You haven't talked to me in a long time.

Sorry, can't talk to you at work. You know that.

I don't like it. Have to be quiet too long. Can't do it.

You have to do it, and so do I. We don't have choices like that. I have to work to feed. If we don't eat, we can't plan.

I like our plans. What's next? I want to do it again.

Iz walked down the hall and entered the bathroom that sat just off the bedroom and dropped the cold clothes to the floor one article at a time. A big sigh escaped. *It's too soon, I don't want to get caught.*

You're too smart to get caught.

No one is so smart that they shouldn't wait.

Turning on the shower, warm water flowed almost immediately, and Iz stepped over the tub into the shower and pulled the curtain tight.

Why do you always make the water so hot? It burns me.

I like it this way. Now hush. At least it's warm water.

How do you know it's too soon?

Iz had been so focused on work that checking the newspaper had been forgotten. Suddenly the shower didn't seem as important. Quickly washing and rinsing clean, Iz fought the desire to stay in the hot shower after remembering the newspaper that now laid on the end table in the other room.

Toweling off, Iz quickly pulled on sweatpants and a sweat shirt, slid on some thick athletic socks, and raced down the hallway. Sitting down on the couch, daylight was just starting to peek through the windows despite the curtains being pulled tightly closed. Iz snapped the rubber band off the end of the bundle and rolled open the paper.

The front page held nothing. There was a story about the mayor sponsoring some fundraiser and another story about the upcoming parades, but nothing about the hooker or the man found in the water duct.

Why isn't there any story?

I don't know. But maybe it's good.

Good? Why is it good? I want to read all the goodie details.

But if there is nothing then maybe it means they don't know anything.

Oh, does that mean we can do it again!!!? Yes, do it again!

Slow down. I didn't say that.

Remember all the things they did, the laughing, pushing, name calling. They stared at you, at us. I hate them, and I know you do too. We shouldn't have to put up with that any more. Don't you remember?

I remember! Okay? I do remember…everything.

Well then act like it. Grow a pair and pick the next one!

Shut up! I will! I will when I'm ready!

Iz stood and began to storm around the room. Pacing back and forth, back and forth, anger bubbled up inside and rage poured out. Beating the newspaper now held in fisted fingers against the kitchen counter, images flashed of memories from both years ago and recent taunts. People laughing, but not just laughing—oh no—mocking, constant heckling everywhere. They'd always been there, but lately it seemed as if everyone stared with an intense desire to hurt. The hatred that began when Iz was just a child now raced out of control.

Keep it together. We have to keep it together.

68

I'm sorry. You're right. Smart, so smart.

Sticks and Stones

Chapter Ten

Kacey walked into the precinct and found Drake sitting at his desk staring intently into his laptop. It was just past seven o'clock, and she knew the chief would be in soon. Drake was tapping away at the keys, and as she walked past she could see the report he was preparing.

"Good morning," she offered, a little uncertain of his reaction. She hated to leave in the middle of the night like that, as it always felt a little awkward doing so, but she's never been able to spend the night at a man's house. The idea of waking in the morning seemed too committed and formal. Drake was the only man she's really ever been comfortable with, but even with him she couldn't manage to overcome that hurdle.

He glanced up briefly, his eyes drifting down her body then back to the computer. "Good morning."

"Sorry...," she started to explain just as two other detectives walked into the room, passing by after grumbling quick morning well wishes.

Drake's broad shoulders shrugged as he waited for the others to pass. "I know your M.O." He offered a smile.

Kacey sighed in relief at his obvious understanding then leaned over his shoulder to read the report. Her hair fell forward and she took a little pleasure in realizing that he seemed to soak in the fresh fragrance of her shampoo.

Drake paused as he waited for her to read the contents, and then leaned back in his seat, both pushing into her and forcing her to stand up. "Chief isn't going to like it, but we got nothing."

"I agree, though. It seems there is no way Fields had anything to do with Parker's death, and that leaves us with no leads."

"So where do we go from here?" Drake asked spinning his chair to face her.

"I say we go through Parker's appointment book and start talking to any client he had contact with over the past month. Someone must have had it in for him."

"Or it's just random, a sadistic killer, and he was in the wrong place at the wrong time."

"Maybe, where was that place? We find that, we find our killer."

"We can follow up with Doc and the crime scene team to see if they have anything, even a fiber to go on. He didn't end up in that waterway on his own, and you can't just carry a body out in the open. So someone carried him, and maybe they carried him in something that left some trace."

At that moment the chief walked in. "Drake, James, my office."

They both stood and followed behind the giant of a man into his office. With the door secured behind them, the chief started firing off questions.

"What have we got?"

"Nothing," Kacey blurted out and then regretted it.

"Nothing? You went out to the nut house, Parker's employer, and you got nothing?"

Drake jumped in after seeing the look on Kacey's face. "We interviewed Parker's employer. He was a solid employee, well respected, he didn't have a beef with anyone. No family to speak of because…, well," he paused not wanting to add that Fields had killed them all. Continuing he added, "His clients liked him. He'd always a bit of a loner growing more isolated, especially after the death of his sister and her children."

Kacey jumped in trying to redeem herself from the prior comment, "We met with Fields. He tried to make us think he had something to do with it. Took pleasure in the story, but had nothing to offer. Random crazy rants, nothing specific. We're certain that if he was somehow the mastermind behind Parker's murder he would have taken pleasure in gloating about it. Best he could say was that he had his ways and gave random possible means that he could have killed Parker. The only thing that was close was that he suggested that one of the ways he potentially killed Parker was by burning him."

"We had the nurse check the logs. Fields has had no contact with anyone other than hospital personnel. It doesn't seem possible that he could have pulled it off, but we left it open for the nurse to contact us should he start spewing details."

The chief's eyes turned to Drake then back to Kacey. "What's next?"

"Canvas everyone on Parker's appointment list, phone logs, texts and see if anything turns up. We're heading over to Doc's to see if there are any fibers or trace on the clothes or body that might give us a clue on where he was actually murdered or how he was transported to the dump site." Drake paused waiting for more questions.

"I need to release something more to the press. They're trying to spin this up into something it's not."

"I would recommend putting it out there that it's not related to the Fields case, to slow them down."

The chief looked at Kacey. "They'll want to know how we know that."

"Tell them," Kacey replied directly, "tell them that Fields has been interviewed, and given the fact that he is in custody and does not possess the means to orchestrate such a crime, we are pursuing other leads."

"They'll want to know what leads," Drake added.

"Yes, and say you cannot elaborate on an on-going investigation, which is true and buys us some time."

The chief ran his thick hand across his chin then nodded. "Okay, but damn it, get this guy so we can stop the chaos."

Before Drake and Kacey could leave the office, the chief barked out one more question, "What about the hooker? Do we have anything on that one?"

"The locals in New Jersey were notified and are handling next of kin. The pimp, John John, was interviewed but he has a solid alibi. It could possibly have been a trick that went wrong." Drake explained and offered a theory.

Kacey added, "The meat around her neck is certainly confusing. Piece of meat as in piece of ass, maybe? Maybe a trick got too caught up on her and got pissed because she was putting out for other men. We'll get Dermot to talk to the other girls, see what he can drum up."

The chief grumbled under his breath and waved them out of the room with one hand.

"Have I ever told you how much I love working for that man?" Kacey asked as they walked down the corridor.

"Yeah, about as much as I love it." Drake replied walking by his desk and grabbing his cell phone, coat, and keys.

Over the next few days Drake and Kacey continued to follow-up on the leads from the appointment book. Everyone they spoke with only had good things to say about Parker. The press continued to try and twist the story, but it was slowly losing steam. Both Drake and Kacey were taking heat from the chief and their fellow police officers.

There was only one person, a man named Harold Sloan, they'd interviewed so far that had given them any possible motive at all–a client Parker had worked with for over three years. The man's business was failing, and it was obvious the financial stress of the situation was getting to him. He was angry, and it showed. What they couldn't figure out, though, was whether he'd blamed Parker in any way. The rotund man had been negative throughout the whole interview, but even so he'd acknowledged that Parker had been a good guy. It didn't seem that Sloan had any motive, just another dead end.

Some nights Kacey went with Drake to his apartment, and after a carry-out or delivery dinner they would spend time reviewing the case files, which would end with very passionate love making. Kacey stayed true to her M.O. and Drake would awaken in the morning to discover she'd slipped out before daylight.

Following each of these events, the next morning they would meet up at the precinct, or at Freddy's café before checking out a car from the motor pool, and continuing to seek some insight into the death of Frank Parker.

There also had been no additional information on the young prostitute or who had caused her demise. Both cases seemed to be going cold, and they were both growing more and more frustrated.

74

Chapter Eleven

Iz came home tired from a long day at work. Stopping on the way home to get something to eat had caused frustration, and after entering the apartment Iz slammed the door and muttered angry words.

Is it time yet?

I don't know! Stop badgering me! Iz shrugged off the coat and tossed it on the couch.

Well, I think it's time. You're itching to do it. I can feel it too, you know.

It's complicated. I need more space, privacy. This small apartment won't let me do it. Have to be careful.

Rent a place, a storage unit or garage.

Iz thought for a moment, pulling the food out of the brown grease-stained sack. Iz's nose wrinkled at the site. Iz was proud of being physically fit, and crappy food like this was unacceptable. Iz's rage grew. That fat guy at the counter had stared, then smiled. No, it wasn't a smile; it was a laugh. Iz had seen out of the corner of the eye, a pink tongue dart in and out of that disgusting mouth, swiping at the chili dripping down dirty fingers.

Iz had seen that guy before and was always repulsed by him. Being clean and fit was important, and disgust and disdain filled Iz with the inability to shed the memory of the guy lapping away at the sauce that covered his fat fingers. But it wasn't just the man's appearance; it was the way he looked at Iz. The pig had actually looked as if he thought he was better than Iz.

The more Iz thought of that man's smug look, the more anger brewed deep inside. *Okay, you're right. It's time.*

Yea! Gonna get us a fat one! Fat pig shouldn't have looked at you like that. Do it tonight. Can we do it tonight?

I'm not sure.

Iz began to pace, the food on the counter growing cold, the smell suddenly filtering in, driving Iz to reach for the bag and pull out the Styrofoam container. Peeling off the seal from the plastic utensils, Iz carried the food to the small table for two near the half wall that separated the living room and kitchen. As Iz ate, the anger continued to grow.

What are you going to do, Iz? Get the fatty, Iz. Get the fatty!

I'm trying to eat here. Can you quiet down, please?

You said it was time. I want to do it. Tonight!

After I eat. Now settle down.

Iz shoveled the food in, chewing aggressively as frustration grew. The flavor of the greasy food was lost in the mounting agitation. Finally, unable to keep the anger at bay, Iz threw down the plastic fork and paced back and forth across the room.

After five minutes of pacing, a headache mounting, and with the constant internal prodding, Iz snatched the coat off the back of the couch, slammed arms through the sleeves, and fisted the keys in the pockets. Moments later Iz was navigating the car through the city streets. It was after ten o'clock. The streets were nearly remiss of people. Iz pulled the car over to the side of the street to think for a few minutes. Pulling back away from the curb, the car headed towards downtown.

Iz reached and turned up the heater fan in an effort to fend off the cold.

How can you be cold? I'm too excited to be cold.

I'm always cold. You know that.

It's not nerves, is it? You aren't going to chicken out, are you?

Shut up! Just watch, okay?

Iz continued to drive the car through the dark streets, and then pulled the car up along the curb about a half a block from a rundown looking bar. With fingers tightly wound around the steering wheel, Iz prepared to wait.

The bar door opened and closed a number of times, but the people that exited were not right. Nearly an hour later, the door pushed open and a very round man walked out onto the sidewalk as he tossed a cigarette into the street. This action disgusted Iz, the anger starting to rise again.

Iz watched as the man practically waddled down the street. Passing two cars, he stopped at the third one, and Iz saw the lights flash as he reached for and then opened the door. Iz resisted the urge to pull the car out until the man started his car and moved nearly a full block away.

Deciding the car was finally a safe enough distance away, Iz pulled out and followed, keeping a good distance between them and pausing before making turns.

The man drove his car into a garage that was attached to a modest and rundown home in a small neighborhood of similar homes.

It's perfect! Go in and get him, Iz.

I have to wait a few minutes. Be quiet.

Did you see his fat ass?

Shhhhh!

He waddles when he walks. Probably thinks he's better than you. Probably thinks women want him like that. I bet he talks to them like he thinks he's all that.

I said hush!

Okay, okay, don't get all worked up.

Sorry, I just need to focus.

Sorry, I'll be quiet now.

Iz parked the car just far enough away that the house was in full view. A half an hour later all the lights went off.

Wait another thirty minutes then go in there.

I know. I've done this before, you know.

Sorry. I trust you. I'm just real excited. Make him pay for all the things they said.

I'm sorry too. I didn't mean to snap.

Forty-five minutes later Iz pulled the coat hood up, concealing face, eyes, and hair, and then stepped out of the car after slipping cold hands into doubled latex gloves and stuffing a syringe filled with 120mg of Succinylcholine a rapid paralytic agent—into a pocket of the heavy jacket. Making sure to be quiet, Iz walked towards the dark house, looked around, and stepped behind a hedge that wrapped around the front yard, and out of the view of the street lights.

Following the line of the house, Iz stopped and peered through the first window. Inside was a small room with a bed positioned between two nightstands. It wasn't possible to see the other side of the room because curtains blocked the view, but it was obvious the room was empty.

The next window was higher off the ground, and Iz recognized it as the kind typically built into a bathroom, usually positioned above the bathtub. Ignoring the window and knowing it was useless as a means of entry, Iz continued around the back of the house and into the back yard. Pausing and listening, the only sounds were those typical of the night—the buzz of the overhead electrical wires, a dog barking several homes away, the leaves rustling against the cold breeze. Feeling confident, Iz approached the back door and peered through one of the six panes that were perfectly spaced in the top half.

Inside a washer and dryer were visible in a small room. Over the appliances, cupboards hung on the wall with a longer cabinet that ran floor to ceiling against the furthest corner. There were piles of laundry scattered on the floor and stacked on top of the dryer.

Iz reached for the door knob and gave it a twist. It didn't budge, locked. Looking around, there was a pile of bricks on the edge of the patio near another very overgrown hedge. On a rusty patio table there was an old towel hanging on one of the two chairs. Iz picked up the towel, walked over and lifted the brick off the ground, and wrapped it in the towel.

Returning to the door, Iz tapped the corner of the lowest window pane to lightly and instantly break the glass, causing a brief noise and shards to fall inside. The sound was muffled as the glass landed on clothes on the floor.

Standing perfectly still, Iz waited and listened. Minutes passed with the wires still buzzing, the barking dog was quiet, and not even a cricket chirped. Iz nearly laughed at that thought, too damn cold for crickets right now.

Reaching through the broken pane and twisting the lock, Iz pushed the door inward and slid inside. Careful not to step on the glass chards, Iz waited until eyes adjusted to the lighting before moving forward out of the laundry room.

Stepping silently through the small room into a hallway, Iz looked both ways. One direction seemed to lead towards the main part of the house, the other towards bedrooms with three doorways in view, two on the left and one on the right.

Thinking back to the outside and the positions of the windows, Iz determined the two on the left were the bathroom and the empty bedroom with the bed and two nightstands. The room on the right was likely the master and certainly where the reward would be.

Iz stopped in front of the bathroom and peered inside. A small nightlight offered a glimpse of the basic room. A tub/shower combo sat at the far end, a toilet on the right, and the sink on the left. There was an assortment of medications on the small counter and clothes hung from the towel rack. A towel hung over the shower rod that was adorned with a curtain with a giant whale on it.

Ha! How appropriate!

Iz resisted the desire to respond, keeping quiet and moving on towards the room at the end. The door was open, and the sound of heavy breathing could be heard coming from inside to the left. Iz could see the end of the bed and moved in, slipping a hand inside the coat pocket and retrieving the syringe.

Stepping forward towards the bed, the sound of the carpet underneath Iz's shoes seemed to scream. But the man in the bed was out cold, as was evident by the constant snoring accompanied by the rise and fall of the blankets appearing as if they were riding the abundant girth.

Standing next to the bed, Iz stared down at the man lying flat on his back with the covers rolled just under his flabby arms exposing big, white, hunks of flabby meat. The thick rolls of the man's neck were squished under his chubby chin. Iz removed the cap of the syringe, returned it to the coat pocket, and then leaned forward and pushed the needle into the rolls of skin, pressing deeply until the syringe couldn't plunge any further. As the man woke to a start, Iz continued to depress the plunger, administering the paralytic, then quickly stepped back and watched as the drug did its work.

The man sat up and struggled under his weight to lift himself off the bed, not a very worthy opponent for a person like Iz who always remained in shape. Before he could even swing his legs over the bed, the drug began to work and the big body slumped back against the pillows, fear filled the eyes bulging from his round face.

With the paralytic fully in control now Iz finally spoke.

"I have a plan for you. You'll be famous, and you'll serve a purpose, something you never thought you'd be able to do. You'll be the example for all the others just like you. Oh, and what I have in store for you. Well, it's going to hurt. Oh yeah, it's going to hurt, but only for a while." Iz sighed and smiled then continued, "Guess we should get started. Unfortunately, we don't have all night."

Ha ha ha! This is going to be so much fun!

Yes, it is. Be quiet and watch.

"Just wait right here. I need a couple of things."

Iz turned away from the paralyzed and frightened man and returned back down the hall. Arriving in the living room, Iz's eyes scanned the room, the kitchen to the left, and the door across from the refrigerator. Iz walked towards that door while being careful to not trip over the stacks of newspapers, a random shoe, or the mismatched furniture.

Twisting the cool, brass knob and pulling inward, the smell of oil and engine grease immediately filled the air as the door swung open. Entering the garage, Iz paused and looked past the car to find the perfect items in the corner on the workbench. After scanning the floor for obstacles, Iz moved forward and collected the items before returning inside to the bedroom.

As Iz returned to the room the man's eyes darted around the room and then dropped to the items Iz carried. Despite being unable to move, it was obvious panic set in.

Iz set the items on the floor against the wall and worked at the bed sheets to completely untuck them from the mattress. Grabbing the corners at the bottom and tugging, the large man barely budged. Iz gave another pull, but despite being physically fit and strong the man's size was too much. Iz stood there and considered other options.

Taking the blanket from the top of the man, Iz laid it out flat on the floor, then went to the opposite side of the bed and rolled the man's body, rocking it side to side until it leaned fully over and fell with a loud thud on the floor.

Walking back around to where the man now lay sprawled out on the blanket, Iz grabbed the corners of the blanket again, this time dragging the huge mass across the floor. It was only a few feet to the hallway and a wooden floor that would be much easier to drag the man on.

Drag him, Iz. Don't let the fat ass slow you down.

Hush, I got this. It's just because he's dead weight.

Dead weight. Not quite yet! Ha! But soon!

Iz tugged again. This time the blanket slid across the floor, and after a few more tugs the massive man was close to the door. Iz rolled the man flat onto his stomach and moved his sprawled arms and legs flat along his body so he could fit through the door.

A few more tugs on the blanket and his body was through the door and in the hallway where the blanket slid much easier. Dragging the mass down the hall, Iz stopped in front of the bathroom door, and then twisted the man to make the turn, stopping again once the body was half in and half out of the bathroom. His head lay in front of the sink while his legs remained outside in the hall.

Iz stepped over his body and went back to the bedroom to collect the items from the garage before appearing in the bathroom again. Iz noticed pictures on the wall that lined the hallway and stopped to look at them. The photos showed the man posed with a few fishing buddies at a lake somewhere, and a couple others were taken at the bar. No apparent family.

Sad, isn't it?

Not really.

You're right. Always right.

Iz took the first item and assessed the size. Four feet was perfect. Taking the other items, Iz began the assembly, and after about thirty minutes the work was done. Iz stepped back to take in the creation.

It's beautiful.

I know.

Iz left the house repeating a whispered taunt over and over again.

Chapter Twelve

The nurse at the front desk reviewed the credentials before locking up the drawers and leading the woman down the hallway. Jessica Sperry's high heeled shoes with a narrow spike clicked as she followed the nurse, each step echoing off the hollow walls.

Random noises followed the women as they passed each door. Pathetic cries fell from somewhere back towards the desk that sounded like a howler monkey haunting and full of angst. Another person laughed uncontrollably and kept calling out "holy mackerel."

Jessica pulled at her coat, wrapping it tighter around her as if somehow that would close out the discomfort she felt in the unusual setting. She had interviewed her fair share of different sorts of people, but this might top it all. For a moment she was questioning why she had come here at all, but before she could reconsider, the nurse stopped in front of a door just near the end of the hall.

The nurse had a radio that squawked on her hip, and she fumbled with the large key ring she'd used to lock up the desk drawers. She selected a gold key and inserted it into the doorknob. "I'll have an intern join you inside. You get no more than thirty minutes, less if he gets agitated and wants you to leave." The nurse stood eyes fixed on Jessica's waiting for acknowledgement that she understood.

"I understand," Jessica said nodding her head as a deep sigh slipped from her mouth.

"You sure you want to do this?"

Jessica wanted to say no but the words coming out of her red lips defied her, "Yes, I'll be fine."

The nurse nodded, her tight bun bobbing with her head. Pushing the door open, she stepped inside. Jessica followed.

A moment later a tall, black male joined them; his muscles rippled under his white medical scrubs. Suddenly Jessica felt both relieved and concerned–relieved that such a big guy was there in case she needed someone and concerned about why she would need such protection. Trying to put that thought out of her head, she faced the man who sat in the corner rocking in a chair that faced the wall.

Jessica recognized Robert Fields from the trial. She covered that story for weeks, and while it had been one of her top stories ever, it also was the one that haunted her more than any other. She had hoped when Fields was institutionalized that she would never have to look back at those stories, and yet here she was in his room.

"Mr. Fields, I don't know if you remember me. I'm Jessica Sperry from the Channel 8 news station. I covered your trial and was hoping you might talk to me about the recent death of Frank Parker."

Fields rocked faster but still faced the wall.

"Mr. Fields, can you tell me anything about Frank Parker? I'd like to get your story before air time tonight."

Fields turned to face her in a sudden and jerky move that caused her to step backwards. A snide grin covered his face that had at least two days of hair growth. "Frank is dead!" Fields shouted.

"Yes, Mr. Fields, he is dead. I was wondering if you know anything about the circumstances that led to his death."

Fields began laughing. Laughing and rocking uncontrollably. Then suddenly he jumped up from his chair and lunged towards Jessica. She let out a short squeak as the meaty intern stepped in between her and Fields and shoved Fields back down into the chair. "Sit down, Robert, or you go into a strait jacket!"

"Frank's dead," Fields said

"Okay, you obviously don't have anything. Thanks, Mr. Fields," Jessica said turning to leave the room.

"He deserved it," Fields said. The rocking stopped as quickly as it started.

Jessica turned back to Fields. "Deserved it in what way?"

"Hypocrite, used to have sex with his sister's kid."

Jessica stood staring at the crazy man in front of her, not sure what to believe. "What are you talking about?"

"Sophie. Oh, yeah he liked her. We did her together sometimes. So, he had to die." Fields laughed a deep, hearty laugh, and he didn't stop for a good five minutes. He rocked back and forth the whole time while Jessica watched.

Finally, he seemed to be calming down and Jessica spoke, "Did you see Parker with your daughter?"

Fields looked directly at Jessica for the first time, and a grin spread over his face. His chin was wet with saliva. "I said we did her together." Stepping forward, Fields lifted his nose in the air and inhaled a deep breath. "He would have liked you too."

A shiver ran down Jessica's spine. The sick pig disgusted her, and she was ready to leave when he added. "Then he wanted her to himself, so I killed her and then I killed him."

"How?"

"I did it, but I'll never tell you or the pigs that came here the other day."

"There were police here the other day?"

With that Fields turned to the wall and resumed rocking.

Jessica waited a few moments then realized he wasn't going to offer any more. She had enough. She had captured everything on her cell phone and needed to get back to the news station to edit the details before the six o'clock news.

Chapter Thirteen

Drake walked into the precinct a few minutes before seven and found Kacey sitting at her desk, head down and pouring over the case files. Her hair was pulled back in a tight pony tail, not her typical style, and he wondered how long she'd been there.

Kacey glanced up at him as she lifted a Styrofoam coffee cup to her lips, her eyes peering over the top as she took a sip of the brew that steamed from inside. Lowering the cup and swallowing the liquid she offered, "Mornin'."

Drake threw her a crooked smile. "Looks like you have been here for a while."

"Couldn't sleep so I thought, what the hell, might as well work. You catch the news last night?"

Drake nodded. "That…," he paused refraining from the name calling he'd start to toss out. "Jillian. What was she thinking?"

"Apparently the same thing we did. Fields was a likely suspect."

Before they could carry on any further, the chief walked in—his face red, his solid jaw jutting forward. He tossed a thumb over his shoulder indicating they report to his office immediately.

They both rose at the same time and sucked in deep breaths before heading that way. They were met with stares from the two other detectives that sat at desks nearby working away on their own cases.

The chief all but slammed the door behind them, threatening the frames hanging on the wall filled with accommodations he'd received throughout the years, causing them to shake in jeopardy of falling from the wall.

"I'm sure by now you've seen the news reports." His face was red and his brow was beaded in perspiration not appropriate for the chill in the air this time of year.

Drake waited patiently for him to unload all the while wondering if his blood pressure had boiled all night while he tried to sleep. As he considered the best approach he watched the chief's body language for signs of whether to embellish in any way. He decided against that. Drake could feel Kacey's stare and knew she was sizing up the situation as well and hoped they were on the same page.

"…the freakin' mayor is on my ass for a resolution now. This case couldn't get any hotter if we stuffed a missile in it and lit a match."

Drake considered the analogy for a moment. "Sir, I think we can safely shutdown the press with the facts we have gathered."

Kacey's gaze turned to Drake, and he could feel her waiting to see where he was headed.

"Oh, yeah and what facts do we have, detective?" The chief's sarcasm was obvious.

"We know Fields has not received any visitors nor been allowed any phone calls. We pulled his financial records, and he has no financial means to pay anyone to pull off Parker's murder. It isn't feasibly possible that he has anything to do with this crime."

Kacey understood now and jumped in, "He is also heavily medicated most days and does not make much sense when you speak to him, nor could he provide any details on how the crime was committed."

"So if not Fields, then do we know who did kill Parker?"

Drake and Kacey exchanged a glance at each other before Drake continued on, "No, sir, we do not."

"So are you saying it is totally random, a pure coincidence that Parker is dead?"

"A coincidence that Parker knew Fields and is dead, yes," Kacey responded cautiously not wanting to close the lid on the theory that Fields had somehow managed to have Robert Parker killed from within the mental hospital just in case a new lead came up.

"Well, that doesn't help us much now, does it?" The chief leaned forward as his large knuckles balled up and pressed down onto his desk. He stood with his broad back arched forward and head down for a few moments, then the phone rang.

Lifting the receiver he didn't respond in his normal manner, barking into the phone, "Yeah?" There were a few moments of silence as he listened to whoever was on the other end, and then he ended the call after saying, "I'm sending a team over now."

Looking up at Drake and Kacey he shook his head. "We've got another murder, and according to the responding officer this one is real bad. What the hell is going on?" After jotting down something on the notepad, he handed Drake the slip of paper. "Get over there now."

Accepting the paper, Drake immediately turned to head out the door with Kacey quick on his heels. They returned to their desks only to grab their phones and coats, and then rushed towards the exit. Both could feel eyes on their backs as they left the squad room.

Kacey drove as Drake was on the phone getting as much detail as he could before they arrived at the crime scene. As he listened and grunted out questions he punched the address into the GPS, an unnecessary step given they both knew exactly where they were headed. Not too many streets were unknown to them.

Arriving at the location of a neighborhood with modest homes, some in better shape than others, they saw several patrol cars and yellow crime tape blocking off the sidewalk and driveway leading to the address of the home the chief had written down.

Kacey pulled the car up alongside the curb facing the wrong direction, somewhat blocking the street in an effort to reduce the onlookers which had already started to surround the sidewalks outside the yellow tape. Craig Dermot was on the inside of the tape controlling the crowd and demanding that people stay back.

Drake sighed when he saw Dermot since he did not want to deal with the arrogant officer this early in the morning. A woman sat inside a patrol car with a blanket wrapped around her. Drake could see she'd been crying.

As they approached Kacey threw on the charm. "Hey Dermot, how'd you catch this one?"

Drake felt a twinge of jealousy as he watched the two interact. For a moment he wondered if they'd ever been intimate, as images of Kacey doing things to Dermot that she'd done with him filtered through his mind in a flurry and setting off an anger he feared he wouldn't be able to hide. Deciding it might be best to step away, he turned toward the patrol car where another young officer by the name of Sparlow according to his name tag stood nearby. Drake recognized the young cop but had never really spoken to him before.

"Officer Sparlow," he greeted the twenty-something man with shining shoes and creased slacks briefly wondering how he kept his shoes that clean in this weather. "She a witness?"

Sparlow looked towards the woman, "Daughter of the victim, just came to check on him this morning. Said he'd been depressed and she was worried so she stopped by on her way to work."

"Is it possible it was suicide? You said the vic had been depressed?"

"No, sir. No way. I've never seen anything like that before."

"You catch the call?"

"Yeah, I'm riding with Dermot. We got the call about an hour ago. Came over here and shit, man, I mean..." Sparlow just shook his head.

Drake noticed the young man looked pale, pretty shook up. "Okay, thanks."

As Drake turned back to where he'd left Kacey, he saw Doc's vehicle pull up. Taking a deep breath, he walked over to Doc and was quickly joined by Kacey.

Doc got out of the car. "Sounds like this one is a doozy."

"I'm getting that feeling," Drake replied as they each ducked under the yellow tape and walked towards the front door of the house.

Drake's eyes scanned the walkway and surrounding bushes and plants. The yard was pretty rundown. The house was in obvious disrepair. The driveway was clear of any cars, and despite the cold the fractured cement had tiny hints of weeds winding through it.

As they approached the door, all three slipped on gloves before entering the house. Drake assessed the door lock and jamb. There was no sign of forced entry. He made a mental note to ask the daughter whether the door was open or closed when she got there.

Another officer took over duty of crowd patrol and Dermot followed them inside, which caused Drake to lose focus for a moment.

Dermot began to recant what they found when they arrived. "The daughter called it in. The 911 call was a mess. She was near hysterics. Rightfully so, we got her out to the patrol car while we cleared the house. Found one victim in the bathroom entry way. Hanging…well, see for yourself." Dermot waited behind the group.

Doc led the way. The living room was overly adorned with mismatched furniture. The curtains were drawn tightly closed, making it seem darker inside than it should. Both the décor and the closed in space was immediately oppressive. The hallway was typical of a home of this size in this neighborhood. Framed photos hanging haphazardly lined the wall. Kacey scanned the walls, no pictures of the woman in the patrol car outside.

"Son of a bitch," Doc said standing with his gloved hands on his hips and his eyes focused on the bathroom doorway.

Kacey could barely see around the coroner, but what she could see was unreal. Her eyes rose to the top of the door frame. She could see hands bound together with a rope and a large eye hook screwed into the frame fed another rope, and a large man hung like a spider in a web.

Doc stepped past the man, giving both Drake and Kacey a full view. Both detectives stood and stared at the unbelievable scene in front of them. A severely obese man hung, the tips of his toes barely scraping the floor, a rope was fed through a pulley system allowing the man to be suspended in the door frame. A two by four was nailed to the man's back just above the tailbone with what appeared to be a stake. The board spanned the full width of the doorway, preventing the body from swinging or crossing the threshold into the bathroom.

"What the hell?" Drake said somewhat under his breath.

Doc was still shaking his head as Kacey just stood and stared.

Drake's eyes scanned the walls around the large man. There were a few scuffs marks. His eyes rose to the jamb at the top of the door frame where the eye hook was screwed in. The wood was cracked as it seemed to be straining under the weight of the body. Drake briefly wondered what would have happened had the frame broken.

***

Kacey's eyes landed on the man's round face, once ruddy pink with years of alcohol abuse, laced with broken blood vessels in his oversized nose, now had a greyish tint. His eyes bulged from their sockets, and his tongue pushed between his fat lips that took on the look of swollen worms.

Typically strong and controlled, she fought a flush of heat that swept over her. Glancing at Drake and not wanting him to see the sweat that she could feel rising on her forehead and the flush in her cheeks, she was relieved to see the pale cast to his skin.

This was like nothing she had ever seen. Adrenaline rushed through her as her eyes scanned the rest of the body. Feet bare, toes with yellowing thick nails barely touching the floor, he wore nothing but a pair of boxers. His large stomach sagged as if suspended a foot above the linoleum floor.

Doc reached in his pocket and pulled out a small camera and began snapping pictures. A crime scene analyst arrived and began following Doc's instructions for recording the scene.

Drake and Kacey each had his and her own requests, and after the scene was properly secured they worked together to lower the body down onto the floor. They realized quickly that it would be impossible to remove the body from the house without removing the two by four from his back. It was not ideal, but Doc began the process of excising the stake from the body. With the spike out they could see it was approximately ten inches long–the type typically used for securing landscaping ties.

Drake and Kacey agreed that Drake would continue to assist with the evidence collection in the house that now focused on how the killer had gotten into the home, and if any prints could be lifted to identify the killer. Meanwhile, Kacey would go out and speak to the daughter, but before they took action Doc asked them to wait and assist with the removal of the body.

A gurney was brought into the home, and it took several people to lift the dead man off the floor for transport back to the morgue. As they rolled the body over it was then that Drake and Kacey realized they knew this man. He was one of Frank Parker's clients—the only client that potentially had an issue with Parker.

***

Drake tasted the burn of bile in the back of his throat. He could feel his pulse quicken, and for a brief moment felt a little light headed. The scene was unreal. How could anyone perform such a sick act? The man had become an ashen hunk of meat now suspended just off the ground. If Drake hadn't known for sure, he wouldn't have recognized the body as the angry client of Frank Parker. Swiping the back of his rugged hand across his forehead then running his fingers through his hair, he took a deep breath forcing himself to focus on the body as a crime scene and not a man they had met just days before nor the father of the woman sitting outside in the police cruiser struggling to come to terms with the vision of her father hanging in the bathroom doorway after having suffered an unimaginable death.

When they had arrived earlier at the scene, Dermot hadn't informed them of the victim's name during his report. Drake stared at Kacey. There was no way this could be a coincidence. Parker and Sloan's deaths were related.

"What the hell is going on?" Kacey asked.

"What's the issue?" Doc asked obviously confused.

"This guy was one of Parker's clients," Drake answered.

Doc let out a low whistle. "Looks like I've got my work cut out for me.

***

Several hours later Drake and Kacey stood once again in the chief's office briefing him on their findings and the connection between Parker and the latest victim.

"Sir, there is no doubt these two cases are somehow connected. We just have to figure out how and why," Drake offered.

"What about the girl? Any way that is connected too?" the chief barked. Dark circles encased his hooded eyes, obvious stress showing on his face.

"It doesn't appear that they are, but we'll look closely at it."

"Both were single men. Maybe one or both tended to favor hookers over committed relationships. We can start there. Maybe one of the other girls has seen them around. We'll get Dermot to go back and snoop around," Kacey offered.

"Do it and keep me posted. The mayor has called me twice today already. After that damn news report last night, and now this, he wants answers and soon. I'm going to call a press conference for tomorrow morning. Try to have me something by then. I don't want the damn FBI coming in here, but if we can't get a wrap on this we'll be forced to."

"Understood," Drake said with Kacey nodding in agreement.

Walking down the corridor without even talking to each other, both detectives naturally headed towards Janet. They needed her skills to try and find any other connections between Parker and Sloan and they needed her to see if any cash withdrawals were made against either man's bank accounts or any late night purchases in the area where Candice Jackson had worked the streets. Maybe if they could put either of them in the area they could tie these all together.

Kacey watched as Drake gave Janet instructions on the searches they needed her to conduct. She could feel a jealous pull inside as she watched Janet's overtly obvious flirtation.

Not wanting Janet to have an upper hand, she tempered her emotions and kept her facial expression and tone in her voice as she added her thoughts into the conversation in check.

Turning away from Janet after a promise of a phone call as soon as she knew anything, Kacey watched Drake from the corner of her eye. He must have noticed and looked over at her with a smile.

"What?" He inquired with a sheepish look on his face.

Kacey rolled her eyes. "Seriously?" she punched him in the arm knocking him off balance and into the wall.

"Easy, tiger," Drake said recovering from the blow.

They walked into the squad room, which was somewhat divided into sections—homicide and vice were on the north side of the room while the drug and gang division was on the south. A vice detective stood near the copy machine and nodded as they walked in. Dermot was not at his desk, but Sparlow, the cop that had partnered with Dermot earlier in the day, was working on the report from the discovery of Sloan's body.

"Hey, where is Dermot?" Kacey asked.

Sparlow looked up from the report. "Oh, hey. We just finished up with the daughter. She's a wreck, but we got her full statement captured. Dermot took her downstairs to get a patrol to take her home. He should be right back."

Dermot rounded the corner just as Sparlow finished his comment. He held a cup of coffee in his hand, and to Drake's surprise he didn't start with his typical cocky comments.

"Hey, Kacey," Dermot said as he acknowledged Drake with a toss of his head.

"Dermot, we need your help."

Dermot set his coffee cup on top of one of the many previously created water stains on the aged wooden desk next to Sparlow. He looked from Kacey to Drake and could see the seriousness in their faces.

"What's up?"

Kacey spoke, "We need you to see if you can turn over anything on the prostitute Candice. As for our other two vics, neither was married. We need to see if any of the other pros recognize either of them. We're hoping you can circulate their pictures and follow up with John John too."

Dermot gazed down at Kacey. "You think Parker and Sloan's murders are connected to the prostitute from the salvage yard?"

"Not sure, but we need to rule it out."

"Sure, you got photos for me to circulate?"

"Yeah," Drake said turning to his laptop. A couple of minutes later he handed Dermot two photographs, one of Frank Parker and one of Harold Sloan.

"We'll head out a little later. No one will be out until this afternoon. I can hit up John John first before the girls hit the streets tonight. As soon as we find anything, well, if we find anything, we'll let you know."

"Thanks," Drake offered remaining professional despite the feeling he had every time he saw Kacey talking to Dermot.

Dermot had turned off his usual annoying flirtations. Drake assumed it was because of the seriousness of a possible serial killer, coupled with the lingering visions of Harold Sloan hanging in the door frame that would likely haunt him for the rest of his life. It was a refreshing change, but one Drake was pretty certain wouldn't last. He pushed back from his chair and stood up to grab his coat off of the back of his chair. Not up to the nonsense right now, he could only be grateful for the moment.

Kacey merely gave Dermot and Sparlow a nod before collecting her coat and phone and followed Drake out the door. Typical of the duo, they didn't need to communicate, as they naturally knew what needed to be done next. Following up with Doc was imperative to learn anything that might help connect the dots. This was getting more confusing and worse, concerning. Three murders in less than a month were alarming, and the pressure was closing in like a heavy cloak, the darkness about to overcome the entire city.

***

The trip over was quiet with just minor exchanges as both Drake and Kacey worked through the details in their heads. For a brief moment Kacey reached across the seat and took Drake's hand in hers. Their eyes met, and a silent understanding was exchanged between them. Within their eyes they each mutually saw pain, worry, fear, and lack of control, but the worst thing was the knowing. Knowing that if they couldn't find out who was doing these things there would likely be more people killed.

Walking into Doc's lab took on a new feeling, one more oppressive than either detective had felt before. Now the residual feelings of failure over Sophie remained and new ones layered on top of those weighed heavier than ever before.

Doc looked up as they entered, removing his bloody gloves and throwing them into a stainless steel trash container lined with a heavy white plastic bag. He immediately pulled on a fresh pair as they approached the table containing a whale of a grayish-white colored body fileted down the middle.

"As always I could set my watch to your arrival time," Doc joked.

"Glad we could be so predictable, again" Kacey replied.

Doc looked at her over his glasses. "Well, I'm sure you want to know the nitty-gritty details. So let's get started."

Pointing to the center of the large man's chest opening, Doc moved a rolling tray over closer for their review.

"No surprise the victim had an enlarged heart. Kind of expected," he said pointing to the first dish on the tray. "Also not surprising are the liver spots likely from excessive use of alcohol. Given that he owned a bar, seems pretty normal. His lungs were also in bad shape, every indication that he was a heavy smoker." He turned over under the light the hand that lay closest to him on the table, showing the yellowish tar stains on the corpse's index and middle finger.

Kacey showed signs of impatience. "All interesting, Doc, but do you have anything that is going to help us understand who might be doing this?"

Doc pumped his hands in the air, palms down, hands flat in a "slow down" motion. "Our victim has an injection site here." He pointed to a spot on the man's flabby neck where a small red circle appeared in the crease of his neck folds. The pin prick stood out with a reddish tint against the chalky skin.

"Do you know what he was injected with?"

"Not specifically but I can speculate."

Drake could sense that Kacey was becoming more annoyed with the pace at which Doc was delivering the news. "Enlighten us."

"Well, there is a fast acting paralytic that is commonly known as SUX. It works very quick and it metabolizes just as fast as the body's enzymes break it down. It makes it tough, but not impossible to detect. It's a smart drug to use in this type of crime. I've run some tests on the metabolites to see if we can prove that was what was used. It'll take a couple of days to get the results."

Drake looked down at the large man and then back up, meeting Doc's eyes. "So he was awake throughout the...," his voice trailed off as the actual visual image of what Sloan must have gone through came to his mind.

"I'm afraid so. The torture caused his already challenged heart to fail. He had a massive heart attack. That is the actual cause of death. I'm not able to tell exactly when he died, but based on the blood vessels in and around the wound in his back where the board impaled him, I would say he was awake though unable to respond during that part. He may have died before he was suspended from the door frame, but it's impossible to know for certain."

"Any trace evidence, finger prints, anything usable?"

"The CSI team is collecting everything. I'd say the rope used to restrain him is a very common twine that can be found at any hardware store," Doc said lifting a sample of the rope from the tray. "They recovered a roll of twine in the garage seems to be an exact match. They'll check it at the lab."

Kacey, who had remained quiet throughout the description of the injection site, now spoke in an almost demanding manner, impatience laced in her tone. "Are you trying to tell us this is an opportunity killer? He came to the house unprepared? There was no plan when he walked into the house? Given the manner in which Sloan was killed and that he has a connection to Frank Parker, that seems completely impossible. There has to be something here." She waved her hands over the body.

"Maybe he'd been in the home before and knew there would be the items he needed," Doc offered with a mild shrug. "I suppose that is for you detectives to figure out."

"Seriously? Rope, pulleys, landscaping ties, he just got lucky?" Kacey rested her hand on her hip shaking her head.

Drake sought out one of the CSI analysts in the adjacent lab, "What are you finding? Are the items common enough that he could have brought them with him and they just happen to match?"

"Well, there weren't any matching pulleys in the garage, so either he used what was here or those are items he may have brought with him. There were more of the landscaping ties in the garage so those along with the rope seem to be items of opportunity," the analyst explained.

Doc reached for the rope having followed Drake into the lab, "While this is a very common kind of rope, the ends are a perfect match. The rope used to suspend the victim was cut for the purpose." Doc showed them the rope ends allowing them an opportunity to view them under a microscope.

The analyst spoke up again, "The board is a standard two by four and, was literally nailed to his back. The nails were ten-inch landscaping stakes. I know you saw them when you were at the house. Both boards and stakes were recovered by the CSI team in the garage, so it would seem your killer just helped himself to supplies found in the garage."

Drake spoke up again turning his question back to Doc, "How hard is it to get your hands on the paralytic?"

Doc thought for a moment then shook his head slightly as if uncertain. "It's used pretty commonly in surgery and lethal injections."

"Lethal injections?" Kacey seemed stunned.

"It's one of the three drugs in the cocktail used in some lethal injections."

"I should tell you that even if we find evidence of SUX it's tough to hold up in court. Both metabolites, succinic acid and choline, are natural constituents of the human body. A good defense attorney will be able to get it thrown out."

"Where can someone get it?" Drake pressed further.

"Obvious places like hospitals, veterinarians, prisons that perform lethal injections via cocktail. There is a cheap generic that can be bought over the internet and, like almost anything, the street."

"Oh, great, so basically anywhere," Kacey said in a very exasperated voice.

"I'm afraid too many to make it easy to track it down."

"What about the impaling?" Kacey asked trying to not allow her frustration to show.

"Well, it's interesting. Give me a hand," Doc said walking them back to the stainless steel table where the body lay, handing them each a pair of gloves while indicating the need for assistance in rolling the body on its side.

It took some effort even with all three of them to roll the large man over where the back was exposed.

"Maybe there's something symbolic with the impaling," Kacey said. "Could our guy be impotent and that was a symbol of penetration?"

Drake and Doc looked at her then back down at the two holes in the back where the spikes had once been.

"Maybe, so we need to look for every impotent man in the city. That should be easy enough," Drake said as sarcasm filled his voice.

* * *

Back at the precinct Drake and Kacey returned to their desks momentarily to gather all their files. A few minutes later they settled into a medium sized room containing a rolling white board on one side that spanned fifteen feet long and four feet high. Drake began on one end of the board drawing out the timeline starting with the death of Sophie, the trial of Robert Fields, and the date of discovery of each of the bodies and the estimated time of death.

Kacey spent the first few minutes at her computer and then left the room for several minutes returning with photos of each of the victims including Sophie, Frank Parker, Candice Jackson and Robert Fields. As the segments of Drake's timeline became complete, she added the photos in the respective locations.

An hour later they had the investigation board populated with specific events from their case files. Stepping back, they stared at the pictorial view, and for a brief moment their eyes each paused on the sweet face of young Sophie.

"What do we know?" Drake asked.

"We know Fields killed Sophie. That is a fact," Kacey answered pointing at the photos.

Drake drew a line between the photos of Sophie and Fields.

"We know John John has an alibi and really had no motive. The girl was producing for him so unless we believe that he hired or ordered her to be killed we can eliminate him as a suspect. Plus, there is no tie between him and any of the other victims that we've found so far."

Kacey's comments reminded Drake that Janet was supposed to be working on connections between Parker, Sloan, and Candice Jackson, the prostitute that had been killed by the dogs. Pulling his phone from his pocket, he punched in a few numbers and waited as Kacey watched.

"Janet, hey, it's Drake. I know you said you would call, but we have got to find something soon. I'm hoping you've worked your magic."

Kacey turned back to her computer and pulled up area maps. After a few minutes she selected what she wanted and sent files back to the printer, leaving the room again to retrieve them.

When she returned Drake was no longer on the phone. He was adding details to the white board from the interviews they had conducted or facts Doc had provided. She went to the right side of the board where a section was clear and began taping up an enlarged map of the city. Using a dry erase marker and red stick on dots she added the key locations, where the bodies had been found, and where Fields had held and tortured Sophie. She added numbers next to each in the order of events.

Drake glanced over at Kacey. Just as the map was nearly complete, footsteps sounded in the hallway outside, and by the sound the shoes made on the floor, it was obvious they were about to be joined by the chief and at least one more person. He raised his eyebrows as a sign of heads up then returned to applying the facts from within the files.

The room suddenly seemed much smaller as the chief and two other people entered the room. Drake recognized one as the district attorney, but the other person was not familiar to him.

"Drake, James," the chief barked as he closed the door behind him. "I think you both know District Attorney Matt Wilson." Not waiting for an acknowledgement he continued, "This is A.D.A. Billie Seals," he said using the abbreviated termed used for assistant district attorneys. "I wanted to give them a briefing, especially since this seems to keep coming back around to the Fields case."

Seals stepped forward and extended her hand to both Drake and Kacey. "It's nice to meet you, detectives," she said in a confident manner, her voice raspy and matching her tall thin frame, large blue eyes, and full lips.

Kacey found herself resisting the desire to look at Drake to see his response to the sudden beauty who had just entered the room.

"Walk us through what we know," the chief requested, seeming anxious to get the pleasantries of introductions over.

"...and we've got one of our guys going back out after dark with photos trying to see if any of the girls on the street can make a connection between Parker and Sloan and the dead prostitute Candice Jackson." Drake wrapped up the explanation both he and Kacey had shared in delivering.

"What has our analyst given us?" the chief asked.

"I just spoke with her a few minutes prior to you coming in. She's still working on it but so far there is no linkage between any of the victims. Bank and credit card records show no common transactions. The only link so far is Sloan was Parker's client, and other than Parker being Fields's brother-in-law we really don't have any connection between them either."

The chief grumbled as Wilson and Seals stepped closer to the board and studied the crime scene photos. Turning back to the group Wilson asked, "Do we need to call in the FBI?"

And here it was—the moment Drake and Kacey had been dreading. Kacey started to answer, but before she could say anything the chief held up his hand with the large palm facing out. "Not yet. Given the timeframe between crimes, we have about a week before we have to start thinking hard about more resources if we still have nothing. We don't need another body in Doc's lab."

Wilson reluctantly agreed to allow the time the chief asked for, but before leaving and taking the sultry A.D.A. Billie Seals with him, he offered a single word of caution, "Mayor."

The chief glanced briefly at each detective before following the attorneys out of the room, leaving Drake and Kacey alone again to continue to work in silence.

"This day just keeps getting better," Kacey said her voice laced with frustration and sarcasm.

"It sure does," Drake responded, and for the first time all day they both smiled.

The smiles didn't last long though as they returned their eyes to the grisly photos taped to the long white board in front of them.

It was after midnight when they were pulled away from the files as Dermot walked into the room. His eyes scanned the board, and his typical cocky self was back as he said, "Looks like you two need my help." Arrogance spilled from his mouth.

"What's up, Dermot," Kacey said, her voice permeating with a strength she almost always used when talking to the cocky young cop.

"Well, I've been across town talking to the working girls and...," he paused, a big grin spread over his face, showing of a mouth full of white teeth.

"And...?" Drake said with an obvious annoyance in his tone.

"Nobody has seen either one of your victims."

"Yeah, and they are always so honest," Kacey replied.

"Well, I think they were being straight up. The girls are scared and that pimp is a punk."

"All the more reason they may have lied."

Dermot stood as the smile slowly vanished from his face, his confidence obviously fading. To compensate for his lack of assurance, he stepped into a more comfortable role. "Hey, Kacey, want to grab a beer? Get away from all these photos for a while?"

"You wish," Kacey countered and laughed out loud.

"Well, when you change your mind let me know."

"Don't hold your breath."

Dermot turned and left the room after throwing a glance over his shoulder to Drake.

Drake shook his head then smiled at Kacey. "That guy is a real piece of work."

Kacey smiled. "Ya' think?" She stretched her lean body, pushing her arms behind her back and lacing her fingers together.

Drake walked over to her. "We need to rest. Come to my place?"

Kacey looked up into Drake's eyes. "Yeah, let's go. Tomorrow is another long day."

An hour later Kacey stepped out of the shower at Drake's apartment and slid her naked body under the sheet and pressed her skin next to Drake's strong, muscular frame.

Drake's arm snaked around her and pulled her near. His lips nuzzled the back of her neck, and he gently kissed her shoulder. She pressed into the warmth of his body and moments later they both fell into a deep sleep.

A rustling sound woke Drake, and he rolled over rubbing at his eyes to catch a glimpse of Kacey pulling on her blouse. Her hair shined even in the mild light that came through a slit in the curtain.

"Kacey, where are you sneaking off to?"

Leaning back over the bed she placed her warm lips on his. "I've got to get home so I can get a change of clothes. Meet me at the diner in the morning, and I'll buy you breakfast."

"Morning? It is morning," Drake replied glancing at the clock on the nightstand. The digital display read 4:20am. "Come on, climb back in," he persuaded, teasing her lips with his tongue.

"Oh, so tempting." After a long kiss she pulled away. "Six thirty. See you there." She turned, slipped through the door, and disappeared. Drake rolled over fisting his pillow under his head.

Chapter Fourteen

Work had been hard the past few days. The hours had been long and right now all Iz wanted to do was lay down, but there was a pressing restlessness inside that wouldn't allow it.

Iz, are you okay?

I'm fine, just tired.

What should we do about it?

Not much we can do about it.

Those pulleys sure were handy. That really made the whole experience the best ever.

I know it was great, wasn't it?

You made him pay. So smart, need to do it again.

Slow down. I have to be careful. If we go too fast, we'll get caught.

You can't get caught. Too smart to get caught.

Everyone can get caught. If I'm not very careful I'll get caught. We'll get caught. We can't take those kinds of chances. You have to be patient and trust me.

I do trust you.. It's just so fun finally making them pay.

Besides, the next one is going to take some time. You had a good idea the other day. We need a private place outside the city to do the next one.

I had a good idea?

Yeah, remember when you said we needed a storage building? Well, I'm thinking something like that. Maybe a barn or a large shed. I have a really good idea for the next one, but it's going to take some special work to pull it off.

This sounds so fun. Can I go with you when you look for the place?

That's kind of a dumb question, don't you think?

Oh, yeah I guess so. Sorry.

I'm hungry. Gonna grab the newspaper and then go out and get some breakfast.

Oh, that sounds good. I'm hungry too.

Iz went into the other room, plucked fresh clothes from the closet while dropping dirty ones in a pile on the floor before stepping into the hot shower.

Iz, I wish you didn't work so late.

As the shower blasted down, Iz tried not to be annoyed.

Why?

I miss you when you are at work. It's so quiet and night time is when we get to have the most fun.

I know but I have to work, you know. How will we pay the bills, buy food?

The mention of food reminded Iz of the hungry feeling again. Finishing up the shower and toweling off, Iz stepped out onto the floor mat and quickly dressed, tucking in the shirt, sliding on a leather belt, and pulling on work boots that had been abandoned only a couple of hours prior.

An hour later Iz walked into a cafe just a few blocks from the apartment. Inside people occupied many of the tables. Iz picked a booth in the back against the wall. The restaurant smelled thick of bacon and toast, causing Iz's stomach to grumble.

Iz tried to remember for a second when was the last time they'd eaten. Unable to recall it, Iz watched closely as the server poured a dark cup of coffee and began to formulate the plan for the next big payback. Unfolding the paper, Iz turned to the classifieds and began to scan looking for the perfect place—a place private, but with easy access to the city.

Chapter Fifteen

Drake walked into the diner, already a buzz with early morning risers. His eyes scanned the room. Two beat cops sat near the door. He gave them a quick nod. He spotted Kacey talking to Dermot and felt his stomach knot up, then chastised himself for letting that pain in the ass get to him. After all, it had been his bed that Kacey had been laying in just a few hours ago.

As he walked forward his eyes met Kacey's, and any feelings of insecurity washed away. She had the sly look on her face that told him she was totally messing with Dermot. A sport for her to torment him. Amusement danced in her eyes.

Dermot turned as he followed Kacey's eyes. "Well look what the cat dragged in," Dermot said to Drake. "Guess I gotta run. Hey, let me know if you need any more help on your case." He slapped Drake on the back as he walked out.

Drake shook his head sliding in next to Kacey on the opposite side of the booth. The waitress appeared from nowhere and automatically poured his coffee, aware of his desires from so many prior mornings just like this one. He nodded his thanks and took a quick sip of the hot drink. The liquid slid over his tongue, and it reminded him of the hot kiss Kacey had delivered just before leaving his apartment.

"Good morning," he said after swallowing the rich fluid.

"Good morning, to you."

He could tell she was in a good mood and relished the moment, knowing when they got to the precinct that would likely change for both of them.

"Wish you could have stayed. It was cold in my bed without you." He smiled across the table at her.

"Yeah, well, I couldn't much show up in the exact same clothes, now could I? We certainly don't need rumors swirling about us."

"No, we don't. The chief would bounce one of us off the case without batting an eye."

Deciding to take a chance on something he'd never attempted before he asked, "Why don't you leave a few clothes over at my place? You can't be getting enough sleep."

Kacey studied him for a moment, but he was unable to read her eyes. There seemed to be a mixture of uncertainty, skepticism, and maybe even a little sadness.

"I'll think about it," she finally responded.

"What more could a guy ask for?"

The waitress reappeared with two plates of food and set them down in front of each of them. "Your usual—hot, sticky and sweet," she said pulling a couple of extra napkins out of her pocket and placing a dispenser filled with syrup down in front of Kacey.

Kacey smiled and said, "You know how to make a girl happy."

"Well, I don't know how you keep your little figure. If I ate what you do I'd weigh three hundred pounds." With that comment hanging in the air the matronly server turned and walked away only to return a few moments later with a fresh coffee pot, which she used to refill both of their cups.

Grateful for the refill, both detectives couldn't help but acknowledge that the comment, however innocent, from the waitress having no idea the impact of her words caused the mood to suddenly take a turn. The case seemed to sit on the table right between them. They could no longer simply relish in the comfort they'd enjoyed hours before, the comment was a giant reminder that they had a three hundred plus pound dead man's killer to track down.

Both ate in what seemed like more of an obligation than desire. Kacey finally spoke. "Any word from Janet?"

Drake shook his head. "Nothing." He glanced at his watch. "It's early. If we don't hear anything by eight, I'll call her."

Two other cops walked in and took a table nearby. Drake looked over and saw that one of them was Sparlow, the young cop that was with Dermot at Sloan's house. He had color back in his face, but he looked away when they made eye contact. Drake imagined it would take him a long time, if ever, to forget the scene at that house.

An hour later with full stomachs and back inside the precinct the pair decided to go up and see Janet directly rather than wait any longer. As they approached it was obvious Janet had been there quite a while and was deep in thought concentrating on her computer intently. She looked up but failed to flirt with Drake as she normally would. Drake looked over at Kacey with concern on his face. It seemed he realized the buxom blonde wasn't her usual self too.

"Janet, is there a problem? Did you find something?" Drake asked.

Janet looked at him and feigned a smile then glanced over at Kacey before speaking. "Good morning. I couldn't sleep. There was just something that was bugging me about all this. You know, with Fields, Parker, the girl, and now Sloan. I kept spinning around and around with it and then I had a thought, so I had to just come back in and work to figure it out."

"And…?" Drake added a hint of frustration in his voice.

"Well, it's not really much but there is something that seems a little strange." Janet stood and motioned for them to follow her. She walked along the tiled corridor until she led them into the room where they had set up the investigation board. Walking up to the board, she pointed at Fields. "Okay, so we all know that Robert Fields shouted out at the two of you in the court room."

Kacey nodded. "That was pretty publicly captured all over the news, so?"

"Well, Frank Parker was his brother-in-law and you interviewed him during the case. He also publicly blamed the police—you guys—for not getting his niece out of that home alive."

"Okay, still not following," Drake said with irritation growing in his tone.

"Then we have Sloan. You also interviewed him right before his death. I read your interview notes. He was a bit nasty with the two of you. Angry at the world, it would seem."

"Yeah, he was broke and tired." Kacey replied, one hand resting on her hip as she pulled her hair back away from her face.

"The part that was bothering me was the prostitute. She didn't seem to fit in, yet the timing was just too…well, ironic, I guess. The irony wouldn't let me sleep. So I came back and looked up her past arrest record. I had just gotten to it when you came in."

Again Drake asked, letting out a heavy sigh, "And…?"

"Well, there was nothing in the notes of the arresting officer that seemed to tie anything together, but I found something. The desk sergeant made a notation on her file. I guess while she was in holding, you were dropping someone off to booking. When you walked by she said something to you through the cell. The note says she yelled out 'hey pig, hey ugly bitch'."

Turning to Kacey, Drake asked, "Do you remember her, Kacey?"

Kacey stepped up to the board where the photo of Candice Jackson was taped next to the other victims. She stared at the photo. The picture was the one from Candice's driver's license. It showed a young, pretty, and clean girl.

Kacey shook her head. "People in the pen say stuff all the time when we walk by. I usually just ignore them."

"So you're trying to say that in some strange way all these people are connected to *us*?" Drake asked, staring at Janet in disbelief.

"I'm afraid so." She continued on, "It could just be coincidence, but it does potentially tie all of these to one killer."

Drake nodded. "Okay, thanks, Janet. Is there anything else?"

"No," she replied seeming almost apologetic. "There weren't any credit card purchases or bank accounts that tied Parker or Sloan to each other in any way we didn't already know, and Candice didn't even have a credit card account."

Drake thanked her again before she turned and left the room, leaving Kacey and Drake alone. "Why do I feel like she is trying to tie this thing to me?"

"I think she is saying this 'thing' is tied to us somehow."

"So are we back to Fields somehow doing this from inside the sanitarium?"

Drake pushed his strong hand through his hair. "We need to go back out there this time with a warrant to search his room and interview every staff member."

"We'd better fill the chief in. This is a pretty big suggestion, and if someone is targeting us for some reason he'll want to know that."

After updating the chief the two detectives were on their way to the district attorney's office to pick up a warrant granting them access to search Robert Fields's personal effects and his room. They also intended to interview every employee at the mental hospital. If Fields hadn't had any visitors other than them and Jessica Sperry from Channel 8 news then the only possible way Fields could be directing these murders was for someone to be aiding Fields from within the hospital. It was up to them to figure out who that person was and the interviews needed to include any outside services as well. If the hospital had a contract for janitorial, laundry services, or any other services that could even possibly have had contact with Fields, they would need to speak with them too.

Before leaving for the DA's they stopped back by Janet's and asked her to pull a complete list of the sanitarium employees' active badges, including those that were from outside companies. Before they arrived at the sanitarium that information would be in their email boxes.

It finally felt like they had a lead. Even though they didn't know specifically who they were looking for, it seemed like they were on the right track. And possibly within the list Janet would soon provide, somewhere lurked their killer.

Chapter Sixteen

Iz, when can we do it again? It's been a long time.

I've already got it figured out. After I clean up, we are going to take a drive. I've got a place picked out. Just have to take a look at it to be sure it's just right.

Oh, can't wait, can't wait. Let's go, Iz. Let's go now.

Shhh...hold on. I need to clean up.

Thirty minutes later Iz collected the keys that had been dropped on the table after work and walked out the front door. The car sat in its usual spot right in front of the apartment door. Iz got in and backed out after firing the engine. With eyes focused on the road, the car turned north and soon entered the highway entrance. The wheels hummed as they glided over the road. Iz reached out and turned on the radio, and music filled the car. Iz smiled and tapped fingers against the steering wheel.

Where we going, Iz?

The country. About ten miles outside of the city. We'll be there soon.

Don't you need the GPS?

Not safe. Can't put this address into the car. Have to be careful and make sure there is no way to trace this to us.

You're so smart, Iz. Always smart. Are we there yet?

Settle down. We're almost there.

Iz exited the highway and turned left at the end of the ramp, then followed directions that had been carefully written on the piece of paper lying on the console in between the seats. It obviously would have been easier to take a cell phone and use GPS but Iz knew that would leave a trail and Iz never left a trail.

About a mile ahead Iz turned the car left once more and then wound through two curves in the road and turned onto a dirt drive. At the end of the lane a big, red barn sat in a pasture surrounded by large oak trees.

A cynical smile crossed Iz's face again. This was even better than expected. Total privacy to do all the things that still needed to be done.

Iz pulled the car to a stop just in front of the barn and exited the vehicle. Standing in the early morning light, a brisk northerly wind forced gloved hands to pull at the collar of the leather jacket. Cautious eyes scanned the pasture and tree line before stepping forward.

The barn had two large rolling doors that rode on a glide rail at the top with a locking pin in the middle that brought them together. The locking pin had a hasp suitable for a padlock. Another smaller walk through door sat on the east side of the two larger doors. Iz walked forward and turned the knob. Unlocked. Pushing the door inward, Iz was greeted immediately by the sweet and musky scent of hay.

Iz fumbled around inside the door on the wall searching for a light switch, and after finding one flipped it into the on position and was immediately greeted with a flood of lights showering down from the beams up high. Wings of a startled sparrow that had been nesting somewhere up in the rafters now flapped overhead. Dust cast small sparkles from particles floating in the air.

The barn was large and held four stalls suitable for horses on each side of the aisle that stretched in between. To the right, a set of wooden steps led to a second floor hayloft. It appeared to be about half full of aging bales.

Iz walked the length of the barn, opening each stall and fingering the assortment of tools that remained abandoned inside. A leather bridle hung frayed and brittle inside one stall. A pitch fork stood propped against a wall of another.

At the far end several farm implements remained stored, rusted from non-use, including two that Iz recognized—a disc with its round sharp plates and a plow with its tines slightly gouging the dirt floor. An old tractor was parked nearby. Iz approached and stepped up, grabbing the steering wheel and swinging into the seat. A nostalgic feeling swept over as a gloved hand reached for the key that dangled from the ignition almost begging to be turned.

To Iz's surprise the engine turned over, but failed to fire. Gloved hands played over the various knobs remembering the purpose of each one. The bucket loader sat flat on the ground, stretching out in front, but had the ability to raise up about fifteen feet in the air.

It needs gas and a good charge.

Probably, but at least it turns over. It might come in handy.

Stepping back down off of the machine, Iz returned to the front of the barn and climbed the steps up to the second level. A barrel hung suspended off the floor by two ropes that ran through a pulley system allowing them to be pulled and forcing the barrel to rock. A saddle was mounted to the barrel, stirrups dangling on either side. Iz smiled, realizing some children had certainly had fun riding that thing.

The hay, though perfectly stacked, showed signs of age, as they were brown in color rather than green when freshly baled. At the end of the barn overlooking the large rolling doors was another smaller door that was held closed by a hasp lock, the obvious point of entry for the hay conveyor.

The sparrow flew out from its nest wildly flapping it wings before returning to its roost once again. Iz could see the small female peeking out of the perfectly crafted nest, and for a moment wondered if she was protecting her young.

Don't worry, I won't be bothering you.

Climbing back down the stairs to the main floor, Iz walked over to the big doors and gave a hard tug on one side. The door groaned with lack of use but gave in and rolled away, letting the morning light in. After giving a tug to the other side, soon both doors were rolled back to give way to ample space to pull the tractor, car, truck, or even a horse trailer inside.

It's perfect, Iz.

Yes, it is.

Iz's eyes landed on the wall next to the open doors, eyes scanning the large array of farming tools, including some pulleys that reminded Iz of the night at the fatty's house. Excitement swept over Iz's body. Those pulleys would help out sometime soon. Iz could picture the perfect scenario. The big doors closed easier than they had opened. The grease in the wheels would soften with each pull.

Iz took one more look around before turning off the lights. Just before exiting Iz picked up an old gas can that sat near the door, and then stepped back outside into the cold morning light.

Turning onto the highway, Iz's mind raced with excitement. The next event was going to be epic.

The sun had come up now and Iz could see a gas station in the distance. Glancing at the time and deciding it was late enough Iz took the exit and pulled into the station. A pay phone stood next to a door marked restroom. Iz exited the car after digging for some coins in the ashtray and grabbing the piece of paper from the console. Picking up the phone Iz deposited the change and punched in the numbers from the paper into the keypad.

The phone rang twice before a man's voice answered. "Hello?"

"Yes, is this Derek?"

"Speaking."

"I spoke to you a few days ago about the farm land you have for lease. I just came from there, and it's exactly what I'm looking for. I would like to secure the lease. I can send the application and a money order tomorrow via FedEx."

"Oh great, I'm glad it's going to work out. I'll look for it. What name is going to be on the lease?"

"The name? Yes, the name is Colton Drake."

Chapter Seventeen

It was after noon by the time Drake and Kacey arrived at the mental hospital. The large mansion, ominous in its own right, loomed at the top of the lane. More ominous was the variety of crazed and dangerous personalities within. Dread filled the car and was masked only by the excitement of possibility. Finally there was hope of narrowing in on a suspect.

Drake parked the car in one of the visitor spaces near the front of the building. Exiting the vehicle, the detectives walked in silence up the walkway and through the doors to be greeted by an unsettling mixture of cold and warm air.

A different attendant than the one they'd met before sat at the front desk. As they approached each produced their badges to the fifty-something man. Drake pulled out the warrant they'd gained to grant them access to Fields's personal effects and room, as well as access to interview employees.

The man looked over his round rimmed glasses after carefully reading the document. "I'll need to get Dr. Ward. He's our psychiatric director. Give me just a few minutes." Turning his chair, the man reached for the phone on the desk beside the computer screen and pushed a couple of buttons, and then spoke quietly into the receiver.

He placed the handset back in the cradle and peered over his glasses again. "Dr. Ward will be with you in just a moment. If you'd like to have a seat," he waved his hand towards a small waiting area to the right of the doors.

"Thank you," Drake offered as he and Kacey stepped back from the desk. Neither made any move towards the waiting area, drawing a frown from the blue eyes that continued to watch them over the tipped glasses.

Several minutes later a tall, slender man approached from a room behind the lobby desk. The man extended his arm and took each detective's hand in a firm handshake. Kacey quickly assessed the man. He wore casual attire—jeans complimented with a buttoned up dress shirt and loafers—all an apparent attempt intended to make the patients comfortable. On his left wrist was a Rolex that spoke of money; it was the only give away that he was different. His smile was perfectly white, yet there was a subtle nervousness that most people would never have caught.

Drake spoke first. "Dr. Ward, thank you for accommodating us. I'm Detective Colton Drake, and this is Detective Kacey James. We have a warrant allowing us access to inspect Robert Fields's room as well as any personal effects he possesses. Additionally, we would like to interview your employees."

"I certainly will accommodate in any way that I can. I do need to respect the patient/doctor relationship, however."

"Yes, we totally understand that. We are more interested in what Fields may be hiding and potentially who he might have been interacting with on your staff."

Glancing between the two detectives the doctor answered, "He would have interacted with most of the staff at one point or another. Whether they merely gave him meds or cleaned his room, or assisted during therapy."

"Doctor, what is the background record process for hiring your staff?"

The doctor relaxed his stance a little and leaned back on his left leg slightly. "Everyone goes through a complete federal and state background check, as well as drug testing before being able to start work here."

"Have you had any recent turnover?" Drake continued to probe in the path Kacey had opened.

"The last person that left was over four months ago. It was an intern that was with us for over fifteen years, and she retired."

"How old was she?" Kacey asked.

"She was turning sixty-two."

Drake and Kacey exchanged a knowing glance. The retiree was a highly unlikely suspect. While neither was a profiler, they'd worked enough cases to know a serial murderer was likely somewhere between twenty-five and forty-five, and while not entirely impossible, the killer was likely a male.

"Have any of your employees either taken a strong interest in Fields or had any employment issues, especially of late?" Kacey asked, wanting to zero in on the employees that might be involved with Fields, so as they conducted interviews they were going after the ones most likely to be suspects. She put emphasis on time being of the essence. Their killer would likely kill again, and she felt certain they didn't have much time.

Dr. Ward thought for a moment. "Honestly, other than myself and the daytime interns, no one has taken a particular interest in Robert Fields. He's...well, difficult for sure. That isn't always something everyone is suited to deal with."

"What is *your* particular interest in Fields?" Drake said with a slight emphasis on the word *your*, a question that undeniably was pointed with intent.

The doctor's demeanor changed slightly; his relaxed stance shifted to being squared off, feet shoulder width apart. "I'm the directing physician in this hospital. In my capacity I meet with the patients, some more than others. My focus sits squarely with the most severely mentally challenged. Robert Fields certainly fits that criteria."

"Aren't all the patients here severely ill?" Kacey pushed, curious to see how he would take the challenge.

Ward paused. "Yes...but, there is some variation. Not all of the patients are murderers. Some will likely be rehabilitated, while others will not. Robert Fields will likely not be rehabilitated."

Curious to proceed with the line of questioning, Drake asked the next question, "Then why bother? Wouldn't it make more sense to expend your talents in a manner that can be successful?"

"One might think so, and at times I ask that same question myself, but let's just say I personally like a challenge. If I can find a way to reach Robert Fields then there is possibly hope for many others throughout the world."

Kacey started to speak, but before she could open her mouth the doctor held up his well-manicured hand. "I know what you're going to say. That all sounds very romantic and arrogant. I would agree, but I became a psychiatrist with an interest in truly learning how a person becomes so incredibly damaged. Call me romantic if you want, but I believe there is a key...an answer. And why can't I be the one that discovers it?"

Drake and Kacey refrained from exchanging another glance, knowing it would only raise the doctor's suspicions, but they both knew this level of arrogance was exactly the type of self value the suspect would possibly possess.

Drake wasted no more time. Within minutes he had questioned the good doctor on his whereabouts on the dates the victims had been murdered.

Without answering, the doctor turned and motioned for them to follow him into the room behind the lobby counter. They found themselves in a large office with several abstract paintings on the walls. The desk was made from a rich mahogany. A large leather desk mat sat squarely in the middle with a laptop centered. A matching pen and pencil holder, stapler, and tape dispenser adorned the desk all perfectly positioned. Two file folders lay on the right corner of the desk, but otherwise nothing was out of order anywhere in the room. Organized, meticulous, perfect.

Ward flipped opened the laptop. "What dates were you asking about?"

Drake recited the dates one by one. In each case the doctor responded that he would have been at the hospital during the day. He had several appointments with patients throughout each of the days. As for the nights, his answer for each was that he would have been home with his two dogs, with no one to confirm his whereabouts.

"Doctor, one last question before we move on to Fields and other interviews." Kacey knew she was pushing but needed to understand this man. "So, you are single. It seems unusual, a talented professional man like you."

The doctor's eyes narrowed a bit, but a sly smile expanded over his face, hazel eyes glistened, white teeth displayed. "Detective, I could probably ask a similar question of you. From the lack of a ring on your finger I would say that you too find it hard to balance relationship and profession."

Ward turned to Drake, his smile persistent. "Same for you, I believe. Work consumes some of us. My guess, we have all fallen victim to it. So to fully answer your question, Detective James, I am single. Nearly married once, several years ago. I guess it just wasn't in the cards. The career won. I suspect, like you, I am a workaholic."

Kacey's cheeks burned, and she hoped the doctor couldn't see.

"Thank you, Doctor. I know this can be uncomfortable, but we must ask these questions."

"I understand, and no offense has been taken." Ward glanced over at Kacey and displayed his picture perfect smile once again, a smile that unsettled her.

Drake's phone buzzed against his hip. He held up a finger as he swiped his finger across the screen and raised the phone to his ear.

"What have you got for us, Janet?"

Kacey watched as Drake listened. His eyes met hers and offered a reassuring smile. Kacey smiled back then glanced back at the doctor who stood waiting patiently on the other side of his pristine desk, that strange smile still plastered on his face.

Drake said thanks and clicked a button on the phone to end the call.

"Doctor," Drake said turning back to face Ward, "We have a list of employees that we will need to meet with. We assume they will each be cooperative."

The smile faded from Ward's face briefly, and then as if he realized the facade had slipped, he reapplied it again. "Of course, I don't believe there will be any problems."

"Great. Give us a few minutes. We'll let you know the order we'd like to talk with people. We'd also like a place to talk with them privately, and we really don't want them forewarned if we can avoid it."

"I can arrange all of that for you."

"First though, we want to search Fields's room and see all of his personal effects."

"I'll have someone escort you now. It will take just a moment to secure Fields."

"We'd like him to be in the room while we conduct the search."

"I'm not sure that is a good idea," Ward said. "It may upset him unnecessarily."

Kacey quickly responded, "With all due respect, Doctor, we have someone out there killing people, and there seems to be a strong possibility that it is connected to Fields. So I'm not sure him being upset is our biggest concern right now."

"I understand, Detective...James, but it is my responsibility to protect him."

"It's not our intention to upset Fields, and we will do everything possible to not let that happen, but his presence is needed."

"Alright, I'll let him be in the room, but if he gets upset, he'll have to be moved."

Fifteen minutes later with Fields in a strait jacket, Drake and Kacey entered the room. Fields rocked wildly until he saw them. Suddenly the rocking came to an abrupt stop and a twisted grin crossed his face.

"How is that hard on, Detective Drake?" Fields asked, the rocking resuming and crazy heckling spewing from his mouth as saliva spilled from the side.

Drake stiffened but stayed focused on what they were there for. He was not going to allow Fields to get the best of him. Ignoring the wild rocking and the slobbering and wild crazy laughter, Drake began looking through the minimal items in Fields's room. For his own protection there wasn't much. The room furnishings consisted of a bed and dresser. The bed had a mattress and a minimal welded frame. On the opposite side of the room there was a small three drawer dresser. It was bolted to the wall, plain with no mirror. There was a closet in the corner and no windows.

Fields sat on the edge of the bed. The rocking slowed as Kacey opened the closet and began going through it after having slipped on a pair of gloves.

Drake pulled open the top drawer of the dresser. Inside were a few pairs of hospital issued light blue clothes similar to scrubs and identical to what Fields currently had on. Underneath were a few hand drawn pictures. They were drawn in crayons, Drake assumed that was all Fields was allowed. Pencils and pens have sharp points, and he couldn't be trusted with those types of items.

The drawings were ominous and dark. The colors were mostly blacks and browns. The actual picture was difficult to depict. Drake bagged the drawings, sending Fields into a rage.

"You can't take those!" Field began rocking back and forth uncontrollably, his head snapping from side to side. "Those are mine. You can't have them!"

Drake ignored the frantic pleas that continued to bleat from the bed as he opened the next drawer. Inside it revealed socks and underwear, nothing more. Pulling the third drawer open, he pushed aside more socks and found a small AM/FM radio.

Turning to Ward who had followed them to Fields's room and remained present the entire time he asked, "Is he allowed to have this?"

Ward looked at the small device. "Yes, as you can see there are no windows or doors for him to escape from. The radio offers a simple pleasure with no risk. It operates on battery only, I'm not sure if it works though."

Drake switched the button on the top to the on position, and a commercial immediately filled the room. "Seems to work just fine."

Drake looked at the small dial next to the volume and saw the dial was set to 104.5 a popular local news station. "How would he have gotten this?"

"Our patients are offered privileges for following their program, taking their meds, and participating in therapy. I'd have to check the logs to see if he earned the radio."

"Do that; I'd like to know how and when, and the crayons for the drawings too."

With nothing left in the drawers Drake turned to Kacey, still avoiding Fields and drowning out the indecipherable chatter that he had dropped into.

Kacey looked at Drake and shook her head. She found nothing further in the closet. "We need you to move him," Kacey said nodding towards Fields. "We need to check under the mattress."

Ward nodded to the intern, the only other person in the room, and the two of them lifted Fields by his arms. He didn't fight, but as he was guided past Kacey he smiled, his lips peeling back to expose yellowing teeth. He hissed at her and said, "Sophie, sweet little Sophie." Kacey could smell the decay of his breath.

It took everything in Kacey not to head butt the bastard and lay him out right there, but instead she turned away from him not giving him the satisfaction and walked over to the bed and flipped the thin mattress up on its end.

Drake approached and assisted. The bed frame was made from welded slats, not the typical removable wooden ones found in a residential bed. Nothing could be removed without a ton of effort and some tools, which Fields would never be granted. There was nothing under the mattress so they dropped it back in place.

Kacey pulled at the sheet corner with her gloved hand then Drake reach inside. Feeling something under the mattress pad, he reached his hand in further. His latex covered fingers poked something smooth that crinkled with his touch. He wrapped his hand around the item and slid his hand back out.

Kacey looked to see what he had found, and Fields went crazy behind them. Ward and the intern immediately responded and pushed him into the corner. He screamed, "Those are mine. I did it! You can't have those. You couldn't stop me. You'll never stop me!"

There were three more drawings. These seemed somewhat different. Still drawn from crayons and some of the same dark colors, these had blues and reds in them too. Kacey took them from Drake and looked at each quickly before dropping them into a large plastic bag that she pulled from her vest pocket.

After checking the rest of the bedding, Drake and Kacey turned to leave the room, but as they did Fields, who had been repeating his mantra and rocking wildly, suddenly jerked free and charged towards the detectives. Drake braced for the oncoming collision when Fields stopped and stared wildly a mere foot from them. His eyes darted from them to the evidence bags.

"Do you see her in your dreams every night, detectives? Little Sophie, sweet Sophie."

Ward and the intern grabbed Fields back and slammed him onto the rumpled bed. "Sit down and shut up Robert," the doctor ordered.

Fields resumed his rocking. Laughter filled the room and filtered out into the hall where Drake and Kacey waited for the doctor to exit.

The next two hours were spent talking with several employees of the hospital. Dr. Ward had provided them with a small meeting room, and employees were called in one by one in the order of most likely being suspected of helping Fields in some way.

The day was exhausting, and the results from the interviews seemed fruitless. Other than discovering that one of the female interns had been providing Fields with batteries for the radio and that Fields had only recently taken up an interest in art and asked for the crayons and paper, they had not learned much.

Most of the employees seemed to genuinely dislike Fields. Many shared stories of the awful things he would say or do whenever they were in his presence. Even Dr. Ward, without disclosing anything confidential, admitted that Robert Fields was typically not a willing participant in his own therapy.

Fields had once again suggested during his interview that he was the killer, but they both knew that was impossible. Or was it? Could Robert Fields be conducting serial murders from inside the mental institution for which he was confined for life?

Sticks and Stones

Chapter Eighteen

Iz sizzled with excitement. It was the first full day off of work in quite a while and night was beginning to fall. Driving out to the barn had been peaceful and yet Iz practically tingled inside. It was time to make another bold statement, and this one was going to be a real doozy.

Drive faster!

I can't. We don't want to get stopped. Can't have anyone notice us. Now settle down already!

Sorry. I'm just so excited. This one is going to be so good. You are really going to show them this time!

Ten minutes later Iz's gloved hands turned the car into the private lane and followed it, stopping just in front of the barns rolling doors. Stepping out of the vehicle with the engine still running, Iz removed a key from inside the front pocket of the heavy coat that was still required to keep the winter's cold out.

A moaning sound came from the trunk. Iz smiled. The cargo that was stowed away with the assistance of the car's tire iron seemed to be stirring. *Perfect.* An alert captive creating a bit of a challenge would make this much more entertaining.

The sun was setting off in the west as Iz slid the key in the lock that was applied a few nights ago, a night when it had been difficult to sleep. The chain slipped loose, and Iz gave the right door a big shove, rolling it open far enough that the car could pull inside.

Returning to the vehicle, Iz could hear quiet moaning coming from the trunk.

What a baby he's being. Dumb ass. He's going to pay. Can't wait. Make it hurt, Iz.

Iz slid behind the wheel and pulled the car forward, stopping about half way down the main aisle of the barn in between the horse stalls. Killing the engine and the headlights, the last moments of daylight shone through the door, affording Iz just enough light to make it safely from inside the car to the main walkthrough door where the light switch was.

Iz flipped the switch and light flooded the barn. Iz walked over to the slider door and tugged it closed. With the light on and the door closed, the solitude and safety of the barn embraced Iz, and for the first time since leaving the apartment Iz's shoulders relaxed.

Opening the back driver's side door of the car, Iz retrieved the tire iron from the back seat then walked to the back of the vehicle and pressed the trunk lid button that was hidden under the hatch.

Iz's stiff gloved fingers wrapped tightly around the tire iron prepared to strike if necessary. Slowly letting the truck lid rise, Iz stared down into the trunk.

The body was still curled in the fetal position unable to move due to the rope that bound his hands and feet in a hog tie and as the light flooded into the cargo area, his eyes blinked open, squinting at the sudden invasion. He tried to push himself up but the bindings made it difficult, and by the way he winced Iz could tell the large lump on his forehead must be hurting something terrible. Iz reached in and pulled the man by his shoulders, and then dragged him forward, leaning him out of the car until he toppled onto the ground.

With a loud thump the man hit the hard floor of the barn causing a deep groan to fall from his gaping mouth. Iz didn't care. Strength would be very necessary later, and there was no reason to be gentle. It wouldn't matter soon anyway.

Grabbing the rope that bound the man's feet, Iz began pulling the heavy body across the floor towards the tractor at the back of the barn.

Leaving the semi-conscious man lying in a heap on the floor just a few feet from the tractor Iz returned to the car. Opening the trunk, Iz removed a box and carried it over to the tractor and set it down near the front wheel, then retrieved a tool box and a bag from the car and went to work on the tractor.

Removing the leather driving gloves Iz had been wearing earlier, disposable latex gloves were pulled on —no sense in getting good gloves dirty. First Iz changed the oil and filter. While the oil was draining, Iz replaced the spark plug and battery.

After about forty-five minutes the tractor had received a pretty good basic tune-up and had been properly fueled with clean gas. Iz slid into the driver's seat and cranked over the engine, pumping the gas and plunging the choke. Several attempts later the engine turned over, spurted, and then fired, but died immediately. Upon a second hard attempt the engine caught. A plume of dark smoke puffed from the small smoke stack, and the tractor shuddered for a few moments then slowly settled down to a steady idle.

Iz smiled then lifted the small bucket off the ground a few inches and turned the tractor to face the man lying in a heap on the floor.

Iz saw the look on the man's face. At first he must have thought Iz was going to run him over with the machine as he attempted to violently squirm away, but like an inchworm he made little to no progress. Iz idled the tractor and then stepped down onto the barn floor, removed the greasy disposable gloves, dropping them into a bucket just inside the third stall, and pulled back on the leather gloves.

Iz could tell he was getting his strength back and realized by the bulging of his eyes and the redness of his face that the man had been shouting. The tractor noise had buried the sounds, and even without the tractor's engine Iz had been so focused on getting the machine started that the noises had been merely drowned out behind the screams that seemed to always play inside Iz's head. Iz might need to knock him out at some point, couldn't have him fighting, but not yet. It would be fun for him to see what was about to happen first.

Iz went about retrieving some items from the side of the barn where the tools were stored and continued to ignore the continuous flow of shouts that seemed to transition from threats to pleading and back again.

Iz assessed the items, first looking over the thick rope, but then pulled at the large reel of barbed wire and decided this was much more suitable for the matter at hand. Taking a pair of wire snips that hung on a rusty nail, Iz clipped off a piece approximately 30 feet long.

Returning to the man, still lying wiggling on the floor, Iz began wrapping the wire around his body and rolling him across the sharp barbs until he was nearly encased in the wire. The barbs dug deeply into his skin, and blood dripped from a number of areas across his neck and arms. The man screamed out in pain as Iz began twisting the ends of the twine together, much the way a farmer would twist the ends of a fence line to ensure livestock couldn't escape.

Make it tighter, Iz!

Unable to resist the cheering, Iz gave the wire another quick turn, causing the man to writhe in pain against the sharp bites. He bled from his side where he was forced to lay on the barbs, his own weight forcing them deeper and penetrating into his tender skin.

Iz spoke for the first time since removing the man from the car. "You really shouldn't tell lies. Everyone knows you don't give a shit and yet you act all holier than thou. Well, not any more. Not after tonight."

The man shouted back, "Let me go! I won't tell anyone, I swear!"

Iz laughed out loud a deep guttural laugh. "More lies! You swear. Really? Isn't that ironic."

"Please, just let me go. I have a family."

"Lying again! You just never learn, do you?" Iz felt the anger racing inside. Returning to the wire reel with quick strides, Iz made another snip of wire that stretched about twenty feet this time, and then a shorter one only about a foot and a half long.

Standing over the man again, the blood weeping from the hundreds of small pricks, Iz smiled down at him. "Since you can't seem to stop lying, I guess I need to shut you up all together."

Shut him up, Iz. Shut him the fuck up!

Iz pulled the man forward with a snap, driving the barbs further into his skin as his weight pressed deeper into the wire. In a single, sudden movement, Iz wrapped the shorter piece of wire around the man's head, forcing the wire into his mouth. The man thrashed his head back and forth trying to resist, but the bite of the wire won out.

Iz made another loop then twisted the ends together at the back of the man's head. The wire ripped into lips and gums. Blood poured from the side of his mouth. He tried to scream, but the wire tore at his tongue, forcing him into silence.

"No more lies for you tonight." Iz slipped the wire snips into a back pocket.

Using the wire to drag the man, Iz pulled him onto the bucket of the tractor. The man struggled, but in his bound state he was unable to resist and soon found himself neatly loaded. Iz raised and tipped the bucket level back so that it faced the ceiling of the barn. This would ensure the man wouldn't simply fall out, and it would make it much harder for him to escape. Given his current bound state, climbing out wouldn't be easy.

Iz retrieved the strip of long wire and carefully wound it into a circle so it could be transported easily and laid it on the seat of the tractor. Iz slid the large barn doors open and backed the car out into the night air, then reached behind the seat and retrieved a pair of rubber boots. Kicking off work boots, Iz slipped on the rubber boots, then removed a watch, and slid it into the glove box.

Iz returned to the tractor to collect the gas can that remained about half full, slid behind the wheel, and then slowly lowered the bucket to a safe traveling height. Inching the machine forward, Iz maneuvered it through the door.

Outside the barn Iz parked the tractor and once more went back to close the barn doors. Although it was pretty certain that no one would be coming around, there was no point in taking any unnecessary risks. No, Iz had plenty of messages to send and getting caught was not in the plans.

Driving the tractor out on the dirt road, Iz kept a careful eye out for cars or a local farmer passing by. It was now after eleven o'clock, and Iz knew farmers went to bed early and were up at the crack of dawn. About two miles from the barn Iz recognized the perfect spot. A small cluster of trees sat just off the road and created what seemed like a picture frame. Iz had spotted it before, and seeing it again caused a shiver of excitement to crawl all through Iz's body.

Iz pulled the tractor onto the shoulder just in front of those trees. A long wire hung low, sagging from years of weather and wind. Iz raised the bucket up as high as it would go and leveled it off flat. It stopped about three feet under the wire.

After ensuring the brake was set hard and the bucket was locked, Iz climbed out over the engine. The tractor's headlights provided just the right amount of light. Stepping into the bucket and making sure the passenger was not in the way, Iz began studying the wire overhead.

Iz, you sure you won't get shocked?

Rubber boots, no watch or rings, and rubber gloves. The only way I can get shocked is if I complete the electrical loop. I've insulated myself. It will be okay.

Well, then what are you waiting for? Light him up!

Hang on a second. I have to be sure he won't fall.

Iz wound around the overhead wire a piece of the barbed wire that was already wrapped around the man, then twisted it tightly, turning it more than ten times to be sure it would not come undone with his weight. The man suddenly seemed to understand what was about to happen, and his eyes were wild with fear.

"Shouldn't have been a liar," Iz said.

Looping the long end of the wire up and over the electrical wire that swung just a few feet over Iz's head, Iz used the wire snips to twist it against itself while being careful to not let it touch the man, which would close the loop. Since Iz was touching him, they would both be electrocuted.

Iz, be careful.

Shhh...I am. Now hush. Just a few more turns.

Iz finally felt certain that it was secured tightly around the barbed trap that held the man to the overhead wire. Assessing the length, Iz climbed out of the bucket to collect the gasoline can and quickly returned. Iz stood gazing down at the terrified man tightly wound in the barbed snare. Eyes darted back and forth, words tried to form on the bloodied lips, but the pain from torn flesh prevented anything more than a muffled scream to escape.

Iz poured the remaining gas over the man's legs, soaking his jeans in the pungent liquid. Shaking out the last drops in the can, Iz could feel skin tingling while imagining the way this would feel. Excitement rose; the thrill of revenge, the teaching, the lesson was ever so sweet.

Iz climb back over the engine and set the can between the rubber boots and slowly lowered the bucket. The wired mess of a man swung slightly and dangled about six feet off the ground. Iz backed the tractor onto the road once more, facing in the direction of the barn, then stepped down onto the road, taking a few steps forward and reaching into a front pocket to remove a small packet of matches with the name of some café embossed on it.

Iz peeled back the cover, ripped off a single stick, and struck the match across the black carbon strip, igniting a small flame. The match burned a bright red flame, turning to yellow, and with a quick flip of the wrist the match was in the air. Taking one more look, Iz marveled at the wire encased cocoon that dangled like an angel in the night air.

A breeze swept through and stole the life from the match. "Shit," Iz muttered in a deep growl, then flipped the booklet open again and struck another match. Taking a step closer, Iz flicked the small blazing piece of cardboard towards the man as he watched on in wild eyed horror as flames engulfed his writhing body. Iz turned, climbed on the tractor and drove off into the night. A swirl of road dust was the only evidence that anyone had been there.

Chapter Nineteen

Drake and Kacey had spent hours pouring over the interview notes from the employees at the mental hospital. For two days they had engaged Janet to run checks on certain people who had shown possible suspicion for one reason or another, but each lead had come up empty.

Frustration had led to exhaustion and finally after going strong for nearly thirty-six hours straight, the chief had ordered them out of the precinct for twenty-four hours of hard earned rest. So far there had not been any more killings, but they each silently knew there would be more. Certainly there had been killers in the past that had somehow gone silent or moved on, killers like the Zodiac that had tormented the West Coast decades before then suddenly just stopped. But this one they each knew deep inside, it was just a matter of time.

Kacey had argued with the chief but ultimately submitted and they had left the precinct to grab some lunch. Laundry had piled high and rest was desperately needed. They'd flirted with the idea of going to Drake's place, but knew that rest would not come if they were together and allowed logic to win out over desire. A few kisses later, Kacey tossed her dark hair over her shoulder, and with a wiggle of her fingers through a teasing smile she said, "See you in the morning." With that she climbed into her own car, and as Drake watched her speed off he fired up his own engine, suddenly aware of the ache in his shoulders. Sleep beckoned him.

Despite the cold air outside, the sun was shining so Drake opened the curtains in the living room of his apartment for the first time in longer than he could remember. The rays cast light on the dust bunnies that were instantly brought into view. He stood looking around and decided he would straighten up before taking a shower. He tossed out three days of newspapers that had never even had the rubber bands removed, then he collected two glasses and a beer bottle left on the bedroom night stand and went room to room clearing items that didn't belong. The laundry basket at the bottom of his closet was overflowing. He pulled it out and quickly sorted it into two different piles and took them into the small laundry room just off the bathroom. After starting a load he returned to the kitchen and washed the few dishes that had piled up, and then removed several carry out containers from the refrigerator, not daring to open any of them. Finally, he took the trash out and spent a few minutes whisking the vacuum around the floor.

Satisfied with the apartments condition now, he went to take a shower. With the hot water cascading over his tired body, he wished Kacey was with him and regretted not insisting on her joining him. Although he knew if she had been here, he never would have gotten the apartment cleaned much less get his laundry done.

He smiled as he stepped out of the shower and toweled off, thoughts of Kacey and the distraction she could have provided flashing through his head. The washer cycle buzzer sounded. He paused and then accepting the fact that he would need clothes in the morning he moved the clean laundry over to the dryer and set the knob. Not even bothering to pull on boxers and still with damp hair he dropped into the bed. The sun had just set, and the bedroom remained dark with curtains drawn.

Despite the exhaustion, Drake tossed and turned as images of faceless bodies lying on the table in Doc's lab plagued him. His subconscious mind would try and lean close to the face of the person, and the closer he leaned in the further the body would move away. Robert Fields came into view as if he suddenly was jerked back into the courtroom. Fields was hurling hideous comments followed by sick and twisted laughter, and then Frank Parker shouted, *"It's all your fault. If you had just..."* Another

136

shift back to Doc's lab; this time a small body lay on the table, draped in a white sheet. Drake could see a hand reaching to pull the sheet back—his hand—and then peeling back the sheet he saw that the small body was Sophie. Her eyes opened, innocent beautiful eyes, asking, *"Why? Why didn't you come and help me?"*

Drake jolted awake, his naked body slick with sweat, the sheets clinging to him. His breath was irregular and ragged, and for a moment he wasn't sure where he was. Casting his eyes to the nightstand, the clock read 2:23. He'd been asleep for several hours, though it felt like it was just moments ago that he laid down.

Swinging his legs out of the bed, he pulled the sheets from the mattress and carried the damp bedding to the laundry. Tossing the clothes from earlier into the dryer, he started the bedding before grabbing another set from the small linen closet in the hall just outside the bedroom.

Ten minutes later the bed was freshly made, and he contemplated laying back down. But instead he pulled on some sweatpants and walked out to the now dark living room, closed the curtains, and flipped on the TV.

Drake sprawled out on the couch and pulled a blanket down off the back and mindlessly flipped stations—a fishing contest somewhere in Georgia, some vampire movie, and a rerun of *Ellen*. He stopped on *Forensic Files* covering a case gone cold since 1979. He thought about Kacey and wondered if she was able to sleep or if she was flipping channels on her couch too.

As the ominous voice narrated the details of the body found in the basement, his mind wandered to Fields. Dr. Ward had been their first suspect. His obvious arrogance and overt willingness to assist in any way possible had made him stand out, but he was not their killer, and he was not working with Fields.

So who was? He wondered. As that thought rolled through his mind, he fell asleep again, this time dropping into a deep sleep. The sound of a neighbor's door slamming woke him. He looked around. It was now five thirty in the morning. He couldn't remember coming out to the living room.

Looking around, he noticed the perfectly stacked magazines on the coffee table and the kitchen counter completely clear of dishes. He tossed back the blanket to get up. For a minute he thought he was losing it. He remembered coming home last night, but for some reason everything else seemed to be a blur.

Drake headed to the bathroom to relieve himself and saw the laundry basket on the floor and flipped the lid to the washer open. *Sheets?*

He tried to compel his memory but failed. He turned to look at the bed and saw that it was perfectly made. Had Kacey been here? No. He was certain if she had been here he would remember that, and yet he really couldn't remember much.

Shrugging it off as sheer exhaustion, he went to the closet and noticed the empty laundry basket. Vaguely remembering putting the clothes in the dryer he turned it on to tumble and quickly brushed his teeth and splashed cold water on his face, then pulled on fresh, warm clothes from inside the dryer. He pulled up in front of the diner. He scanned the parking lot looking for Kacey's car, but he came up empty. She usually beat him here, so he decided she must be sleeping in. He'd give her another thirty minutes before calling to make sure she woke up.

Inside the diner at the far corner table were the beat cops. He saw Dermot and the kid–*what was his name? Sparlow, that's right*–sitting with two other cops. He couldn't remember their names. He nodded to a fellow detective that worked human trafficking. Not feeling social, he made his way to the counter and took a stool on the end.

Moments later he had a steaming cup of coffee, and the fog that had followed him all morning seemed to slowly lift. Someone had left the morning paper lying on the counter. He picked it up and scanned the pages for anything about the case and almost smiled when he found nothing. Instead there was some scandal about the public water department that filled the headlines.

While checking his watch, he felt a hand slap down on his back. Dermot stood there with his typical thrown back shoulders and cocky smile. "Hey, where's my girlfriend?"

Drake feigned a smile not wanting to let Dermot see how much he'd like to punch him. "Getting some well needed rest would be my guess."

"Damn, I'd like to help rock her to sleep, if you know what I mean." Dermot made a fist and pumped his arm in and out.

"Hey watch it, jackass," Drake warned.

Dermot could see the sour look on Drake's face and threw his hands up palms out. "Whoa, easy, Drake. You gotta admit you'd like to tear up that little fire cracker too."

Drake started to stand up, but then a smile crossed over his face as Kacey punched Dermot in the arm. "Like he said, watch it, jackass."

"Ah, shit. Sorry, Kacey, I was just messing around." Dermot squirmed turning to face her.

"Yeah, well you couldn't handle it anyway." She wiggled her pinky finger at him, tossed her dark hair to one side and heartily laughed as she slid in beside Drake.

Dermot's group of buddies had gathered around and a howl of laughter followed the cocky, red-faced cop out the door.

Drake shook his head and laughed as he took another sip of coffee. "Well, good morning to you. Looks like sleep did you some good."

"Fire cracker, huh?"

"I didn't say it, but it might just be on the mark."

"Yeah, well don't ever call me that, or I'll punch you too."

"Deal."

"Did you order yet?" Kacey asked changing the subject.

"Not yet, was waiting on you."

Judy appeared out of nowhere, ripping a pen from her beehive hair, and dropped an order pad on the counter. "The usual?"

"I'm starving. Can you add a side of biscuits and gravy for me this morning?" Drake asked.

"Will you share?" Kacey questioned in a teasing manner.

"Of course."

Judy laughed. "You got it, Detective."

Kacey sipped on her coffee and asked, "Did you get some rest?"

"Some," Drake answered hesitantly.

"Uh oh, that doesn't sound very convincing."

"Yeah, I passed out on the couch. I got some shut eye. Doesn't seem like I got as much as you, by the way you put Dermot in his place." Drake smiled at her, trying to shrug off the fact that he couldn't really remember his night very well.

The food arrived, giving him a reprieve from trying to figure it out or explain it. The smell was amazing and Drake dug in. He was really hungry, but didn't think he should be. The last thing he'd done was eat with Kacey before going home, but after glancing at his watch he calculated that it had been sixteen hours ago. Realizing that made him feel better.

Judy came to clear away the dishes and pour more of the dark brew that was not the best, but certainly better than the so-called coffee at the precinct. At about the same time both Drake and Kacey's cell phones buzzed. As Drake swiped the screen on his phone to read the text, he threw down a twenty-dollar bill on the counter, plenty to cover the tab and leave a decent tip.

"Bye, guys," Judy called after them as they headed out into the morning sunlight.

Something in the air felt different, like the first hint of spring. Drake sucked it deeply into his lungs; it felt cleansing and refreshing. He figured he'd need that because today was about to get unclean.

The text message pinged both of their phones at almost exactly the same time and included an address outside of the city. Somewhere out in the country. After agreeing to take Drake's truck, they took off. Drake drove and Kacey called the chief.

After about five minutes on the phone, she hung up and turned to Drake who was focused on weaving in and out of the traffic. Ten minutes later they were on the highway and Drake pressed the accelerator down.

"Chief and Doc are going to meet us out there. We don't know much other than a local farmer found a body hanging from a telephone wire. The victim had been burned."

Drake asked, "What makes them think it's murder? Could it have been some sort of farming accident?"

"The unusual circumstances, it sounds like the farmer was pretty shook up."

"So assuming the victim was intentionally strung up and burned, why do we think it is related? The M.O. is all wrong. It's unusual for a serial killer to change his method of killing so drastically."

Kacey shrugged. "Someone must think so, or we wouldn't be heading down Highway 95 at a speed faster than your truck wants to run."

Drake gave Kacey a sideways glance, shaking his head and cracking a smile. "You know one of the things I love about working with you is the fact that you find the fun in just about anything."

"What's that supposed to mean?" Kacey asked with a cocky grin on her face.

"It means, even though we are on our way to what sounds like a gruesome scene, you have time to crack jokes about my truck."

"It's what happens after rest and food. You should be used to it by now," she tossed back then settled back into the seat and stared out the window, watching the scenery outside go by.

The trees were finally starting to show minor signs of the season changing, as there were suddenly sprigs of life. Grass sprouts were popping up in a few spots, working hard to pop their heads out past the dead remnants of last year. Life...there were signs of life, refreshing and liberating. They passed a field that had yet to share the signs of spring, and just around the corner the doom that would be facing them in just a few minutes flooded back in. Kacey sighed in anticipation.

"You said our killer wouldn't change M.O., but he hasn't followed a single M.O. yet. In fact if the victims weren't all somehow tied to Fields we would never think it was the same killer."

Drake answered as he exited the highway, "True, but there are too many coincidences for this to be multiple killers."

"I agree, but that means the M.O. is not the important part of the killing."

"What are you saying?"

"I'm saying there must be some other reason to kill these people. Maybe they all pissed him off in a certain way, and the way he is killing them is revenge for whatever he thinks they did to him."

"So nailing a board to someone's back is revenge for what?"

"I don't know, but maybe he is motivated by hate for something done to him or something he thinks was done to him. Setting us up because he's angry is only part of it. We've been so focused on figuring out who Fields has doing this for him that we have missed being focused on the actual motive." Drake pulled onto a dirt road following the directions of the female GPS voice from his cell phone.

Kacey considered what Drake was saying as she watched the dirt road spotted by trees pass under the road. She saw a couple of old farm houses and then saw an old barn sitting back in the trees that looked like it hadn't been used in years. She stared at the old building. The road curved to the right, and then they could see cars and lights. The dirt crunched under the truck's tires as they rolled up to a stop. Yellow crime scene tape was wrapped around several of the trees, cordoning off a section just off the left side of the road.

Kacey's eyes followed the tape and landed on the unimaginable. She opened the door and stepped out onto the soil, her eyes still fixed on the body dangling like a burnt shish-kabob suspended several feet off the ground.

Drake stepped out from his side of the truck, and true to his normal style, his eyes closed in on the surroundings first, avoiding looking directly at the body until he'd taken in most of the crime scene.

Ducking under the yellow tape, Drake flashed his badge and then averted his eyes, allowing them to finally land on the body. Stepping closer, both he and Kacey walked a near full circle around the body, careful to not step on anything that appeared to be evidence. Despite the breeze, the smell of burnt flesh hung in the air causing both detectives to gag back bile that naturally rose in their throats.

As they worked their way around the body they could see the barbed wire wrapped tightly, biting into the burnt flesh while suspending from the electrical wire.

Doc and the chief walked up just moments later. The chief had a grim look on his face. He shook his head as he walked up to them. "What have we got?"

"Just got here, crime scene is setting up. Cordoned off a pretty good section, doesn't appear the area has been tramped down by the locals. We haven't had a chance to talk to anyone yet," Drake answered.

"The body is burned from the bottom up," Kacey commented, noting the fully charred feet and mostly intact upper torso and

142

making a point that the victim had not just fallen onto the telephone wire. If that had happened the expectation would be that the body would be burned the most at the nearest point to the wire.

Despite the observation it was hard to tell if the body was that of a man or woman. The hair had been burned off and the clothes melted, flesh hung in charred hunks.

"Kacey, you take the local interviews," the chief nodded towards the county patrol car sitting at the edge of the road with a uniformed officer standing nearby. "Find out if the body was still on fire when he arrived."

Doc jumped in. "It doesn't appear that there is any fire retardant on the body or the ground. The smell contains an oil scent. I'm thinking an accelerant was used, probably diesel fuel. Of course I'll know more once I am able to take some samples at the lab."

"How soon before we can take the body down?" Drake asked.

"CSI will need to get all their photographs done and samples of soil and tree leaves first. Then the fire crew can help us cut the body down. Once I get it back to the lab I'll see if there is any way to lift prints, but at first glance, it doesn't look good. Otherwise we are looking at dental records."

Kacey looked at Drake, nodded to the others, and turned to walk over to the sheriff's cruiser that sat out on the road. As she approached she saw the officer was young and was obviously shaken. Small town cop probably thought he was going to get a ton of action, never did. Not until this. Likely his fantasy wasn't quite panning out to be the excitement he had pictured.

"Detective Kacey James," she introduced herself offering a hand.

Despite the fact that he was physically shaken, he received her hand in a strong grip and met her eyes. "Different circumstances, I'd say it was a pleasure to meet you, detective. Officer Jenks," he said tapping the name badge over the left pocket on his jacket.

Kacey didn't respond, just offered a smile. "Can you tell me how you came upon the scene?"

"I was just out patrolling. Old man Reardon down the road lost the wife a couple months back. I run by and check on him most mornings. Nights are the worst for him, you know."

Kacey shook her head, though she could only imagine. "Was this on your way to or from Mr. Reardon's?"

"I came from town, opposite end of the road about four miles in, went by and made my check, then came out here and was about to loop back around this road to the highway. I would have taken that on back into town, possibly catch a speeder or two." He shrugged his shoulders.

"Is that your usual path?"

"Pretty much every night, give or take an hour or so."

"Is tonight on the give or take side of the hour?"

"Take, I was a little late. My little sister went into labor last night. I ran by the hospital before heading out here, took a look at my little nephew."

"What time was it, do you think?"

"I stopped by Hank's, uh, Mr. Reardon's about seven o'clock, I guess. We talked for a bit, maybe thirty minutes or so. He made me a cup of coffee. I had my radio with me, not a lot going on."

"So that puts you out here at what, seven thirty or eight?"

"That's right. I called it in at," he leaned inside the cruiser and looked at the monitor on the dash, "seven forty-two."

"When you got here, was the body still on fire?"

"No, ma'am, about the same as it is right now."

Kacey glanced back at the body hanging from the telephone wire. The body seemed to smolder slightly. She glanced down the road and turned her body to approach from the direction the officer had indicated he was coming from. The body hung squarely in view as the officer's patrol car would have come around a very slight bend in the road.

"Did you get out of your patrol?"

"I started to walk up to the body. Pulled over right where I am parked now, walked about half way," he said pointing to a place in the dirt in between where they stood. "But then it was obvious there was nothing I could do, and I thought there might be some evidence. Didn't want to ruin it so, I came back to my cruiser and called it in on my radio. Then stayed here and waited."

"That was some quick thinking, officer." Kacey said offering him praise for the way he handled the situation, as the only means of comfort she could provide.

144

"Thanks." He shook his head. "Honestly, I almost lost my cookies while I was waiting. The smell…" his words trailed off as he kicked at the dirt with his shiny black shoe.

"I know. It's not something most officers will ever experience, and well, those of us that do, never get used to it."

"Thanks, Detective James," he shook his head.

"Anything else you can remember? Any cars in the area? Anyone that seemed out of the ordinary?"

"Honestly, after the hospital I never saw anyone at all once I made the turn onto 420 Road, which heads out into the country."

"Thanks again, Officer Jenks."

He nodded his head and leaned back against his car. Kacey shook his hand and then turned and walked back towards Drake and the rest of the team. Now the area around the body was being reviewed by a CSI team. Small yellow markers sat in various places in the dirt, and a photographer was taking pictures.

"What did I miss?" Kacey asked.

Drake stood up from a place near where the burnt body still hung dangling above the ground, grotesquely swaying with the morning breeze. Despite the time that had passed, the air still held a strong odor from the charred flesh.

Rubbing his nose with the back of his gloved hand, Drake spoke, "There are tire tracks in the dirt. Based on the size of the tire tread and wheelbase, it seems like it might have been a tractor. The CSI team isn't sure whether they will be able to identify make and model, which might narrow it down, but my guess is a lot of farmers out here have tractors."

Kacey's eyes scanned the horizon before she nodded. "So our guy drove a tractor with the body on it then somehow suspended it from the wire?"

Drake tipped his head to one side and shrugged his shoulders. "Looks like fence wire is what is wrapped around the body. Again, probably pretty generic to this area."

"Please, tell me they've found something we can use."

"Maybe, they took some samples of soil, burnt wood on the telephone pole, and leaves on the trees nearby. That should tell us what kind or if an accelerant was used. Initial thought is that it is likely diesel fuel."

"That won't help us."

"I know."

Doc had been working with one of the CSI techs and walked over to Drake and Kacey. "We're ready to take the body down. "We'll lower it down onto a tarp. I'll take everything with me back to the lab. The CSI team will recover the clothes, wire and any debris that comes off the body onto the tarp."

"Can we look for identification once the body is down?" Drake asked.

Doc's eyes moved to the body. "We can try but not sure there will be much to recover. The clothes are pretty burnt. Like I said before, I might be able to get a print or two. The fingers are pretty burnt, but we could get lucky. I'll work on dental identification immediately if I can't get prints."

Chief Dalton joined the group, "Drake, James, anything you see here that makes you believe this is the same killer for your ongoing investigation?"

Drake shook his head. "Unless this...person is somehow connected to our other victims, I would say no. The sooner we get an identification we'll know more."

The chief nodded his chin up at Kacey. "You agree?"

Kacey shrugged. "Other than the very strange way this person was killed, and truly this could just be a case of Hatfields and McCoys, local farmers getting pissed off at each other. Nothing would indicate this is related."

"Doc, how quick before we get identification?" the chief asked, his frustration showing.

Doc held up his hands, his latex gloves facing palms out. "You will get it as quickly as I can get to it. We are going to pull the body down now. I doubt any identification is left on the body, but we'll look before we remove the body from here. As I explained to these guys," gesturing towards Drake and Kacey, "I will attempt to get prints, but I can't say whether there is enough material left on the hands to take an impression. Without that we'll be left with dental impressions, and we need to know who we are trying to compare them to. Bottom line, until someone comes up as a missing person, we could have nothing. "

"Shit!"

Pumping his palms at Dalton, Doc continued, "Let's not jump off yet. Give me time to examine the body."

146

Doc pushed passed the group and began working with the CSI analyst who was struggling to pull a large yellow tarp open on the ground under the body.

A few minutes later after the fire department had the power turned off, the body was cut from the power line and lowered face down onto the center of the tarp.

Doc carefully stepped onto the tarp next to the body and examined what was remaining of the clothing. The pants were burnt almost entirely and melted, nearly fused, to the body. Motioning to the CSI that had been assisting with the tarp, Doc asked, "Help me turn him over."

Kacey stepped forward. "Him?"

Doc nodded. "Yes, definitely a male."

As the body was rolled over, the dead man's left arm fell away from the body, and Kacey caught a glimpse of a watch.

Drake stepped forward as did the chief, all leaning in, careful not to step on the tarp for fear of destroying any fibers or other evidence that may have fallen onto the tarp.

Kacey pointed. "Doc, is that watch a Rolex?"

Doc rolled the arm so that the wrist faced upwards. "Yes, gold. It's still ticking."

"Drake I think it's Dr. Ward."

The chief was the first to speak. "What makes you say that?"

"Ward wore a gold Rolex. I saw it when we interviewed him. Thought it was odd how he tried to be all casual, but the watch gave away his wealth."

Drake nodded. "I noticed it too but didn't think much about it."

Doc carefully opened the clasp, allowing the watch to fall from the partially charred wrist. Parts of it were scorched with black smoke. Flipping it over in his palm, he rubbed at the back of the dial until the initials T.W. were displayed.

Drake was dialing his phone before anyone could even move. "Janet. Hey, real quick, can you pull up Dr. Ward from the mental hospital and tell me what his first name is?"

All eyes were on Drake as he waited. "Thanks," he said and disconnected the call. "Dr. Timothy Ward."

Sticks and Stones

Chapter Twenty

Drake tossed his cell phone and keys on the desk and looked over just as Kacey ran her hands across her face. Before he could say anything to her, she turned to walk away, and he watched her go out the door. Through the glass windows at the end of the room, he saw her enter the ladies room on the left of the hall. This case was certainly taking its toll on both of them. Despite the rest he'd gotten the night before, he felt more tired now than he did after they'd pulled nearly three days straight.

While he waited for her to return he made a call to Janet to ask for the next of kin information on Dr. Timothy Ward, thinking a family member may be able to offer positive I.D' from the Rolex watch.

A few minutes later Kacey walked back in the room. Drake sat at his desk staring at a few photos he'd printed out from the burn site where they assume it was Ward that had been literally barbequed. Looking up at her, their eyes met. "You okay?"

"Yeah, I just had to get the smell out of my head. Now I smell like burnt soap, but it's better, I guess."

He nodded in understanding, his eyes returning to the photos.

Kacey walked around to where he was seated and leaned in to look at the photos over his shoulder. He could feel her breath on his neck and for a moment found his mind drifting to the last time they were in his bed.

Hearing footsteps, Drake looked up and saw Craig Dermot enter the room. Dermot seemed to be in rare form this morning, his shoulders thrown back in a cocky display, and his hand rested

149

on the gun holster that sat high on his waist belt. "Hey, Kacey, I heard you two caught another fun case. The guys in the locker room this morning were wagering on whether you're going to catch this guy. They even had fun names for your vics too."

Kacey snapped back at him, still unable to shake off the acrid smell of burnt flesh that hung in her sinuses. "What are you spouting off about, Dermot?"

"You know, they came up with some good ones. You better hope the press doesn't catch wind of them."

"Really? And what, pray tell, could the rookies in the locker room have to say that I'd be worried about?"

Dermot had an arrogant grin on his face. "The Burner for today's body. Flat Ass for the vic with the two by four nailed to his hind side. The Floater for the first one, which obviously wasn't very imaginative, but my personal favorite was the hooker in the junk yard—Bacon Bait." He laughed then continued, "Get it? She was young like jail bait and had a pork chop around her neck. Bacon Bait."

Drake pushed his chair back hard from his desk to stand up, causing the chair to nearly topple over, with two steps he crossed the room. His chest instantly pressed against Dermot, and his eyes narrowed in and fixed on the young officer. "I've had about enough of your smart mouth, Dermot. You know you have the makings of a good cop, but this kind of shit is gonna get a cap in your ass. Now get your punk ass out of our investigation room and tell your friends if they've got any more clever names they'd better run them past us before spoutin' off."

"Dude, chill out," Dermot responded to the sudden outburst. "We were just having some fun."

"You think this is fun? You little son of a bitch, I seem to remember one of your little flunkies, what is his name?...Sparrow, losing his cookies at one of our scenes and you, big man, weren't too far behind him."

Chief Harding entered the room and took in the scene. "We have a problem in here?"

"No, sir. I'll see you later, Kacey," Dermot offered before pushing off of Drake and intentionally bumping his shoulder against the detective as he walked away.

"Yeah, thanks for the warning," Kacey popped off before the young cop was out of ear shot.

"What was that all about?" the chief demanded.

"Dermot was out of line, Chief. It's all under control," Kacey commented as Drake pulled his chair back up to the table and took a seat.

"We don't have time for you two to be distracted by school yard games."

"Chief, there is no problem, and we are not distracted."

"Good. Now what have we got?"

"We're waiting on a call from Doc to see if he was able to lift any prints. We need something besides the watch to confirm that the latest victim is in fact Dr. Ward."

"I called the hospital, his cell phone, and his home on the way back from the scene. Cell went directly to voicemail, no answer at home, answering machine picked up, and the hospital wasn't expecting him until around two today." Kacey raised her left arm and looked at her watch surprised at how much time had passed. "That's in about twenty minutes."

"Did you inquire about any other methods they might have to contact him?"

"Yes, they said they would typically call his cell phone, and he would respond almost immediately. I asked them to try and reach him and if they did to ask him to call me directly."

Drake seemed to have his composure back and finally spoke, "We asked Janet to find next of kin. Worst case, someone in his family may be able to make a quick positive I.D. based on the watch."

"When will we have that information?"

"Within the next few minutes. She just started working on it about one o'clock."

As if on key, Drake's cell phone rang. He reached and picked it up. As he listened he jotted some information down onto a notepad that lay on his desk. After a quick thank you, he set the phone back in the cradle.

"That was Janet. She gave me parents and a brother, his only living relatives. No children, no wife or ex-wife."

"Do you have a photo of the watch?"

"Yes, we do. Parents live out in Greenwood." Drake answered, referring to a suburb about two hours south of the city. "Brother is local. I suggest we see him first. If it is Dr. Ward he may be able to help break the news to the parents."

Chief Dalton nodded his head and walked away without another word.

Drake stood as he scooped up the photos and slid them into a file. "Let's go. I've got an address and place of employment. The brother owns a night club. My guess is his house is the best place to find him this time of day."

Kacey swept her coat off the back of her chair and was in motion without another word.

Thirty five minutes later after pulling through a drive thru to grab a couple of sandwiches and a coffee, they arrived in front of a two story brownstone that had once been an industrial building but now had been divided into a duplex. A Hummer sat parked on the street with a vanity license plate that read "THE HUMP" on it.

Drake pointed to the plate. "That's his vehicle. He owns the Hump Bar downtown on 37th and Washington."

Kacey knew of the bar, though she'd never personally been inside. It was a local hotspot for the twenty-something crowd that like to dance until dawn. The bar had an after hour license allowing it to remain open until four o'clock in the morning. The bar closed for thirty minutes at two and reopened as a coffee house at two thirty. The music kept pumping, but the alcohol sales ended after the one thirty last call. It was a pretty good setup for a bar owner, allowing the sales to keep flowing and the patrons to sober up before stepping back out onto the streets and into their cars. For the most part the bar had a pretty good reputation. The biggest excitement was an occasional bar fight, but the patrol cops picked up those calls.

Stepping out of the car into the late afternoon air, the sun was shining and it seemed oddly in contrast to the call they were about to make on Tony Ward.

Kacey led as they walked up the narrow sidewalk to the front door of the duplex marked with an "A." She pushed on the button located to the left of the storm door that encased a larger wooden door behind it.

After a few moments she pushed the button again and heard the distinct buzzer sound inside the apartment. After one more push they were about to give up when they heard the sound of movement inside. A raspy female voice said, "Who is it," through the speaker that was installed above the button.

Kacey responded, "Detectives James and Drake. We'd like to speak with Tony Ward."

The sound of a chain being removed from the inside and the hammer sliding out of the lock was followed by the door cracking open slightly. Inside a tall blonde woman with hair pulled back in a messy ponytail peered through the crack. She rubbed at her eyes as the light violated the dark interior.

"You got any I.D.?" She asked skeptically and sounding slightly annoyed.

Kacey held up her badge for the woman to inspect, and after a few moments she pulled the door open further then unlocked the latch on the storm door and pushed it open.

"What's this all about? Tony's sleeping, and he don't like to be woke up."

"We're sorry to bother you, ma'am," Kacey said although she didn't quite feel the sentiment given the rude demeanor and the obvious lack of education demonstrated in her grammar. "We need to speak to Tony regarding his brother Tim."

Seeming surprised, the women looked at them each before disappearing somewhere into the house without saying anything. Kacey took her departure as an invitation and pushed the door open and stepped inside as Drake followed her.

The interior was lit by the glow from the hallway where the woman had flipped on the switch when she retreated back into the home. The furnishings were high quality and neatly appointed. The walnut floors had a brilliant shine. The foyer opened into a formal sitting room on one side with a fireplace. A painting hung over the mantel that seemed so familiar to Kacey that she couldn't quite place it but was certain it was worth thousands of dollars. On the opposite side of the foyer was another room complete with a flat screen TV mounted on the wall that must have been at least seventy inches. It was obvious Ward was doing pretty well with his business.

A few moments later a dark haired man wearing Joe Boxer pajama bottoms and a t-shirt appeared in the hall and walked towards them. The blonde was not with him.

Approaching them, though obviously having just awakened, the man's face showed concern. "How may I help you?" he asked in a raspy voice with the sounds of sleep and the hangover of cigarettes and alcohol.

"Mr. Ward, we're sorry to wake you, but we are here because we have reason to believe your brother Tim may have been involved in a crime."

Ward laughed out loud. "You can call me Tony, but umm Tim, involved in a crime? No way. My brother squeaks when he walks."

Drake realized he'd misunderstood the implication as to the nature of his brother's possible involvement in the crime, but used it to his advantage. "Could you please take a look at a photo and tell us if you recognize it?"

Ward looked confused but shrugged his shoulders. "Okay, yeah, sure."

Drake pulled the photo out of the file folder he'd carried with him inside. He handed the photo of the watch over to the puzzled man who now seemed completely awake and alert; both Kacey and Drake watched to see his reaction.

Ward looked at the photo and immediately his head nodded. "Yeah, that's Tim's. My parents gave it to him as a graduation gift when he graduated from med school. Did someone take it? It looks messed up."

"Mr. Ward, Tony. I'm afraid we have some bad news. This watch was found on a body recovered in what we believe to be a murder."

"Murder?" It took a moment for the gravity of what was being proposed to sink in. Shaking his head, Ward stared back at Kacey then looked to Drake as if seeking more information.

"Yes, I'm afraid so."

"Are you telling me my brother was murdered?"

"We can't be 100% sure, but this watch was found on the victim's left wrist."

"Where is he? I want to go see. I can tell you if it's him."

Ward was in motion, grabbing a pair of perfectly placed shoes from a chrome shoe rack near the front door. He scooped up a pair of keys from a matching key rack that hung on the wall.

"Tony, unfortunately, it's not that easy. You see, there was a lot of damage to the body. The coroner is working on making an identification, but we might need Tim's dental records for comparison."

"Dental records? What do you mean by a lot of damage? Was there some sort of car accident?"

Kacey looked over at Drake. Her stomach churned, but she knew she had to continue. "Tony, I'm sorry but the body suffered burns that have made it impossible to say for certain who the person is."

"Jesus Christ." Ward walked over to one of the chairs in the room with the big TV and slumped down into it. His hands trembled, and the keys he grabbed from the key rack were now gripped in his clenched fist. In his other hand was the cell phone he'd been holding the entire time.

"Who would do such a thing? Tim didn't have enemies. Unless..." his voice trailed off.

"Unless?" Drake probed. "You were about to say something. Is there someone you know that might have wanted to harm your brother?"

Ward shook his head. "Unless one of those crazy people he spent his entire life trying to *fix* did something to him." He nearly spit out the word *fix* as if he hated the idea.

"You didn't approve of your brother's profession?"

Ward's head raised and he looked at Drake, his eyes moist. "Being a doctor was awesome. Working with those nuts was different. I mean, let's face it, they're crazy. He tried to make them better. Some of them actually got out of there. Anyone of those could have done something to him."

"Do you know how we can get his medical and dental records?"

"I can't even believe this." He sat staring at the detectives.

"Again, I'm very sorry," Kacey continued. "The sooner we can make a positive identification the more likely we will catch the person responsible for this. I know this is a lot to ask right now."

Ward shook his head and stood up. As he did the woman that had disappeared stuck her head out of a door down the hall. "Baby, are you coming back to bed? It's cold without you."

"Unless he changed for some unknown reason, he has gone to the same place for years. My whole family goes there." He said ignoring the woman

After punching a few buttons on his phone he turned it to face the detectives. The screen displayed a dental center located in mid-town. Kacey snapped a photo of it with her own cell phone then thanked him.

"How will I find out if it is Tim? I mean, maybe it's not. Maybe someone stole his watch and then they got burned. I mean, shit, what do I tell our parents?"

Kacey was cautious to offer any hope to him, knowing instinctively given the other victims and their connection so far to Fields and to her and Drake that was not likely. "With dental records we will get a positive identification very quickly. If you want to come down to the coroner's office we can get these records sent over to him and should have an answer for you."

"Then I'm not telling my parents anything until I know for sure. I'm not sure my mom can take it."

"I understand." Kacey placed her hand on his shoulder, and when she did the man broke into tears. "We need to go now. Is there anyone we can call for you?"

As Ward considered the question the bedroom door swung open and the blonde stomped toward them brushing by, yanking the front door open before slamming it behind her after shouting "asshole" over her shoulder.

Tony didn't even seem to notice. "No, I'm fine. I'll get dressed and meet you there."

Kacey nodded and handed him her card before turning to leave with Drake following.

Outside the sun had dipped behind a layer of clouds that seemed to roll in from nowhere, giving the afternoon a gloomy feeling and making Kacey wonder if spring would really ever grace the city. She briefly considered the irony of the sudden dark sky and the notification they had just given.

Drake was already on the phone to Janet requesting her to get a warrant and have the dental records sent over to Doc for Dr. Timothy Ward. Although in his mind it was a mere formality, he already knew instinctively that the body they found was that of Ward.

Drake tucked his cell phone into his pocket as he opened the driver's side car door of the police cruiser. "We've got to figure out how Fields is getting to these victims."

Kacey slid into the passenger seat next to him and turned to ask, "Don't you mean if he's getting to them?"

Drake studied her face for a moment and the seriousness in her question before he replied. "How can anything else make sense?"

"Drake, we've worked plenty of homicides that didn't make sense. There is a piece of the puzzle we are missing, and when we figure out what that is we get our guy."

Drake nodded then turned the key in the ignition, bringing to life the car before pulling away from the curb. "Well, we'd better hurry up before the chief hands our asses to us."

"Has Doc found anything yet?" Kacey asked switching gears.

"Yeah, he told me to stop on by. Hopefully by the time we get there he'll have the dental records too."

"What judge is on duty?"

"Klassen," Drake answered. Obviously he already asked Janet the same question.

"Good. He's usually quick and hassle free," Kacey said referring to the difficulties some judges presented when requesting a warrant for information. "I'll call the chief and fill him in."

"Knock yourself out." Drake smiled knowing the conversation would be an abrasive one.

Several minutes later, Drake pulled the cruiser into a spot in front of the coroner's office. Before exiting the vehicle, he sucked in a deep sigh, the familiar doom of the lab already bathing him in its medicinal smell, as images of Sophie flitted through his mind. A glance in Kacey's direction proved that he could almost read her mind, as similar thoughts displayed in the furrow of her brow.

"Let's go see if Doc can help shed some light on this," Drake offered, sounding more encouraged than he actually felt.

Kacey nodded then pulled the lever on the car door.

Inside the building the smells and feelings already assumed in the vehicle flooded both detectives as they walked through the corridor and entered the lab where Doc was bent over the burnt body they had removed from the side of a country road just hours earlier.

"Well, my two favorite detectives. I received the dental records via fax. I was just comparing them if you'd like to see."

Drake and Kacey approached the table and leaned in, the smell of burnt flesh assaulting their noses. Each struggled to focus closely on nothing other than what Doc was saying and showing them.

Doc had the dental x-rays up on a lighted display. He pointed to one of the slides. "See this here? The doctor had a very expensive bridge covering teeth 16, 17, and 18." Moving the light over the body and pulling down the jaw that hung by partially blackened flesh, he pointed to the lower left jaw. "Teeth 16, 17, and 18 also have a bridge. And," he continued, "there is a filling on tooth 3, also a match." He pointed back to one of the slides. "I can positively say this is in fact Dr. Ward."

Drake and Kacey looked at each other. Silence filled the room for a moment, and then Drake spoke first, "What else can you tell us about the body?"

"Well, I'm certain there was an accelerant used. The lab is working on exactly what was used, but my initial assessment is diesel fuel." He leaned in and sniffed the body near the legs. "You can smell it."

Kacey raised her hand in protest. "Thanks, I'll take your word for it."

Doc shrugged and continued on, "The accelerant seems to have only been poured onto the lower part of the body. Likely the pants were the point of origin. We did recover a few scraps of the clothing. The lab should be able to confirm this as well."

Drake thought for a moment then turned to Kacey. "That seems intentional."

"Why?" Kacey asked seeming confused.

"Well, imagine you have a hostage. He is bound. Usually the perp would have him kneel on the ground and pour the accelerant over his head."

Kacey stared at the body that lay on the table in front of her. "But in this case, the victim… Ward was possibly lying on the ground, assuming he was wrapped in the barbed wire prior to the accelerant being applied."

Drake considered her assessment and nodded in agreement. "So it's just coincidence that the accelerant was applied primarily to the bottom part of the body?"

Kacey shrugged her shoulders and nodded. "Maybe."

Drake shook his head. "I don't know why but it feels off to me." He began talking it through, "I'm a sadistic killer. I want my victims to suffer. I'm going to burn them, and they know it. What better way to scare the shit out of them, intensifying their suffering–their fear– than pouring it over their head, into their face, eyes, nose, and mouth?"

Kacey countered the theory. "Maybe the point was to make him know he was going to burn slowly, that his death would take longer because the accelerant was only applied on his legs. I'm a sadistic killer and I take my time explaining to my victim how the fire will crawl slowly up his body until it finally reached his head. All the while he will watch and feel the most pain from the entire experience. Death will be certain but slow."

Drake looked at her and nodded, seeming to accept the possibility, then turned his eyes to Doc. "How long before death?"

Doc held up his index finger on his gloved hand and curled it twice, motioning to the detectives to lean back in. They both complied by following the doctor's lead and leaning back over the area near the head. Doc focused the light again into the mouth of the victim.

"The inside of the mouth is blackened, and the esophagus is scorched with a good amount of charring."

Drake spoke first. "So he was alive long enough to breath in a good amount of the smoke."

"Yes," Doc confirmed.

So Kacey's assessment could be correct. Our killer wanted our victim to watch the flames crawl up his body, making the suffering last longer."

"It's possible. Although why killers do what they do will forever be a mystery to me." Doc shook his head and let out a deep sigh.

"Did you find any other things that will help us?"

Doc shook his head. "I'll call you if the crime team comes up with anything unique, but this guy is smart."

A half an hour later Dr. Ward's brother arrived. Kacey and Drake shared with him the information they had learned from Doc regarding the dental matches to confirm the body was in fact his brother.

He stood with his shoulders slouched and head bowed slightly forward as he listened. After swiping at his eyes he asked, "Can I see him?"

Kacey glanced at Drake. "It's not recommended. You don't want that image in your head."

"You don't understand. My parents will never believe it. They will need to know that I saw him, confirmed it. They may never get closure. He's their golden boy, you know. Yeah, I own my own business, maybe even a fairly successful one, but it doesn't quite measure up to being a doctor."

Kacey nodded before asking him to wait a moment while she talked with Doc, leaving Drake with the grieving brother..

A few minutes later she returned and explained that his brother's body would be moved to the viewing room—a room that allowed for viewing from behind a glass window, keeping contaminates out of the laboratory and away from the body. Since Doc was still examining the body and because it was evidence in a crime, family could not be allowed access to touch the body. Kacey felt relief because there were other more personal reasons to not allow a family member close to a loved one that had suffered in such a tragic way. She knew from personal experience the image of seeing a body like this would never go away.

After the viewing was complete the younger Ward brother left visibly shaken without accepting any assistance from the detectives.

"You handled that really well," Drake said to Kacey, knowing the death notifications always affected her.

"Thanks," she replied before turning towards the exit in an anxious attempt to get out of the building.

Sticks and Stones

Chapter Twenty One

The next two days were spent going over and over the information for each of the murders. Both Drake and Kacey were exhausted from not having rested. The wall was now covered with more photographs, including those from the Ward crime scene.

The table they worked from was littered with Styrofoam cups, some still half filled with coffee. Kacey stood up and began clearing away the mess. It was nine-thirty at night, and the last food they had was breakfast burritos more than twelve hours earlier.

"I need food, a shower, some sleep, and fresh clothes. I'm out of ideas." She pushed at her hair, tangling it behind her neck in a dark twist and then releasing it before pushing her hands through it again with obvious exhaustion and frustration.

Drake stood to help her clean up the mess as the chief entered the room. His square shoulders filled the door frame.

"Let me preface this by saying the decision has already been made," he started, a grim look covering his always serious face.

"Chief?" Drake inquired, confused by the abrupt entry and odd disclaimer.

"Tomorrow morning you will get some additional assistance. You've done a good job, but we need a fresh set of eyes before someone else is killed."

Drake and Kacey exchanged a glance and waited for Dalton to continue.

"The FBI is sending in two agents tomorrow. A profiler and a psychologist."

"Come on, Chief," Kacey began to protest.

"I knew you wouldn't like it, but we have no choice."

Drake continued where Kacey left off. "The Feebs? Seriously?" He referred to the agents in commonly used slang amongst local police authority.

"They'll be here at o-ten-thirty. Get some rest so you're fresh to brief them. The case is still yours. They'll be here to consult." Before leaving the room he added, "For now," then disappeared as quickly as he had appeared, leaving a gaping hole in the door frame.

"Shit!" Kacey muttered under her breath.

Drake grabbed his jacket off the back of one of the chairs, slammed the files into his brief case, and said, "Let's go. Dinner at my place. We've got to solve this before they take it from us."

Kacey grabbed her coat, slipping into the sleeves before collecting the rest of the files and copies of photos that matched those hanging on the board in the room.

When they got to his truck Drake asked, "How does delivery sound?"

"Okay, but can we swing by my place so I can grab some clothes?"

Drake glanced over at her and a smile covered his face for the first time in days. "Detective James, does this mean you might actually stay the whole night?"

"Slow down, big boy. We've got a little over twelve hours before the F...B...I," dragging out the letters as she spoke, "descends upon us. We need to use every minute of it."

Drake nodded a slow, deliberate nod, and the smile stayed on his face. "Yeah okay. I understand your logic."

The truck roared up in front of Kacey's apartment building. Drake started to get out and follow her, but she waved her hand at him. "I'll be right back—two minutes tops."

Pulling his door shut again, he settled back in the seat and watched her disappear into the night, then saw lights come on inside her apartment.

He closed his eyes and waited, taking advantage of the silence in the vehicle to allow himself to relax. He nearly nodded off so he shifted in the seat to force himself to stay awake. Glancing at his watch he suddenly realized Kacey had been gone for nearly fifteen minutes. Something wasn't right. He pulled the door handle and exited the truck. As he took quick, long strides up to her apartment he could hear voices that seemed to be arguing. He immediately recognized Kacey's voice and the voice of a man that seemed familiar, but he couldn't place it right away.

He approached the door and tapped on it with his thick knuckles. The door swung inward. Inside he could see Kacey pushing against a male. "What the hell is going on in here?"

The man swung around and staggered, nearly falling over the coffee table. "Oh looky, the partner comes to the rescue," Craig Dermot said with an obvious slur in his speech.

"Dermot, get the hell out of here," Drake said pulling him away from Kacey.

"Screw you, Drake."

Kacey pushed at the inebriated man. "Get the hell out of here and go sleep it off in your car."

Drake gave Dermot another tug and forced him out of the front door as the man reached inside his coat pocket to fish out a set of car keys. Nearly dragging him away from the doorway, Drake pulled him along all the while Dermot spouted off about Kacey being a cock tease and how he was going to get him some of that.

Doing all he could to not pop the guy in the face, Drake shoved him hard into the side of his car, pushed the fob button to release the doors, and shoved Dermot inside before closing the door behind him. "Sleep it off, Dermot, or I'll report this to the chief." Drake shoved the keys he'd recovered from the drunken officer into his own pocket as he pushed the lock button on the car, locking Dermot inside.

Kacey appeared behind him with a small overnight bag over her shoulder. Drake led her away from Dermot's car. Once back inside the truck he asked, "What the hell was that all about?"

Kacey turned in her seat to face him, "Hell if I know. I was getting my stuff together, heard a knock at the door, and thought it was you. When I opened it, that drunk asshole pushed his way inside."

"Did he hurt you?"

Kacey laughed out loud. "That punk ass. No, I was just trying to get him back outside, but he was all hands and talkin' shit. Trust me, if he'd tried anything I would have dropped him like a rock."

Drake glanced over at the car. Dermot's head was rolled back on the headrest. He was obviously passed out. After reaching into his pocket he held up Dermot's keys. Do we leave these here or take them with us?" A big grin covered his face.

"Take them. If he wakes up before he's sober and tries to drive, he could kill someone." She shared the smile. "Besides, make him figure out how he's getting back home. Dumb ass. Serves him right."

Drake laughed out loud and shoved the keys back in his coat pocket and turned the engine over on the truck.

As Drake drove towards his apartment, Kacey called for carry-out to be delivered. After she'd completed the order and hung up the phone, Drake glanced over at her and asked, "How does Dermot know where you live?"

Kacey shrugged. "Heck if I know. He is a cop, ya' know."

Drake nodded. His face, now covered with nearly two days of beard growth—making him look even more ruggedly handsome, had a sullen look on it.

Kacey watched him for a moment and then teased him, "Aw, you're jealous. How cute."

Drake shook his head. "I am anything but cute."

"Yes, you are and you are jealous. Dermot is a ball bag. Don't worry about him. Not in a million years would I sleep with that arrogant jerk."

"Then why do you tease around with him?"

"Because I can, silly."

Drake muttered a slight, "Hmmm," under his breath.

"You really don't understand women, Colton. You see the one big hold we have over men is sex, well, and intelligence, but we'll leave that alone for a moment. A guy like Dermot can be manipulated by the *idea* of sex so easily that, well, it's nearly impossible for a woman to leave alone. Taunting him is totally entertainment for me, and frankly, for all the other guys to watch. So that is why I do it. Because I can."

Drake pulled the truck into a parking space and shook his head again "You are really remarkable, you know that? So is that what you're doing with me? Using sex?"

The sideways smile on Kacey's face turned to a complete grin. "You really don't get women. If I was toying with you, do you think I would allow you to do *things* to me? Never mind. I'll just have to show you the difference, I guess." She reached over and ran her hand slyly up his thigh and across his groin, offering a gentle squeeze, and then pulled on her door handle and hopped down out of the truck.

Drake groaned as he followed her up to his apartment. He inserted the key into the lock, turned the doorknob, and pushed the door inward. He followed Kacey inside. After dropping his computer bag containing the files they had brought with them, he grabbed her arm and pulled her back to him. "You know that wasn't very nice of you."

"Really? I thought it was incredibly generous." She giggled then leaned up to him and teased his lips with her tongue while wrapping one arm around the back of his neck and sliding her free hand over the front of his jeans again. Feeling his obvious erection, she continued caressing him. "It would seem you thought it was pretty nice too…unless you'd like me to stop."

Abruptly removing her hand and pulling away, Drake groaned again and he reached for her to pull her back to him just as there was a knock on the door. Kacey laughed out loud as Drake groaned even louder. "Seriously?"

Kacey went to the door and allowed the delivery man in to set the bags on the counter across the room. She reached in her own computer bag to retrieve her wallet and handed the young blonde teenager a credit card. After applying a tip, she let him back out the door and turned back to Drake with a huge smile on her face.

"Shall we eat?"

Drake shook his head with a tormented look on his face. "You are ruthless, you know?"

"Maybe so, and I'm starving." She walked towards the kitchen to gather a couple of plates and glasses.

Chapter Twenty Two

Drake and Kacey spent much of the night reviewing files, numerous photos, interview notes, and Doc's medical assessments of the victims. Frustration and exhaustion finally led them into the bedroom where Kacey finished what she had started before the food delivery had arrived. Their lovemaking was slow, purposeful, yet less demanding, allowing them both to fall into a deep sleep, their bodies curled around each other where they remained until Drake's phone alarm sounded at six o'clock in the morning.

Kacey stirred first stretching her lean legs and pressing into Drake. He moved next to her, pulling her body further into his. Kacey opened her eyes and found Drake looking at her.

"You're still here," he said with surprise in his voice.

"Well, you had me all tied up with your legs all night. I couldn't get away even if I wanted to."

"Oh, so you tried to leave?"

"I was too tired to get free," she smirked then leaned in and kissed his cheek.

"I see. Well, I'm glad you're here."

"You know what today is, right?"

"Ummm, please tell me I'm not forgetting your birthday. I'm not good at that stuff."

"No, worse than me getting older. It's Feeb day."

"Are you trying to piss me off this early in the morning?"

Kacey's phone rattled from the bedside nightstand where she'd laid it before falling into Drake's arms the night before. She stretched over Drake's chest to grab the phone and slid her finger

169

across the screen without looking at the caller ID. "James," she said into the microphone.

"You bitch!"

"What the hell? Dermot?"

"You left me in my car and took my goddamned keys."

"Hey, stop yelling at me. You should be grateful. If I'd let you drive you'd be sleeping it off in a cell, giving up your badge, and that is best case scenario."

"I want my keys now!"

"You've got a lot of nerve, Dermot. You come to my house drunk, trying to force yourself on me, and now you think you can just demand me to jump? Well, guess what, asshole, take a cab."

She pushed her hair back as she slammed the phone onto the nightstand and then slid off the bed.

"Hey, slow down," Drake said grabbing for her.

"What an asshole he is."

Drake watched her sleek lean body as she faded into the bathroom. He heard the shower turn on and slipped from beneath the covers to follow her.

Joining her in the shower, he poured shampoo into his hand and slowly massaged it into her dark hair then allowed his hands to slip down to her shoulders, massaging until he could feel her relax.

She turned to face him. She smiled as she rinsed the soap from her hair, then proceeded to soap his chest, rising to her tip toes to kiss his lips.

***

Freshly showered and rejuvenated from the passion that seemed to continue from the night into the morning, Drake and Kacey stood side by the side in the kitchen. Drake washed and Kacey dried the dishes from the breakfast they'd shared.

Kacey placed the last plate in the cupboard above her head. "You know, I am very surprised that you have a decently stocked refrigerator. Those eggs were great."

"There is a lot about me you could still learn, if you choose to." Drake teased her with a twinkle in his eyes; the corner of his mouth turned up on one side.

Kacey placed her hand on his chest and pushed him back. "Really? Slow down, big boy. We need to get into the department before the FBI takes over our whole case."

Drake groaned. "You had to say those three ugly letters, didn't you?"

"Sorry, but we really do need to go."

"I know. It's just been nice enjoying having you here and blocking out the case even for just a few hours."

"I know, but now let's go get the bastard that's doing all this."

Drake smiled. "And that is why I love having you as my partner."

Kacey pushed her hair back over her shoulder and smiled. "Then let's go."

Drake smiled as he leaned in and kissed her tenderly, and then turned to the living room where he began gathering up the files that remained spread out on the coffee table.

Chapter Twenty Three

Upon arriving at the precinct, Drake and Kacey walked into the office and immediately saw Dermot sitting at his desk nursing a cup of coffee with his head resting in the palm of his hand.

Kacey walked right past him without saying a word. Drake stopped next to his desk and glared down at the junior officer as he threw down a set of keys. "You screwed up last night. Do it again and you'll be sitting here wishing you were dead. Are we clear?"

Dermot never even raised his head, and Drake didn't wait for an answer. He just followed Kacey into the investigation room. She was already in the process of setting up the photos they'd removed to take with them the night before.

Drake began to assist and looked up at the clock that hung on the wall over the white board. It was nine o'clock. If they were on time the FBI agents would be in within an hour. His stomach knotted up on him. He was not looking forward to their arrival. Dermot crossed his mind again too. Stupid bastard.

Kacey looked at him. "You okay?" she asked.

Not realizing he'd been standing there staring at the clock, his eyes met hers. "Yeah, just not thrilled about the FBI coming in. We can catch this guy ourselves. There's something in these files. We just have to figure it out."

"I know. I don't like it either. So let's get started. I keep thinking each time we go through the files something will jump out. We just aren't seeing it."

Nodding his head in agreement, Drake pulled out one of the chairs at the table and sat down. As they were just about to settle in, Dermot appeared in the door. He held two cups of coffee in his hands. He walked over and sat a cup in front of each of them. "Thanks for not ratting me out. It won't happen again."

Kacey looked at him. His eyes were red, and his clothes were rumpled from sleeping in the car. "Better get out of here. Chief will be in here in a few."

Drake just stared at him, though he picked up the coffee and took a sip as he watched Dermot over the steaming brew.

Once Dermot had left the room Drake asked, "Why do you put up with that asshole?"

"He's young, dumb, and full of himself. Don't you remember those days?"

Drake chuckled. "I was never like that."

"Really?" Kacey laughed at the irony of the comment. "Still full of yourself, maybe?"

"Yeah okay, you might be right."

Sliding out a chair, Kacey joined him at the table and pulled her laptop from her computer bag. She sat staring at the screen as the machine fired up. After the page loaded she then randomly began searching on the Internet for combinations of the victims' names. It was a long shot, but she couldn't think of anything they had not yet tried and wondered if there was some way Janet could have missed something.

An hour passed and suddenly there were voices in the hallway. Both detectives looked up from their fruitless searches to see the chief entering the room followed by two others. The first was a woman in a black pencil skirt, her chestnut brown hair neatly fashioned into a bun. She was tall and lean, her dark and intense eyes masked by dark framed glasses. She quickly scanned the room before assessing the pair sitting at the table.

Following her was a man, also tall with dark hair and dark eyes. He carried himself with confidence, and his broad shoulders filled the door way as he entered. Despite his perfectly pressed suit he had a ruggedness about him that seemed in almost contradiction to the rest of his demeanor.

Drake and Kacey rose from their seats in unison. The woman out stretched her hand first to Drake and then to Kacey. With each she made eye contact as a thin smile crossed her lips. "Agent Spinelli. Thanks for allowing us in to assist."

The male followed suit and took the same actions introducing himself, "Agent Connor." His eyes locked in on each detective and his rugged face held a serious look as he shook hands with the two detectives.

The chief took over once each of the detectives had returned the introductions. "Agents, thank you for coming in. We welcome your input and will openly share our case files with you. My detectives obviously keep control of the case, but anything you can do to help us catch this sick bastard is welcomed."

Drake and Kacey knew the comments were intended for their benefit. He had just set the stage for how this would work. Neither was happy with the fact that the case had lingered open to the point of needing assistance, but at least for now they still had control of the situation.

Agent Spinelli spoke first. "Thank you, Chief. We are here to assist not take over. We will attempt to aid in developing a profile which should help in narrowing the search efforts. It would be especially helpful if you could walk us through what you have uncovered so far."

Agent Connor walked over to the white board that contained the timeline and photographs. He stood in front of each photo for several seconds before moving to the next.

Kacey watched and wondered if somehow he thought those photos would speak to him as if reading tea leaves. Deciding to join him, she walked up beside him and began back at the first photograph. Spinelli joined them, all three standing in a row as Kacey outlined the discovery of each of the bodies, the subsequent autopsy findings and the linkage back to Robert Fields, the sadistic killer who sat in a mental hospital after killing his family and torturing his young daughter Sophie. The two agents listened intently as Kacey completed the overview.

Agent Connor spoke for the first time since his introduction. "He's methodical. The fact that his method of killing changes with each murder says he is sending a message."

Kacey tried not to show her annoyance at the generalization. "Right, but what is that message?"

175

"I don't know, but when we figure it out we will catch your guy," Agent Connor said turning to face Kacey.

"One more thing," Agent Spinelli chimed in, "he won't stop until his message has been fully delivered."

Drake, who had been standing back observing during the entire exchange, chimed in, "Or until he's caught."

Spinelli shrugged her shoulders. "Yes, or until he is caught."

"We'd like to talk to Fields. He seems to be the only connection here." Connor paused to seemingly choose his words carefully before continuing, "Besides the two of you."

"Look," Kacey started to interject but was cut off by Spinelli's hand raised in the air.

"We are not here to investigate you, but we have to address the fact that in some way you are both tied to this case. If we choose to ignore those facts we may overlook important details that could potentially damage the investigation."

Kacey relaxed a little, though her mind was still reeling. *Seriously, could they be considered suspects?* Kacey refrained from allowing her eyes to land on Drake and kept her eyes on Spinelli, making sure that she maintained contact. She could sense Drake was doing the same even though she really couldn't see his face.

Drake's voice came from over her shoulder. "Well, okay let's head out to the hospital. I'll pull the car around." He looked to Kacey. "Mind calling ahead and letting them know we are coming out and will want to see Fields?"

Connor nodded to Drake and turned to the chief. "We'll give you a briefing at the end of the day."

The chief grunted in response before turning and leaving the room.

Chapter Twenty Four

Walking into the kitchen and dropping keys onto the counter, Iz went directly to the refrigerator, opened the door, and scanned the contents. The shelves were stocked, but not wanting to cook a container holding some leftovers was worthy of the microwave.

A few minutes later, Iz sat satisfied on the couch with legs stretched out, feet propped up on the coffee table. A sigh escaped and within minutes sleep came.

Two hours later waking with a start, Iz stretched and stood, heading back towards the bedroom.

Iz?

Iz didn't respond at first, continuing to the bedroom and beginning to strip off clothes and crawling into the bed and pulling the covers up.

Iz?

What?

When can we do it again?

Not now.

Why, Iz? Why not now?

Lots of reasons.

Like what?

Well, first of all, I am too tired to do anything. Work has been hectic. I've barely had any free hours. More importantly, there is too much attention right now. It's too risky. We need to wait.

But, Iz...no one has come looking for us.

I know, but we can't get over confident.

Do you think about it? Them?
Yes. I think about it.
Me too. I think about it all the time. It is so exciting.
I know.
How long do you think we have to wait?
I don't know. Now go to sleep.
Iz?
We have to go to sleep!
But, Iz?
Damn it! What?
I'm sorry, Iz. It's just...I need to do it again.
We'll do it again when it is safe. Now go to sleep.

Chapter Twenty Five

Drake stepped out of his truck into the parking lot at the precinct and walked towards the front entry. He heard a whistle from somewhere off to the left and turned to see Kacey walking towards him.

"Good morning. Did you get some rest?" Kacey smiled looking somewhat refreshed.

"Some, I guess," Drake responded, a sour look on his face.

"What's up?" she asked reading his mood.

He shrugged. "I dunno. I guess the Feebs have me rattled."

"I know, but hey, they got nothing more from the visit with Fields than we did."

Drake shrugged. "Yeah, I guess so."

Kacey studied his face, noting the day old beard growth. Worry filled her, but before she could say anything out of the corner of her eye she saw the two FBI agents, Spinelli and Connor walking towards them.

Not wanting to draw any attention, she smiled as they approached and pulled the door open, holding it for Spinelli to enter. Drake took the other door handle, allowing Connor to pass in front of him.

Spinelli acknowledged the gesture offering a quick "Morning" as a greeting.

The group walked the marbled hallway to the investigation room.

Drake opened the conversation, "Fields gives us nothing. The man is crazier than a mad hatter."

"I agree, Detective," Connor responded. "However, if he is somehow behind this we have to figure out how he is orchestrating this from within the hospital. We need to overturn every stone on whom, if anyone, he was ever close to. It could be someone as far back as a childhood friend."

"How would he be manipulating that person to do these things from within that hospital? He has no means to contact the outside. He's had no visitors. I think that is a waste...," Kacey was arguing and got cutoff.

"It is possible that someone he was close to in the past feels compelled to do these things on his behalf without his input. It's a long shot, but we have to eliminate it as a possibility."

Drake shook his head, his hands placed on his hips.

"There's more," Connor continued. "We told you yesterday that you are not under investigation, but we do have some things we need to clear up so that we have it on record."

"Oh, here it comes?" Drake scoffed.

"Detective, it's necessary. It's not intended to degrade you, but quite the opposite. It's intended to support you and ensure no one challenges the integrity of the investigation or you being part of the investigation." Spinelli stated in a matter of fact tone.

Kacey turned from Drake and responded, "What do you need from us?"

"We need to show that you each have an alibi for at least one of the nights of the murders. We know you responded to the scenes, but in each case several hours had already passed."

"Yeah, enough time for someone to go and get cleaned up. You think we don't know what you are inferring?" Drake said.

"Well, let's get to it and see if we can't quickly close this out so we can move on."

"Does the chief know you are asking this?"

"Yes. Yes, he does. We explained what we needed to do when we debriefed him last night."

Kacey shrugged and gave Drake a look that said he should drop it. "Okay, let's do it."

"Great. Let's just walk through the timelines of the night of each death, starting first with the murder of Frank Parker, Robert Fields's brother in law." Spinelli fished through some papers in a file folder that had occupied the table moments earlier.

"Parker was found floating in the water under a bridge overpass, and the autopsy revealed that he had a needle embedded in his eye."

"We can check our badge scans, motor pool, and case files to tell me what time we left here that night."

"Where were you when you got the call to come out to the crime scene?" Connor inquired, his face maintaining the seriousness he had held since they'd met.

Kacey glanced at Drake. "I was in bed. It was the middle of the night."

"Were you alone?"

"Ah shit, this is ridiculous," Drake said slamming one of the chairs into the table.

Connor stepped forward. "Look, I understand how this might feel, but the reality is we need your cooperation so we can get back to what is important, and that is finding the man that killed those people." He pointed at the white board with the photos of the murdered victims.

"Drake, it's okay," Kacey said before continuing. "I was alone. I live alone."

"What about you, Detective Drake?"

"I was in bed. Alone!"

"You remember this explicitly?"

"Yes."

"How?"

Drake sighed in frustration before continuing. "I leave my cell phone next to my bed on the nightstand. It rang. Remember being in bed."

Connor and Spinelli's eyes moved to Kacey. "Same. Cell phone rang, I answered."

"Okay. What about the other murders?"

One by one they walked through each time of the murders. Candice Jackson, the young prostitute found in the salvage yard ravished by dogs; Harold Sloan, Frank Parker's client found in his home suspended from his bathroom door frame, a board nailed across his back side; and finally, Dr. Timothy Ward, the director of the mental hospital where Robert Fields remained imprisoned for his heinous crimes, suspended and burned out in the rural area outside of the city.

Neither detective had an alibi, and in each case the calls had come either in the middle of the night or at a time when they were together, but for the estimated time of death, neither could specifically claim any real alibi.

Drake piped up after thinking for a minute, "Our research analyst can pull the GPS on the cell phones for the nights of each murder. It will show that when the calls came in we were each in our homes and will show our recollection is correct. I know that doesn't one hundred percent say where we were when the crimes happened, but it certainly says we have a good memory of the events immediately following the murders."

Connor nodded. "Let's have her do it. Everything helps."

Drake placed a call to Janet and after just a few moments disconnected. "She'll send it over as soon as she has it pulled. It shouldn't take too long."

"Okay, let's re-focus. We'd like to see the crime scenes. Being able to see the places the un-sub has chosen may help with a profile. It could be symbolic and meaningful in the message he's trying to send," Connor stated.

"I can stay here and keep hashing through the data," Kacey offered. "I keep feeling like there's something very simple we have missed, and I think one of these times it is going to jump off the page at me."

"Okay, let's move. It won't be long before he acts again and we need to figure out his next move before that happens," Spinelli stated already turning to the door.

Kacey watched the trio leave the room then sat down and opened her laptop. As the machine powered on she considered what it was she wanted to search.

Several hours later the two FBI agents and Drake returned to the precinct to find Kacey hunched over her laptop deep in concentration. When she heard the footsteps she looked up.

"How's your search going?" Drake asked.

Kacey shook her head. I've searched on everything I can think of. There have been previous murders where a needle was inserted into the victim's eye and, of course, thousands of fire related crimes, but I got nothing but a bunch of recipes when searching on the pork chop crime. I also tried to find a correlation to the salvage yard. There have been others where bodies have been discovered in salvage yards, but nothing even close to the bathroom scene. And in none of these were there common threads between a salvage yard and the fire death or any other combination."

"So our killer has not perpetrated these crimes in another city and just suddenly moved here starting up again."

Kacey leaned back in her chair and sighed, pulling her hair into a pile at the back of her head.

"This is good," Spinelli stated.

Drake turned to her. "How so?"

"A drifter is harder to find. They come and go and don't leave a trail. If your killer is from this community, he is less likely to move on to another location."

"What if he just stops? Or even gets scared and just decides to lay low. Or maybe he's already completed the message he was trying to send," Kacey speculated.

"He won't just stop until the message is not only delivered but understood. The symbolism in the killings is just as important as the killing."

"So what could be the potential motives?"

"Well," Spinelli started then walked over to the white board. "The typical reasons people commit murder include," she wrote a list on the board as she spoke, "*Revenge, Jealousy/Sex, Greed, Hate, Property Dispute, Drugs, Initiation, Urge to Protect, Protect a Secret, Class Conflict, Personal Vendetta,* and *Politics.*"

Spinelli stepped back from the list as the others stepped forward and stared at it.

"So which ones can we eliminate?"

Drake spoke first. "Greed. There has been plenty of opportunity to take from the victims, but nothing has been taken and Candice Jackson didn't have a pot to piss in."

"Okay," Spinelli stepped forward and put an X over *Greed.*

"I can't say jealousy doesn't apply, but *Sex* can be struck off. Even though Candice was a prostitute there were no signs of sex

183

prior to the murder. None of the other victims had any signs of sexual trauma either. And given the fact that we have both males and female victims, it seems that sex is out."

The foursome stood, considering the proposal for a few moments, and then in silent agreement, Spinelli put an X through the word *Sex*, leaving *Jealousy* still in the list of possibilities.

"*Property Dispute* is out. There's no tangible evidence tying these people together," Kacey stated.

"What if the property is not tangible?" Connor asked.

"Like?" Kacey inquired.

"Like a child, girlfriend, love of a parent."

"Wouldn't that fall into the category of *Jealousy* or *Revenge?*"

Connor conceded, "Okay, as long as we all agree that is how we are considering it. Property is tangible."

The others all nodded in agreement as Spinelli crossed off *Property Dispute* from the board.

The process continued and ultimately *Class Conflict, Politics, Protecting a Secret, Urge to Protect,* and *Drugs* were also removed from the list. They all stood before the board and considered the remaining items: *Revenge, Jealousy, Hate, Initiation,* and *Vendetta.*

Spinelli, who had remained quiet as they had one by one reduced the list, now spoke. "I think *Hate* can be removed too."

The others each started to debate the comment. Raising her hand she continued, "Hear me out. Yes, the crimes are violent, but typical hate crimes are bloody and consistent. A killer takes a hatchet and repeatedly chops at his victim. In this case there is a story being told. We don't know what the story is yet. I would argue that, yes, he hates these people in the moment, but these victims are more about the message than the source of the hate."

"I see what you're saying, but we can't be sure," Kacey countered.

"Okay. You're right," Spinelli conceded. "How about this, we start to break down these and prioritize them in the order of the most likely reason."

"Well, I would say *Revenge* is first if we really think Robert Fields is somehow orchestrating this from inside his hospital room," Drake said.

"Or if someone is orchestrating this on his behalf," Kacey added.

Connor had been deep in concentration for a while. "What could he be jealous of? Harold Sloan was a terrible drunk, significantly obese, reclusive, and Candice was a street worker."

"Good point," Kacey stated. "You're right, Drake. Nothing indicates our killer is trying to be like these people or that he is angry over the lifestyle they've led. He doesn't seem to desire to have any material objects, as nothing of value is missing. Candice didn't have anything of value. He also doesn't seem to be trying to take on the personality of any of our victims."

They spent another hour further talking through the possible motives and narrowed the list to *Revenge, Vendetta, Initiation,* and *Hate.*

Looking at the list, Connor spoke up, "He's angry about something. It could be past or present and when that boils up into hate, he kills. His victims are both random and chosen. This makes him highly unusual and means he's organized, thoughtful, and controlled. He's sending a message and he wants to be understood."

"I'm stuck on initiation as a motive. This could mean we have multiple killers," Kacey said, a concerned look on her face.

Drake spoke up shrugging his shoulders. "This could explain the random methods of murder."

"It could also explain the seemingly taunting message to the two of you. Possibly a specific gang trying to tell the two of you that you can't stop them," Connor stated.

"Wouldn't it make more sense for the targets of the message to be detectives in the gang division if that were the case?"

"Possibly, but we can't be sure." Connor agreed then continued, "Have either of you had any dealings, even brief encounters, with gang members?"

Drake and Kacey looked at each other, considering the question, and after a couple of moments Drake said, "Well a couple of years ago there was a seventeen-year-old boy killed by a gang member. We arrested the shooter."

"Any idea where that shooter is right now?" Spinelli asked.

Kacey shrugged. "No, but we can find out."

Drake's cell phone rang. He quickly answered the call after seeing Janet's number pop up. "Drake."

"I just forwarded over all the GPS phone dumps from your cell phones. Just letting you know it all checks out."

"Thanks, Janet. We'll pull the files. Can you do something else for us too?"

"Shoot."

"Kacey and I worked a case a couple of years ago involving a seventeen-year-old murder victim. The shooter was a gang member by the name of Fats, real name was Bellows. Can you find out where he is now? I think they shipped him upstate."

"I'm on it."

"Hey, Janet. We need it fast."

"Your wish is my command."

Drake ended the call. "The GPS files are in our email boxes. She said everything checks out."

Connor and Spinelli nodded.

"How soon before we have info on your gang shooter?"

"Knowing Janet, a few minutes," Drake answered.

"Good," Connor said just as Dermott walked into the room.

Everyone turned to face the younger officer. "What's up?" Kacey asked.

"You might want to turn on the tube. Jessica Sperry is live right now."

Drake reached for a remote lying next to them on the table they'd been working on and punched the power button, bringing to life a TV that sat on a stand in the far corner of the room.

Everyone moved over to face the TV and watched as the reporter stood in front of the mental hospital where Robert Fields resided and Dr. Timothy Ward had worked.

Photos of the victims were on the screen next to the woman, then quickly changed to photos of both Drake and Kacey.

"...FBI agents have been brought in to assist these two detectives who have been unable to stop the killer that has been terrorizing our city streets for weeks now. So far four people are dead and all seem to be related back to the preventable and senseless murder of young Sophie Fields. Are the very detectives assigned to find the killer somehow involved? Hopefully, the FBI will be able to identify the connection and catch the killer before *he strikes again. Jessica Sperry reporting live from Channel 8 News with another update at ten o'clock."*

The screen switched to an image of a retail store, and the story changed back to the education budget at a local school. Drake punched off the TV and let out a big sigh. "That little…"

Kacey held up her hand to stop Drake from finishing the sentence. "Ignore her. Let's get back to what we were doing and just prove her wrong."

Drake's phone rang and broke the mood. Janet's number appeared on the display.

Chapter Twenty Six

It had been another long and frustrating day at work. Iz struggled at times with being pushed so hard, but even on difficult days enjoyed the work. It was well after eight o'clock when Iz walked into the dark apartment and navigated from memory down the hall and back to the bedroom.

Dropping onto the edge of the bed and kicking off boots, Iz was immediately greeted with questions.

Iz, you've been gone so long. I missed you.

Long day at work, but I'm home now.

I've been waiting, hoping we could do it again. We've waited long enough. It's dark. Perfect, right, Iz?

I'm tired. It's still too soon.

NO, Iz, it's NOT too soon!

Don't raise your voice to me!

Sorry. I just miss it. We can't let people treat us like they do.

Iz sat silently considering this. After a few moments and ignoring the desire to lay back on the bed and sleep, images began to form and overcome the weary feeling that had been obvious when first entering the apartment just a few minutes earlier.

Iz's eyes glanced at the clock on the nightstand next to the bed. There was time. It was late enough but relatively early. Reaching to the nightstand and pulling the top drawer open, Iz retrieved an older Polaroid camera. A required item for the idea Iz had been thinking of for days.

Are we going out?

Yes, just settle down.

Okay, I'll settle down. Thank you, Iz.

An hour later after changing into dark clothing and collecting some items, Iz was driving down the street navigating the city roads carefully, comfortably cloaked in the darkness that only was violated by the city lights. The roads were light of cars, which allowed Iz to relax back into the seat. The camera was in the back seat along with a few other important items hidden inside a black bag.

Iz's eyes shifted to the clock on the center dashboard as the car settled to a stop at a light. The green digit numbers read 9:46. A smile crept over Iz's mouth.

Iz, are we almost there?

Yes. Just two more streets.

I'm so excited now, Iz. I can't wait.

The light changed, and Iz continued to navigate the car to the desired destination and pulled into the parking lot, scanning the best location to park where there was good visibility to the doors. Iz continued until finally spotting the Mercedes, selected a space at the rear of the lot, and backed in facing the car, settling in to wait.

How long will we have to wait, Iz?

Shhh, quiet now.

Ten minutes passed before one of the side doors to the well-lit building opened. Iz leaned forward in the seat, squinting over the steering wheel. Realizing the person was a male, Iz settled back low in the seat, low enough to not be seen. A car engine fired somewhere a few vehicles away. Iz sat still and waited, listening until the car could be heard driving away.

Sliding back up in the seat, Iz's eyes settled on the Mercedes and released a low sigh. Another door opened and a figure began walking through the cars. Iz narrowed eyes in again, watching closely. A breath caught in Iz's chest, a flutter of excitement coursing with each step the body took towards the Mercedes. Iz glanced quickly at the clock—ten thirty— right on schedule.

The Mercedes door opened, and the woman slid inside. Iz watched steadily, patiently waiting before starting the vehicle.

Get her now, Iz!

No, not here. It's not safe. Now hush.

The Mercedes pulled away from the space it had occupied, and Iz fired up the engine, pulling out and leaving the headlights off until safely onto the street. The Mercedes slipped through the dark unaware it was being followed. Iz kept a safe distance as the driver ahead made her way to a residential street a few miles away in a posh neighborhood.

Iz killed the lights again and followed the car into the neighborhood, stopping next to the curb a few houses away. Grabbing the bag behind the seat, Iz stepped out of the car and slipped along the walkway, avoiding street lamps and stepping into the shadows next to the home as the Mercedes waited for the garage door to open. As the car pulled in, Iz slipped inside stepping over the sensor and staying tucked close to the corner right before the door rolled closed. The driver turned off the car and the headlights dimmed which left the garage lit only by the overhead garage door opener light.

Iz set the black bag down on the floor and flexed gloved hands, adrenaline pumping, waiting for the car door to swing open. As the driver stepped out with her hands filled with keys and a purse, Iz stepped forward. Before recognition could even set in, Iz wrapped both arms around the woman. One hand coved her mouth and the other squeezed tightly around her neck. The woman fought but moments later went limp.

Iz allowed the purse and keys to drop to the floor and then dragged the unconscious woman across the garage floor and through the unlocked door that connected the garage and the interior of the home. Once inside Iz scanned the room, eyes quickly adjusting to the ambient lighting from a glow somewhere off in the distance. Even in the dark Iz could see that the home was lavishly decorated.

After dropping the woman's body onto the thick carpet in the open expanse of the living room, Iz returned to the garage to retrieve the black bag containing the Polaroid camera and other items needed to execute the plan.

Oh, Iz, this is going to be the best one ever. She's pretty. We're going to show her. Right. Iz?

Oh, yeah we're going to show her.

Yeah, we're going to show her.

Iz retrieved the black bag from the corner of the garage where it had been abandoned after entering the garage. The garage was almost entirely dark now, but Iz easily navigated back into the living room. The woman was just beginning to stir. A smile crossed Iz's face.

Fumbling with the zipper on the bag through gloved hands Iz opened it to remove the camera, a roll of duct tape, and a small pair of scissors. Peeling back a strip of the heavy tape, Iz carefully cut the strip then wrapped the woman's hands tightly behind her back.

Next, Iz cut another piece of tape and applied this one over the woman's mouth, making a complete loop around her head and ensuring it wouldn't come off as she would, no doubt, fight her situation as soon as she fully awoke.

Just as the woman opened her eyes, Iz completed the task of wrapping a third strip of tape around her ankles, securing them together. Grabbing the woman's long locks of hair, Iz dragged the woman over to a coffee table that sat in front of a large leather sofa. The coffee table's base was solid marble. Iz removed a bundle of rope from the bag and tied the woman's bound hands to the base, making it impossible for the woman to move about the room. She was now properly secured.

After assessing the surroundings more thoroughly, Iz twisted on the switch of a small lamp that sat on the table next to the couch, then lifted the camera and began snapping off photos of the woman. She was now fully alert and struggled against her confinement. Her mouth only made gurgling sounds as she tried to speak, the tape preventing anything intelligible from being said.

Iz barely noticed her talking at all, continuing to snap pictures and laying each one out on the coffee table while the images slowly appeared. As the woman continued to struggle, Iz stopped and stared at the images on the table, admiring the strange expressions captured in each. As the photographs polarized, they showed expressions that depicted fear, recognition and anger.

With attention aimed around the house, Iz turned away from the woman and walked across the room towards the kitchen. Slowly opening a few of the drawers, Iz worked through the kitchen collecting a couple of items before returning to the room.

Iz held a knife, and even in the low lighting the blade glimmered, catching the woman's eyes and causing her to instinctively attempt to recoil, pushing deeper into the hard stone of the coffee table. She shook her head violently, and her eyes were wild with obvious fear. More unintelligible noises spilled from her terrified face.

Cut her, Iz. Cut her good. Make her pay. Make her pay for all the things she says.

Iz walked forward and slid the blade of the knife down the woman's face. Crimson red flowed from the cut and dripped onto the white carpet.

Cut her again, Iz. Cut her.

Iz took the tip of the knife and from the navel cut open the dress exposing her full breasts that seemed to overflow from her bra.

The woman was near hysterical now, but the tape was tight, holding her in place unable to push away from the knife. Iz stared at the woman's exposed torso and then went to work with the knife.

Five minutes later Iz stepped back and admired the work.

It's beautiful, Iz.

Thanks.

Now kill her!

Not quite yet.

Iz lifted the camera again and took several more pictures, laying each down on the table next to the others. Minutes later the pictures had developed and Iz stared at the collection. Gathering them all up, Iz laid them out all around the floor near her then stood back making eye contact with the woman for the first time. Leaning in, Iz whispered quietly in the woman's ear, "Bye."

Iz pushed the knife against the woman's abdomen, and then pressed hard until the knife was buried in the soft flesh and met resistance. Iz stepped back to avoid the blood that began to spill out. Iz twisted the handle a full turn to the right then watched as the woman's terrified face slowly grew pale and went slack.

Iz, we did it! I feel so good. Do you feel good too?

Yes. I do feel good. She was a little bitch.

Can we keep some of the pictures?

No! It's not safe.

But they are so pretty.

We can't. Now stop! Don't spoil it.

You're right. I just hope I can remember what they look like forever.

Iz stood and stared at the woman and the living room that had become the scene. The previously pristine room was now shiny with dark, coppery stains and littered with photographs. Iz placed the duct tape and camera back into the bag and turned to leave. Before exiting through the garage door, Iz turned back and took one more look at the scene with a feeling of satisfaction.

Leaving through the garage, Iz followed the same shadows back to the car and quietly opened and closed the door, then pulled away and slid off into the dark night. The clock on the dash read just after midnight.

Iz, thank you.

Okay, calm down now. We need to get home and get some sleep.

I'm not sure I'll be able to.

Me either.

Chapter Twenty Seven

Drake, Kacey, Connor, and Spinelli had closed up shop around eight o'clock that night and had agreed to meet back up in the morning at eight. Drake and Kacey had agreed to go their own ways despite the desire to go together. Everyone needed a good rest so they could each come back fresh.

With the FBI in town it was decided that Kacey would arrive first, walking past Dermot's desk on the way to the investigation room. She resisted the temptation to just walk past him without even acknowledging him, but realizing that would likely just fuel the fire with him, she greeted him, "Hey, Dermot."

Dermot looked up and their eyes met briefly. "Good morning," Dermot replied. Then his eyes skirted the room. "Where's your boyfriend?"

"Shut up, Dermot," Kacey tossed back at him, frustrated with his eager attempt to return their relationship to one of jokes and jibes. Without looking at him any further, she continued on to the investigation room to drop off her laptop bag before she went to the room just down the hallway and began making coffee. As she was pouring her first cup of coffee she heard Spinelli and Connor's voices.

Poking her head out of the room, Kacey gave a call out to the pair, "Coffee's ready if you'd like some."

"Oh, great, thanks," Connor replied, entering the room with Spinelli on his heels.

Each of the FBI agents filled their cups, mixing and stirring the cream and sweeteners to their respective satisfaction.

About fifteen minutes later and right at eight o'clock, Drake entered the investigation room where the others had settled and were each studying a file in an attempt to put the puzzle together.

"Good morning, Detective," Spinelli offered.

Drake nodded in response as his eyes darted reflexively to Kacey. Kacey looked at him and noted the tired look on his face and the light stubble of beard. He looked like he hadn't slept all night.

Kacey tried to cover for him, hoping the FBI agents wouldn't notice, given their lack of time working with him. "Coffee's ready in the break room."

"Great, thanks." Without saying anything else Drake walked out of the room, leaving his coat and laptop lying on the end of the table.

Kacey swallowed the last sip of coffee from her Styrofoam cup and stood up. "Anyone want a refill?"

Spinelli and Connor each shook their head in decline of the offer. Kacey shrugged before following Drake to the other room. Stepping next to him at the coffee station, she gave a sideways glance as he poured coffee into a cup. "You okay? Looks like you didn't get a wink of sleep."

Drake took a sip of the dark brew before turning to her and responding, "I never get good sleep when you aren't there."

"Actually, you don't get good sleep when I am there." Kacey gave him a seductive smile. "Seriously, Drake, you look like hell."

"I know." He shook his head. "This case has me all twisted up. I can't stop thinking that we are missing something and because of it more people are going to die."

"Well, let's go find that missing piece so we can find this guy."

"I wish it was that easy."

"It is, Drake. We just have to focus. Now come, let's go do this so we can get these Feebs out of our asses and get back to normal."

This made Drake smile. "Okay, you're right. You're always right, Kacey."

"Well, I don't know about all of that, but hey, you can keep the compliments coming all day."

Drake took another sip of the coffee and followed Kacey back to the investigation room, but before they could even settle down at the table to begin digging through the files yet again, the chief entered the room.

"What have we got?"

Kacey took the lead. "Not much, sir. We've been working on a profile."

"Well, what is that doing for us? Do we have a name? Address? At least tell me we have a list of potential suspects to interview."

Connor stood up. "It's not that easy. I wish it were, but we have narrowed this down some and I believe we have a reasonable profile. We believe our killer or killers are white male, thirty to forty-five, organized, and motivated by one of four reasons: revenge, vendetta, initiation, or hate."

"Wait, you said *he or they*? Are you trying to tell me we could be dealing with multiple killers?"

"Given the unusual nature of the murders, we are investigating the possibility of gang initiation as a credible motive. Your analyst confirmed that the convicted gang lord by the name of Fats was killed in prison. He was shanked while in the shower. Your detectives were responsible for his imprisonment. We can't rule out the possibility that someone in the gang is trying to settle up the score by making your detectives look like they might be responsible for these murders." Connor stopped and continued to face the chief without even a blink before he continued. "Chief, it is one possibility, and we have to rule each of them out to prove there's no way either is involved."

Without even responding Chief Harding grunted and left the room.

Connor exchanged looks with the others. "Let's get back to work."

The next several hours were spent continuing to fish through the evidence, the reports from Dr. Ward, and the possible connections to the gang lord Fats. Without being able to disprove the connection, they agreed to continue to pursue the idea as a viable one.

At a little after one o'clock, lunch was brought in and they all nibbled on sandwiches from a local deli as they read, continued to study the white board, and toss out possible theories. The room had settled into silence; the only noise was the occasional sound of one of them taking a bite out of a sandwich.

Suddenly, the room came alive with the ringing of Drake's cell phone. Looking at the screen, his brow furrowed as he swiped the screen and held the phone to his ear. "Drake," he said answering the call.

All eyes were on Drake as the others watched and listened to the one-sided conversation.

"What's the address?" There was a pause as he grabbed a pen and jotted down some information on a small notepad from inside his shirt pocket. "Has Doc been contacted? We're on our way." He punched a button on his phone.

"We have another body." He paused before looking at Kacey then back to the others. "It's Jessica Sperry, the Channel 8 News reporter."

Kacey had turned to put away her laptop but quickly spun back around. "What?"

Drake stared at her and nodded.

"Shit, what is going on?"

Connor and Spinelli stood up and were in motion right behind Drake and Kacey. As they walked out of the precinct Connor probed.

"What do we know?"

Spinelli dangled a set of keys in the air. "We'll drive my car. We don't have time for motor pool."

The four poured into a black sedan that seemed typical of a fed's car, and Spinelli sped away as Drake gave directions.

"She didn't report to work for a lunch meeting with the station director. That's totally out of character for her. She never missed an opportunity for attention." Drake nearly stuttered, realizing he was speaking ill of the dead.

"What else do we know?"

"The director sent someone over to her home to check on her after making several phone calls that she never answered. I don't have any other details, but apparently the woman he sent called 911, but had to be taken to the hospital after collapsing."

"Is Doc on his way?" Kacey asked.

"Yes, they called him right before calling us."

The car was quiet the rest of the ride. They pulled up to the curb in front of an impressive home in an affluent neighborhood. There were three patrol cars positioned to block the street and news vans from Channel 2 and other stations that were already starting to crowd in, pushing their way in an attempt to breach the barricade.

Drake looked at the reporters and shook his head. "Vultures, even when it's one of their own."

Kacey looked away from them. Disgust filled her.

The foursome walked towards the house, up the drive, flashing their badges as they ducked under the yellow tape that cordoned off the home. An officer stood at the front door and nodded as they passed. Kacey recognized him but couldn't remember his name. She was just glad it wasn't Dermot; she didn't think she could deal with his banter right now.

Inside the front door they immediately were greeted by a large living area and open floor plan that flowed into a kitchen and trailed off down a hall into other unknown parts.

Kacey's eyes immediately landed on the body grotesquely tied to the coffee table. Blood pooled around the body and soaked into the carpet. The crimson color faded and was now dark and sticky looking. Surrounding the body were at least two dozen Polaroid photographs. The scene was unbelievable. Jessica's face, typically beautiful and perfectly made up, was gaunt and pale. Her lifeless eyes stared as if admiring the photographs around her.

Drake walked through the home studying the floor and the surroundings.—his typical M.O. He never went to the body first. He pulled on gloves and opened the dishwasher. It was empty. His eyes scanned the kitchen counter and inside the sink. Next he stepped on the canister inside a small door at the end of the kitchen, popping the lid open on the trash can. Peering inside he saw the trash was also empty except for an oatmeal package. Finally he returned to the living room, allowing his eyes to see the dead reporter.

As Drake approached, Doc entered the home through the front door carrying his satchel, his glasses perched precariously on his nose. Drake nodded to him as he placed the satchel on the floor next to the body.

Conner and Spinelli went through the entire home. Spinelli looked at the answering machine that sat on the counter. The red light flashed. With a gloved finger she pushed the button and soon the house filled with a voice. *"Hey, Jess, call me."* The caller hung up. Another message played. *"Jess, you're late. I'm worried. Call me."* The machine went silent. Spinelli made a note of the number that had shown on the caller ID.

Connor opened the door that led to the garage and reached along the wall until his hand found the light switch. Inside, a car took up one side of the two car space. His eyes scanned the area looking for anything that might give insight into how someone had taken control of the reporter.

Kacey joined Connor, leaving the body to Doc and the CSI team that had already begun to catalogue and collect the photos that littered the floor and body.

She walked to the other side of the car and looked around the open space. Nothing seemed out of order. "Looks like she arrived home, parked her car, and went inside just like any other day."

"No signs of forced entry. Maybe she knew her killer and let him in," Connor speculated.

"Maybe," Kacey shrugged as she continued to look around. She checked out the tools that hung on the peg board, looking for a possible murder weapon. It was obvious Jessica had been stabbed several times. Doc would be able to tell them just how many and with how much anger and force. Kacey ran questions through her head, trying to align the scene to their narrowed list of possible motives. She pictured the list they had on the board back at the precinct. *Did this look like a hate crime, revenge?* Jessica likely had a number of people she'd reported about in the past that might have a score to settle with her.

Kacey turned to walk back towards the door. "Hey, Connor? Does this look like drag marks?" She kneeled down near the front of the car and close to the door.

Connor joined Kasey, kneeling next to her. The dust on the floor appeared to be disturbed and light skid marks were visible. "It does appear as if something was dragged across here."

"Given the distance of the marks, it could be consistent with heels dragging on the floor." Kacey stood, pushing open the door, careful not to step on the area they were studying. Peering back

200

inside the house, she looked to see Jessica's feet. Her shoes were still on her feet–dark blue pumps.

"Hey, can we get a CSI out here?" Kacey called out.

Looking back at the marks on the floor, Kacey pointed to Connor. "High heels likely caused the marks."

The CSI agent appeared in the doorway. "What have we got?"

"Possible drag marks here," Kacey said pointing to the floor.

Drake appeared in the door frame. "What'd you find?"

"Looks like maybe Jessica was dragged across the floor."

"So her killer was either inside her car with her, waiting inside when she got home, or someone managed to get inside the garage without tripping the safety when she was pulling in."

Spinelli joined the trio. "There doesn't appear to be any signs of breaking and entering. All the windows and doors have been checked and are secure."

"I'm surprised she doesn't have an alarm system."

Connor looked around. "It is odd given the neighborhood. You'd have thought she'd have taken more precautions."

"She couldn't be that popular either. She had a special knack for getting under people's skin," Drake added.

"She get under your skin, Drake? Spinelli asked.

"Yeah, more than once," Drake answered honestly, then turned and walked back into the house.

Kacey added, "She got under my skin more than twice." She followed Drake, stepping past the CSI who was taking pictures of the scuff marks on the floor.

Inside Kacey approached Doc who was busy assessing the body. He had a liver probe in his hand and looked up at Kacey as she inquired, "Do you have a time of death?"

"Based on body temp, rigor, and lividity, she's been dead between ten and fourteen hours. See the bluish color of her skin where the body has been in contact with the floor, and what appears to be bruises on her wrists around the area where the ropes secured her to the table? This would have passed within eighteen hours," he said pointing his gloved finger at her wrists and rolling her slightly to one side showing her bare back where he'd cut open her dress to expose her bare skin. A blue hue was obvious in the areas he pointed.

Kacey looked at her watch, reading two thirty. "So you are putting her T.O.D.," referring to the time of death, "as somewhere between one thirty and five thirty?"

Doc made an attempt to flex the reporter's left arm. "Yes, I'd say that is as narrow as we'll get."

Kacey nodded. "What about cause of death?"

"Exsanguination, she bled out. There are multiple stab wounds."

"Do you know how many?" Kacey continued as Connor, Drake, and Spinelli joined the conversation.

"I'll need a more thorough examination, but it appears there are at least four."

Drake looked at Kacey. "Weapon? Knife?"

"I'll have to take impressions at the lab, but yes. The cuts are thinner on one end, consistent with a knife blade."

Drake turned to one of the CSI agents. "Who is the lead?"

The middle aged man turned and pointed to a woman at the end of the hall. "Agent Drummond."

Drake nodded and turned, walking towards the woman. Introducing himself first, Drake asked, "How soon do you think it will be before we can get some information on the photos? We need to know the type of camera, film, or anything that might give us a lead."

"It will probably be a couple of days," she responded. Her long ponytail bobbed from side to side.

"Great," Drake replied before turning away and walking back to the living room and out the front door.

Kacey followed him. "Hey, what's up with you?"

"This case, this whole case, just has me frustrated. It seems like we can't catch a break, and Spinelli questioning whether Jessica had pissed me off before is frustrating. I don't like feeling like a suspect, but damned if someone isn't doing a great job of making both of us look bad."

"Who gives a crap, Drake? Let them think whatever they want. We need to stay focused on finding the killer. That will be all that matters in the end."

Connor approached the pair as they stood on the lawn still surrounded by reporters and onlookers, the yellow crime tape separating them from the mob that awaited any tidbit of information about what was going on inside the home.

"Is everything okay out here?"

Drake turned to the FBI agent. "Yes, everything is fine," he lied, trying to hide how annoyed he felt.

"We have everything here we can get. We need to interview co-workers and try to identify any enemies she may have made. We've got a couple of possibilities to follow up on, including the gang angle. Let's get to work quickly to identify any possible leads."

Kacey continued as Spinelli joined them, "Our killer is working faster these days and each one of these killings contains some sort of message. We have to understand what that message is. I'm starting to feel like he's just toying with us. He's literally taunting me and Drake."

The foursome returned to the car while each ducked under the yellow tape and ignored the chatter of questions from the reporters.

Once inside the car Spinelli stated, "It's time to narrow down any enemies the two of you may have created. If the mission is to destroy your careers then we have to find out who that is."

"The only thing all of the victims have in common is us. They all somehow tie back to us and Fields," Kacey stated.

"So let's map out what we have. We have the possible connection with the killing of Fats, the gang leader in jail. There is the possibility that someone is killing on behalf of Fields. It's possible though not likely that this murder is unrelated or that they are all unrelated. The unusual changes in the killings suggest the possibility of multiple killers. We need to split up these theories and begin working each of them until they can be excluded."

The car fell silent.

Kacey finally broke the silence. "Drake and I can work the idea that Jessica's murder is not related."

Drake looked over at her as a puzzled expression fell over his face.

She continued on, "I think we need another set of eyes on Fields, and if there is a connection to Fats we can't be the ones to make that. I say, we ask the chief for some additional resources to conduct those interviews and let Spinelli and Connor focus on Fields."

Drake nodded his head. "Okay." He surrendered, realizing her recommendation would protect them from an accusation of police cover up or corruption.

Connor and Spinelli agreed. "Let's split up the tasks when we get back to the precinct."

Two hours later after briefing the chief, the team split the tasks as agreed. Dermot and Sparlow were assigned the task of tracking down leads on the gang members that worked with or for Fats. Meanwhile, Spinelli and Connor were continuing to work on the possibility that someone was contracted by Fields. They had shifted their focus onto any friends, past co-workers, or distant relatives that Fields may have encouraged to continue his pathological and ruthless desire to kill.

Drake and Kacey pulled out of the police precinct with a car from the motor pool and were now on their way to interview Jessica Sperry's boss and co-workers.

Kacey reached over and took Drake's hand. "It's good to be alone with you."

Drake squeezed her hand and looked at her as they exited the precinct parking lot. "Did you...?"

Anticipating the rest of his question, she responded before he could finish, "Yes, the main reason I offered to split up all the work was so that we could have just a few minutes. You seemed so out of it this morning. I just wanted to reconnect, make sure you are really okay."

"I'm okay. It just feels like we aren't making any progress, and I don't know why but Spinelli and Connor get under my skin."

"I know, but they're just doing their jobs."

"I guess," Drake agreed as he navigated his way to the news station where Jessica Sperry worked.

"I know the Feebs have these three potential motives for the murders but I just don't see the connection with Fats. If they wanted to get back at us for the murder of Fats in prison, they would have just taken us out, gang style. You know they would have just shot us down on the street. This idea that they would create these elaborate scenes to make it look like somehow we are involved is not consistent with gang related crimes."

"I'm not following that one either, but my heart isn't broken that Dermot is out chasing down leads on gang turf. He's probably shittin' his pants right now, serves his scumbag ass right." He laughed for the first time in days.

Kacey laughed with him. It felt good to laugh. Their amusement at Dermot's expense fell away and Kacey continued, "I do think there could be some connection with Fields. However, I can't make a connection on how he could be getting someone to do his dirty work, but he's crazy enough to pull it off."

"Do you think he's cognitive enough to orchestrate these murders from within a mental hospital?"

"I think he's sick enough and he would like nothing better than to continue to torment us. It's like the only thing left for him is to ensure our suffering never ends, constantly reminding us of the power he had over us when he had Sophie."

Drake glanced her way as he turned the car into the news station parking lot. "Maybe, I wish…" His words trailed off, and the end of the sentence hung in the air.

Kacey knew what he wanted to say. He wished they had killed Fields that day. It was the only way either would ever have peace. Sophie would still be dead, but there would be some relief in knowing they killed Fields and ended it once and for all. She had thought of revenge for Sophie more times then she could possibly ever count. She knew they both wished him dead. Both had regrets of not killing him on the spot. So what if there was a reprimand. Suspension maybe, but no one would have held their badges for long—not after what that man did. The department had a code, and under certain circumstances, heads would turn. Fields was one of those circumstances.

"I know. Me too." Kacey responded after a long pause, then pulled on the door handle and stepped out of the car, releasing Drake's hand that she had been holding the whole time they drove.

Inside the building Drake presented his badge at the front desk and introduced each of them. A young, fresh looking woman, no more than twenty-five, sat at the desk twirling her hair around her index finger. She smacked on gum, her tongue occasionally poking out of her mouth. Kacey wondered if she was flirting with Drake or just truly that dumb and obnoxious.

Responding to Drake's request to speak to the station director, she pushed a couple of buttons on a phone that sat in the middle of her desk and leaned back in her chair, perky breasts popping up almost at attention. Kacey turned away not wanting to grant her the attention she so desperately was aiming for.

Drake turned away too, raising his eyebrows in acknowledgement of the odd and immature behavior, and grinned at Kacey.

A few moments later a door opened from the left end of the short, white hallway, and a tall, slender and slightly balding man approached the two detectives and extended his hand.

"Detectives Colton Drake and Kacey James," Drake offered, accepting the man's extended hand. "We'd like to talk with you about Ms. Sperry."

"Yes, please follow me this way." Before starting to walk back towards the door he came through he asked the young receptionist, "Hold my calls, Cindy."

"Yes, Mr. Trainer," Cindy replied popping her gum out of her mouth from the right corner.

Kacey forced the shake of her head down, purely disgusted by the young woman. Drake stepped back and let Kacey go in front of him as they followed Trainer through the door into a large room that had several desks. A lot of lights were mounted overhead, and a small stage off in one corner with a podium was the obvious center of attention for the six and ten o'clock news.

They followed him under the lights to another door to the right, of the stage which led past a viewing booth. They continued walking as they went by two offices on one side of the hall and another large office in the opposite far corner. Trainer's name was plastered on the door on a shiny chrome plate. Underneath it read 'Station Director".

The office had been professionally decorated with stylish chairs and a large matching desk. The walls had artwork that looked like it could have been painted by Picasso, but much more childlike with brilliant colors and strong lines.

Trainer's desk was mostly neat with a few papers lying in the middle and a folder off to one side that said "Top Stories" on it.

Trainer offered them each a seat which they accepted. "Sorry, for your loss. It must have been quite a surprise," Kacey offered.

"Yes. When Jessica didn't show up for our luncheon I got very worried. After a couple of hours and her not returning calls, I knew something must be wrong. I just didn't expect..." his voice trailed off sounding a little choked.

"How long have you and Ms. Sperry worked together?" Drake asked.

"Jessica worked here for over five years. I was once an anchor and about two years ago promoted to Director. We worked together that whole time."

"Can you tell us your relationship with Ms. Sperry?" Kacey asked.

Trainer looked taken back. "Are you inferring that we were more than colleagues?"

"We have to ask," Kacey replied and patiently waited for his response.

Trainer seemed uncomfortable. "We were colleagues."

"Did Jessica have a romantic interest with anyone here at work?" Drake continued to press, "With you at any point during her career, or with anyone else here at the station?"

Trainer seemed to squirm again. "Look, I'm married, have been for twelve years. There was a period when Jess and I worked together that we got close. We spent a few months working long hours and, well, things happened. It didn't last long, and once I got promoted it ended. It was never serious for either of us. A fling, and my wife doesn't know, and I'd like to keep it that way."

"We don't have any reason to inform your wife unless there is a connection to you and how Ms. Sperry met her fate."

"There is no connection," Trainer replied, obviously annoyed with the questioning.

"What about any other romantic involvements?"

Trainer shook his head. "Jess was pretty focused on her career. She's divorced and she ended up that way because her career was more important to her than family or friends."

"Was Ms. Sperry interested in the job you got?"

Again Trainer looked really uncomfortable. "Listen, I'm not going to explain this again. Jessica and I were friends, close for a while. She was too new to the station to even be considered for the job at the time, and while she likely aspired to a promotion one day, it was never an issue with us. We had a very good working relationship, and there was no conflict."

Drake held up his palms. "Look, I know this is uncomfortable, but we have to ask these questions in order to rule out any possible connection to you or others here at the station. Our goal is to find her killer, not turn your life upside down."

Relaxing back into his chair, Trainer nodded. "Okay. I don't know of anyone here that was gunning for Jessica. She was aggressive, and most people stayed out of her path. They knew she was good at her job and let her do it. The younger reporters watched and learned from her."

"So there was no one that may have been jealous of Ms. Sperry for always getting the good stories or wishing they had more screen time? You know, the good top stories," Kacey asked leaning in and nodding at the file folder lying on Trainer's desk.

"No." Trainer shook his head with certainty.

"Who will benefit from Ms. Sperry's death? I mean, I assume someone will receive a promotion."

Trainer thought for a moment. "Yes, I suppose so. I haven't considered that in detail yet."

"But there must be someone that is next in line for the top stories," Kacey continued to push on the topic of the folder.

"Yes, Jake Thunder. He is next in line for the six and ten o'clock anchor position."

"We'd like to speak with Mr. Thunder."

"Thunder is not your guy. We all know there is a maniac out there killing people, and you are doing nothing to solve it. You're wasting your time here while the killer is considering who next to kill."

"One more question before we meet with Mr. Thunder. Was Ms. Sperry working on a particular story now that was about to explode, or did she have any enemies that might have wanted her dead?"

Trainer laughed. "The only big story she was working on is the serial murderer that seems to have chosen to incorporate the two of you as possible suspects. And as for any enemies, Jessica probably has a dozen enemies with the stories she has covered in the past. In fact, you two would be likely top picks for people that disliked her."

"Thank you, Mr. Trainer. We'd like you to compile a list of people Ms. Sperry might have given cause to want her dead and the related stories that each would be associated with. We appreciate your time today," Drake stated as he and Kacey stood to leave.

Trainer followed the detectives out of the office then led them back towards the studio with the stage and lights. He waved to a man standing near the podium and motioned him over to them.

"Jake, these detectives would like to ask you a few questions about Jessica."

Jake raised his eyebrows and nodded his head. "Oh…kay," he said dragging out the word.

"Use the office next to production," Trainer offered before giving one more assessment to the detectives and turning, disappearing back into his office.

Drake and Kacey exited the building with their interview notes and a list of potential people that may have wanted Jessica dead.

Sitting back inside the cruiser, Kacey reached up and pushed the button lighting the inside of the car since the sun had set long ago. She leaned toward the middle of the car and shared the list with Drake. They looked it over and discussed the names. All had been major headlines over the past couple of years. Kacey pointed at a name about half way down the page. Ironically, Fields was on the list.

Drake nodded. His face looked grim. "Damn it to hell, that guy has to be connected to all of this somehow."

"Spinelli and Connor will, no doubt, find this interesting."

"I'm sure they will."

"I wonder what they found today?" Kacey pondered.

"I assume nothing or they would have called us gloating that they'd solved the case, or at bare minimum had a suspect."

Kacey nodded. "Well, I'm starving. Let's go grab a bite and I wish we could get a beer, but we're still on the clock."

"You don't have to ask me twice."

"While you drive I'll call Connor and check in. We need to appear collaborative and open to any turns in the investigation."

Drake smiled and turned the key in the ignition, backing out as Kacey punched in Connor's contact number on her phone.

They pulled back into the precinct and turned the cruiser into the motor pool. "I left my computer bag inside. I want to run in and get it," Kacey said.

"Yeah, okay me too, but then food."

Kacey grinned and bounded up the steps towards the front door.

Inside they walked through the long corridor and wound through the hall, entering the investigation room. The lights were off. Connor had explained that he and Spinelli had hit dead ends and cut out about a half hour earlier.

After collecting their personal items, Kacey walked out of the room, flipping the lights back off, and bumped directly into Dermot and Sparlow.

"Hey, good lookin'. I knew you missed me," Dermot chimed at Kacey.

"You wish, Dermot," Kacey tossed back.

Drake made an effort to turn the young buck's focus back to work rather than his obviously very overactive hormones. "What'd you guys turn up today?"

Sparlow replied as Dermot stood there with a stupid grin on his face, "Nothing."

"Nothing? You must have talked to a few people."

Dermot spouted off, "Yeah, we got stonewalled in most places, but it seems there was no love loss for Fats," referring to the dead drug lord.

"How's that?"

"Fats being dead afforded a lot of other people opportunity. Seems like most of his cronies are dead or gained a promotion from his death."

"Okay, well write up your report. We're going to need a briefing in the morning," Kacey directed.

Dermot cocked his shoulder back and placed his thumbs on his gun belt. "I'll give you a briefing right now if you want one, lil' mama."

Sparlow clicked his tongue. "Man, you are cruising to get your clock cleaned."

"She can clean my cock…I mean, clock too." Dermot laughed at his so called slip of the tongue.

In a swift movement Drake had Dermot slammed against the wall with his forearm pressed tightly against Dermot's throat and his hip shoved up into Dermot's groin. "You little son of a bitch, apologize right now."

"Dude, you are nuts. I'm just messing around. Take a chill," Dermot choked out in ragged breath.

"Now!" Drake demanded, not letting loose of his hold.

"Alright, I'm sorry."

Kacey stepped forward. "Drake, let the boy go."

Drake looked at Kacey then slowly released Dermot and backed away.

"Let's go." Kacey shoved Drake towards the door. "Dermot, we need our briefing in the morning. Get busy."

Kacey heard him mumble something about a crazy bitch as she continued to push Drake down the hall to the exit.

Outside the air had turned colder and the wind had picked up. Kacey hugged her police-issued jacket against her. "What the hell was that?" she said turning to Drake.

"Sorry, but I am sick of that asshole's shit."

"Yeah, well, I don't need a hero."

"I know you don't but I couldn't stop myself."

Kacey shook her head, obviously angry. "It's not cool, Drake. This is my job."

"I'm sorry. I just…" Drake's voice trailed off.

"You know, I think I'm just going to go home and shower. It's been a long day. Hell it's your job too!"

"Kacey, don't do this."

"I'll catch you in the morning, Colton."

Drake watched her walk away. She rarely called him by his first name. In fact, she only used that name when they were making love or when she was mad. He was certain they would not be making love tonight.

Chapter Twenty Eight

Shhhh... I need to sleep.

Iz, you have to do it. You know we have to. We need to.

Iz tossed and turned, finally throwing the covers back. Sleep was obviously not going to come tonight.

Pacing through the apartment, thoughts rolled through Iz's head. Thoughts of that bitch of a reporter staring back. More images swirled through Iz's brain that nearly conjured up the smell of burnt flesh and that arrogant doctor swinging in the wind, flames engulfing his body, and the sound of the fire as the tractor's engine drowned out the screams.

Iz paced faster, finally deciding to go out. Maybe the night's air would stop the thoughts prodding from within. Iz slipped into dark clothes, shoes, and zipped on a thick coat. Before stepping out into the night, Iz grabbed car keys and a black bag that was stored deep in the back of the closet, the same bag that held the Polaroid camera from two nights earlier.

Where are we going, Iz? Are we going to do it? Do it, Iz. Please, can we do it?

Shut up. I don't know. I just need to get out for a while.

But I don't want to shut up. I WANT you to do it.

Locking the apartment and walking out to the car, Iz tried hard to ignore the constant chatter. Sliding behind the wheel, Iz dropped the bag onto the backseat, and cranked the engine over. After waiting a minute or so for the car's heating system to kick in, Iz backed out of the space and turned out of the parking lot onto the road.

213

Iz drove for over an hour. Ultimately, the car seemed to have a mind of its own, weaving through the bare streets. Iz glanced at the dashboard of the car. It was nearly two o'clock in the morning, and Iz had passed only a couple cars during the short drive.

It's easy, Iz. So easy.

Iz's heart rate increased. This was going to be easy.

About two miles away Iz pulled into a dark, empty parking lot and reached for the bag in the back seat. Peeling the zipper back, Iz fingered around inside the bag, feeling the items until each of the desired objects had been confirmed. A smile settled on Iz's face.

Feeling good, Iz pulled away from the curb again and continued down the street, navigating familiar roadways until the car rested in a parking lot of a housing division dotted with small affordable homes.

Iz's eyes scanned the parking lot for any signs of life or movement. It was dark and clear. Pulling the hoodie up over rumpled hair and sliding hands into dark gloves, Iz pulled on the car door handle, grabbed the black bag, and stepped quietly out of the vehicle.

Iz walked across the parking lot, winding in between the cars, silently sliding up the sidewalk that led to a plain, grey house with little other than grass for landscaping. Once at the front door, Iz hesitated and looked around once more.

Do it, Iz. Knock on that door.

Iz listened then pressed a gloved index finger against the doorbell button and waited.

Moments passed and Iz pressed the button again. This time a stirring could be heard from within, followed by the sound of feet approaching, and finally the lock turning in the mechanism.

The door opened a few inches.

There was a glow from a light that had been turned on somewhere deeper in the home that allowed Iz enough light to see the surprised look on the occupant's face.

"What are you doing here?"

"Can I come in?"

The question was followed by a slight hesitation, but then the homeowner stepped back and opened the door, allowing Iz to enter.

Chapter Twenty Nine

Drake stepped into the steaming hot shower without turning on the lights. His head pounded from frustration and lack of sleep. The beads of water seemed to be crashing against his body. He ignored the stinging sensation and focused on the heat that relaxed his taunt muscles. Grasping through the dark, his fingers wrapped around a bar of soap and the razor. After nearly slicing his finger, his trembling hands dropped the sharp tool on the floor, making a clattering sound. He bent and lightly slid his hand across the floor, his fingertips colliding with the sharp edge of the blade. He swore under his breath and allowed the hot water to wash away the blood. Although he couldn't see it, he could feel it trickling away from the raw flesh. He applied soap and scratched away at the two-day stubble that had formed on his chiseled chin.

Part of him wanted to say to hell with it and throw the razor down and ignore the way he looked, but Kacey's concerned eyes seemed to be staring at him in the dark and he knew he couldn't walk into the station house another day looking like he had the prior day, especially not after the way things had ended with them the night before. He had lost his cool with Dermot and made Kacey angry. Somehow he would need to make that right. He definitely didn't want Kacey to turn away from him again. They had finally gotten back on the right track and then his temper had gotten the best of him.

Finishing up quickly, he turned off the shower and stepped out into the cool air and toweled off. A thought suddenly hit him; since Kacey had left angry they had never eaten so he hoped maybe he could catch her at Freddy's to talk before Connor and Spinelli were around.

A few minutes later Drake took up a stool at the café counter. His eyes immediately scanned the parking lot and the restaurant when he walked in. Since it was early, he ordered a cup of coffee and pretended to look over the menu, which he knew by heart, delaying ordering food as he waited to see if Kacey would show.

A few minutes passed, and he heard the door open. Resisting the temptation to turn and look to see who had walked in, he waited. His spirits lifted when he heard someone take a seat next to him, but immediately fell again when he saw it was Sparlow.

"Hey what's up, Drake?" The young officer asked.

Drake glanced at the young man. "Nothing, I guess."

"Boy, you sure lit up Dermot last night."

"Yeah, well, someone needed to," Drake tossed back.

"He's a good guy, just a little bit of a player at times."

Drake gave him a look and picked up his menu again pretending to read it.

The waitress came over and took Sparlow's order. The young cop looked at Drake. "Aren't you gonna order?"

Drake grunted. "Not sure what I want yet," he lied, still trying to buy some time. He glanced at the clock over the pass-through kitchen window. Being almost seven o'clock, his spirits dipped even further as hopes that Kacey would come in became more distant.

The bell over the door rang again and Drake sipped his coffee.

"Well, look who we have here," Sparlow piped off.

Drake took it as a signal to turn and look. He immediately felt an incredible relief wash over him as he saw Kacey approach and slip into the seat on the opposite side of him.

"Hey, sorry I'm late. I guess I had a hard time dragging myself out this morning."

Drake offered a smile, hoping she would be able to see that he was sincerely sorry for the outburst at the precinct the night before. "Good morning."

She gave him a sideways glance and returned his smile.

The waitress approached and placed Sparlow's food on the counter in front of him. "See, you should have ordered when I did. Now you'll just have to enjoy the smell of my food."

Drake shrugged as Kacey ordered a coffee.

She looked over at him. "You gonna eat something?"

"Yeah, just couldn't decide."

Moments later the waitress had taken both of their orders, and they sat quietly sipping on their coffees as Sparlow mopped up his plate with the last bit of toast.

"Well, I guess I am out of here," he said tossing some money on the counter and standing. "I'll see you two later."

Neither responded to him, just nodded in agreement. With the young cop gone, Drake turned slightly towards Kacey. "Hey, about last night, I messed up. That guy just really hacks me off."

Kacey looked at his face, studying the rugged lines and the sharp edges of his jaw then stated, "I don't need a partner, friend, or... you know, anyone else that doesn't trust me or doesn't believe I can handle myself. Christ, Drake, I'm a cop too."

"I know and this has nothing to do with your ability to handle yourself. Honestly, I might have backed that jerk up against the wall for talking like that to any woman."

Kacey tipped her head at him. "Really?" Sarcasm filled her voice.

"Okay, almost any woman."

They both laughed, and Drake could feel himself relaxing. "Look, I won't do it again. You have my word. I'll never let Dermot get to me again."

"Where is the little jerk anyway?" Kacey inquired.

Drake shrugged "Who knows? Sparlow never said, and I never asked."

The food came, and they both devoured the meal while exchanging small talk about the FBI agents and what the day might hold. After paying they returned to their vehicles to make their way to the station.

"Good morning," Spinelli stated as Drake and Kacey walked into the investigation room. Connor looked up from his computer and nodded, his cell phone balanced between his shoulder and his ear.

"Good morning," Kacey replied, dropping her computer bag onto the table next to Spinelli.

"I called the chief on my way in. Figured he'd want an update. He said he'd be in here around nine."

"What's he got going on?" Kacey tipped her head towards Connor.

"Briefing our director."

"Got it."

"Did Connor fill you in?" Drake asked Spinelli before continuing. "I filled him in on our interviews last night with the news station."

"Yeah, interesting that Robert Fields comes up on the list. Seems he just keeps tying all of this together."

"So it seems, but everything keeps coming up a dead end on how he could be orchestrating this from inside his nice little padded room."

"We've requested records going back farther. Visitor lists, phone records. Maybe we just haven't looked back into the past far enough," Spinelli shared. "It's a long shot but the best we have."

"Oh, and we ran into the officers that were going to do the leg work on the Fats connection last night. They hit a dead end too. Seems most people are pretty happy Fats is dead. Dermot is supposed to get us a complete report this morning. In fact, he should have brought it over already," Kacey stated.

"Let me go check on it," Drake offered.

Kacey looked at him with a puzzled expression.

Drake glanced at her, giving a nod indicating that she needed to trust him. "Sparlow was at the café earlier but Dermot wasn't with him. Maybe he was working on his report and just hasn't finished it up. I'll get a status. Hopefully, he'll have it before the chief gets here."

Connor ended his call and stood up. "Well, that was fun," he said obviously sarcastically. "Where's Drake off to?"

"He's checking with the guys that were running down the leads on the connection to Fats, and the chief will be in shortly for a briefing," Kacey explained.

She continued handing them the list Trainer had provided them during his questioning. "We've got a complete list of possible enemies Jessica Sperry may have created. As we explained last night, any of them could have been her killer, but we did find it incredibly interesting that Robert Fields seems to turn up around every angle we run."

"How'd the interview with Trainer go?"

"He seemed appropriately effected by Jessica's death. We did get an admission to an affair that lasted a short time when Trainer was an anchor. He claims it ended when he got promoted."

"Is he married?"

"Yes. He said his wife doesn't know."

"Any chance Jessica was blackmailing him in any way?"

"It's possible, I suppose, but we didn't get that sense. He said she was too into her career to want more of a relationship. Frankly, what I knew of Jessica, that's true. She was somewhat ruthless. It was all about the story and how that story made her look on the tube."

"No way to ignore the fact that you and Drake are listed on the possible enemies," Spinelli stated in a matter of fact kind of way.

"Nope, can't ignore that." Kacey pulled out a chair and sat down.

Connor raised his hand. "Can we get a search on related crimes? Eventually something is going to tie these together. I'd like a region-wide search on crimes committed where a Polaroid was used—anything where photos of the victim were left behind or even mailed afterwards."

"On it." Kacey got up and headed out of the room to go see Janet.

As she rounded the corner she nearly bumped directly into Drake. He caught her, and for a very brief moment they were caught in a collision embrace.

"How's Dermot coming on the report?"

"He's not in. Sparlow hasn't heard from him. Thinks he may have tied a good one on last night. He's running over to his house to check on him."

"Chief is going to be pissed."

"Yeah, I told Sparlow to use the lights. Where are you headed?"

"Janet. Connor wants her to run a list of any murders where pictures were taken of the victim and left at the scene or mailed in anything similar that we can connect to Jessica. Want to tag along?"

"Sure." Drake walked alongside her as they worked their way through the halls.

*＊＊

After visiting Janet, Drake and Kacey re-entered the room where Connor and Spinelli occupied the long table. They both looked up from their computers.

"Okay, Janet will have something for us soon."

Drake's phone rang. He looked at the face and swiped the phone. "Doc, please tell us you have something." He punched another button, putting the phone on speaker and setting it down in the center of the table.

"I have the results of her blood work. Jessica did not have any drugs or alcohol in her system."

"I didn't expect that she would. What else have you got?"

"There was no sexual assault, and I don't find any trace evidence on her other than carpet fibers, which are consistent with that in her home. She had some dirt on her legs. It appears to be transfer from the garage floor. I've sent it to the crime lab to look at."

"What was the cause of death?"

"She had five unique stab wounds. They were all pre-mortem. The first two were superficial. The next two were deeper, but non-fatal. The final was deep, directly inserted into the lungs and then given a hard twist to the right."

"So the final one was the fatal wound?" Drake continued to probe.

"Yes. The killer is likely right-handed based on the direction of the twist in the wound."

"What weapon are we looking for?" Connor asked.

"It appears to be consistent with a common kitchen knife. Four- inch blade with a serrated edge."

"So like a steak knife?"

222

"Yes, that would be consistent with the wound."

"Anything else, Doc?" Kacey probed.

"No, I think that's it."

"Did the lab say when they will have their results from the photos and dirt samples?"

"Probably a week," Doc replied reluctantly.

"We can't afford a week," Connor added. "Is there any way to escalate those results?"

"The chief would have to make the request for overtime. Not sure he would get it, but worth the ask."

"Ask the chief what?" Dalton's thick frame filled the doorway. He stood with his hands on his hips.

"Thanks, Doc." Drake said and ended the call.

"A request for overtime of the lab to get the items analyzed from the Sperry murder."

"Tell me they have some DNA."

"Well, no, sir. They've got carpet fibers, dirt, and the photos. The carpet and dirt are probably not going to give us anything, but maybe the photos will give us a tip on what the killer's message is, or maybe the killer got sloppy and left a print behind," Connor answered.

"Were there any witnesses at the reporter's house?"

"Nothing, beat cops have been going door to door and so far no one saw or heard anything."

"So basically, we still have nothing."

"There seems to be a positive connection to Fields. The news station director provided a list of people and the respective cases that Jessica Sperry had been the investigative reporter on and may have pushed a little too hard. Fields is on that list," Drake added to what Connor had already shared.

"Then we have to figure out how the hell he is committing these crimes from within that facility."

Kacey added, "There's more, Chief."

He turned his attention towards her. "I'm listening and I have this bad feeling I'm not going to like what I hear."

"Drake and I are on the list as well."

"What?" The chief look perplexed.

"Well, Jessica never gave us any slack. She was too often way up in our grill. Always pushing on us, saying we weren't doing enough. Lately, she'd been making accusations that we are somehow responsible for the recent murders."

"We need to make progress. That news station will run with it, especially with Jessica dead. If we don't find something I'll be forced to take you off the case and open an internal investigation against the two of you."

"Where is Dermot on the gang lead?" the chief asked changing the topic.

"He's working on the report, but it looks like a dead end."

"Well, that doesn't help us either. He needs to get that report in pronto. Lean on him."

The room got quiet.

Drake finally spoke up, "You can't honestly think…"

The chief held up his hand. "Of course not, but we may need to eliminate the two of you. And the best way to do that is through an official investigation."

"Sir, we need a few more days," Kacey stated.

"You've got however many days the press stands down. After that I won't have a choice. I'll call and ask for the overtime on the labs, and you better keep your fingers crossed they find something." He turned to leave then paused briefly, glancing once more back at the group before walking away, his large frame creating a void in the doorway.

"Well, that's just peachy," Kacey said sarcastically and slammed her hand against the table. Her jet black hair pulled tight at the base of her neck bobbed with the motion.

Drake was obviously angry and left the room abruptly.

"We need to regroup," Connor said.

"Regroup against what? We don't have anything."

A noise at the door stopped the team in mid conversation.

"Am I interrupting?" Sparlow was standing in the door frame.

Kacey turned to the young cop. "What's up, Sparlow?"

"It's Dermot. I couldn't reach him on the phone. I figured he tied one on last night following his run in…well, you know. So I ran over to his house, and his car is in the garage. I can see it through the window, but I can't get him to answer."

"Maybe he hooked up with someone?" Kacey said not showing any real concern.

"I know he can be a jerk but I've been working with him for three months, and he's never just not shown up for work and he's always answered his phone. He may appear to be immature in a lot of ways, but he takes his job very seriously."

Kacey sat still for a moment contemplating what Sparlow had just shared. "Did anything look suspicious beside the fact that his car was in the garage?"

Sparlow thought for a brief moment. "No, nothing that I noticed."

"Okay, let's give him a couple of hours then if he doesn't show up we'll find a way to get inside his house."

"Okay. I'll keep trying to call his cell phone to see if he turns it back on. Right now it just goes to voicemail."

"Let us know if you reach him and tell him to get his tail in here and get that report to us."

"I'll start working on the report. Our interview notes are on his desk."

"Thanks, Sparlow." Kacey said as the young cop turned and left the room.

***

Drake approached Janet. "Tell me you have something for me. I mean, even the slightest tidbit of information would be helpful right now."

Janet smiled and started to do her usual flirting, but upon a deeper review of Drake's face she checked herself. "The heat turned up pretty high on this one?" she asked.

"That is putting it mildly."

"Okay, here's what I have so far. I pulled Jessica's phone records. A complete dump of the past sixty days, I've matched up those that are frequently dialed and given you the cross reference to who they belong to. Not much, but a start. Here's a copy, and I've emailed it to you just now as well."

Drake took the copy she handed him and scanned the page. He noticed lots of phone calls and texts to Trainer. "Get anything on the pictures?"

"I thought I had a couple of leads. There were two murders in adjacent states where the killer had left behind photos, but in those cases both have been incarcerated. I'm afraid it's a dead end at least nearby. I'll expand the search to the whole U.S."

Drake was about to turn away when she stopped him.

"There is one more thing. I'm not sure it means anything but I've been thinking about the random methods of killing. So I ran a search just typing them all into one string, and the weirdest thing pops up."

"Okay. Lay it on me," Drake leaned back in and rested his arm on the counter.

"Well, you know how in grade school kids tease each other?"

"Yeah, so?" Drake wasn't following her, and it showed in his eyes.

"If I type the following words of fire, needle, two by four, pork chop and pictures, I get a list of childhood taunts."

"I don't get it." Drake shook his head.

"Okay, so one of them is *Liar Liar Pants on Fire*, and another one is *You Are So Ugly Your Mom Had to Tie a Pork Chop Around Your Neck to Get the Dog to Play with You.*"

Drake stood tall. "I see what you're saying."

"There is literally a match to all of them."

"All of them?" Drake asked with surprise in his voice.

"All of them. And there are more."

"What do you mean *more*?"

"Well, there's one that says *Step on a Crack Break Your Mother's Back*, and *I'm Rubber You're Glue, Whatever Bounces off of Me Sticks to You.*"

"Can you email me the whole list?"

"Sure." Janet was tapping on the keys already.

"Thanks. Oh, and hey, can you keep this between us for a little bit? I just want to look it over first before we go announcing to the world there's a connection. We can't afford to look stupid on this one."

Janet held up her hands and then put her index finger and thumb together with her right hand and made a twisting motion in front of her mouth indicating her lips were sealed.

Drake thanked her again, and with the Jessica Sperry phone records in his hands, he turned and walked down the hall back towards the investigation room.

***

Drake entered the room and saw Connor, Spinelli, and Kacey all gathered around the white board. The photos had lines drawn connecting them together. "What are you working on?" he asked as he joined the group.

"We're trying to see where we have all the connections. And quite frankly, there are a lot. But oddly, not everything connects together," Connor answered.

Drake stared at the board and realized that Jessica's photo had been added to the array of other victims. His eyes suddenly fixed on two names at the bottom of the board–his and Kacey's. Lines were drawn to their names, and the thing Drake noticed immediately was every photo on the board had a link to both him and Kacey's name. His jaw tightened.

"What's that all about?"

"It's a map of any connections," Spinelli stated in a matter of fact tone.

"I see that. What's the point?"

"We wanted to see how at risk we are if the press runs with their angle on this."

Kacey added, "It looks bad, Drake."

"Yeah, well your little map can say whatever it wants, but we are not involved with this." He slammed the copy of the phone records down on the table.

"What's that?" Connor asked as the papers slid across the table.

"Jessica Sperry's phone records," Drake replied, pulling out a chair and dropping into it. "Janet dumped her phone records for the past sixty days then referenced the names to repeat or frequent callers."

"Anything interesting?" Kacey asked.

"I haven't gone through it in detail, but Trainer is on there a whole bunch. He's her boss so maybe that's expected. She

227

emailed the dump, which should include the actual text messages. It might tell us if they really had cut off their relationship. There are a couple of calls out to the mental hospital where Fields is housed. Not sure what that is all about, but she did go out there not too long ago. The others, I don't recognize."

"Okay, well let's work that list to see if there are any other names on there we need to focus on," Kacey said.

"Nothing came up on the photographs. She ran adjacent states and found zip. Two serials that used photos in their crimes, but both are locked up."

"Can we ask her to expand the search to the whole U.S.?"

"She's already on it," Drake responded running his thick hand over his face.

"Okay, let's have a look at the phone records."

"Let me forward them to each of you. Janet sent them to my email box," Drake offered logging into his laptop.

An hour passed as they worked together to scan through the text messages trying to correlate the level of risk that might be associated to each news report Jessica had worked.

They had mapped them down to the top three cases that each held a legitimate amount of conflict between Jessica and the person in her sights. One of the cases involving an alleged pedophile even included what could be considered threatening language and was worthy of following up on.

Spinelli and Connor agreed to go talk to the suspect in that case. Jessica had been pressing him for an interview during the trial. He had adamantly denied the allegations of the assault on the child, his own daughter. Ultimately, the child had recanted her accusations, but only after the man had been discarded from his job and his home had been spray painted by vandals.

After searching for and viewing the footage it was pretty clear Jessica had run a smear campaign on the guy, probably had ruined his life. Trainer's list included him as well, so Spinelli and Connor took off to interview him.

As soon as they were gone, Drake motioned for Kacey to come over to him. "Janet ran into something. I wanted to share it with you before letting the Feebs have a look at it. Could be a long shot, but it is pretty interesting."

"Yeah, what you got?" Kacey asked, joining Drake and leaning in over his shoulder.

Drake explained to her about the childhood taunts and showed her the examples and the list of others. "It's a pretty good match."

Kacey clicked her tongue in her cheek. "We need to show the chief this before our friends take credit for it."

Before they could say anything else Sparlow appeared in the door. "Hey, guys. Still haven't heard from Dermot."

Drake looked up from the computer. "What's up?"

"Demot no showed for work, not answering his phone, and when Sparlow went to his house his car is in the garage but there is no answer." Kacey shared what Sparlow had told them earlier.

Drake leaned back in his chair. "That doesn't seem like wonder boy."

"No, it's not like him at all," Sparlow stated.

"Maybe we should head over there and check on him."

Sparlow was shaking his head. "Yeah, man, I mean it's not like him. The dude is an idiot about a lot of things, but not being a cop. If he's scheduled he's here."

"Okay, let's go," Drake said standing up and grabbing his jacket off the back of his chair where he draped it earlier.

***

Kacey rapped her knuckles on the door of the small house. The living room curtain was drawn, and the door had four window panes at the top that spanned out like a fan. "Dermot, open up. You're late for work, and if the chief finds out he'll have your hide."

There was no answer, nor any movement from inside.

"Sparlow, try the side gate and see if you can go around to the back door," Kacey directed, but Drake was already heading that way.

Both Kacey and Sparlow followed. Drake started to reach over the wooden door to the fenced back yard. "Does he have a dog?"

Sparlow shook his head.

Drake fumbled around on the other side finding the slide bolt and pulling the gate open.

The three walked around the back and found a window that was pretty far off the ground, likely that of a bathroom. Continuing on they passed another window. The curtains were drawn, making it impossible to see inside. Once they got to the back yard. They approached a sliding glass door.

Sparlow reached for it and gave it a tug. Open.

Looking at each other they nodded in agreement that they should enter. Pulling the door open wide enough that they could each slip through, Sparlow led the way inside where they entered into a small dining area, next to the kitchen that had a pass-through counter with a couple of barstools.

Continuing on they turned slightly and entered the living room. There were a few newspapers on the coffee table, but otherwise the room was neat. A flat screen television mounted on the wall was turned off and the house was quiet.

"Dermot, you better not be hung over in here," Sparlow said, his voice sounding both nervous and pissed.

Drake and Kacey followed Sparlow down the narrow hallway, past a bedroom on the left, and on the right a bathroom that belonged to the window they passed outside. There was one more room on the right with the door slightly ajar. Sparlow knocked.

"Dermot, you better not be with some girl."

Drake glanced back at Kacey. She cocked her head to the side as she continued to follow. Sparlow pushed on the door.

The scene inside was unreal. Sparlow pushed back past Drake and Kacey, barely making it to the bathroom, retching over the toilet.

Drake moved forward into the room that Sparlow fled. Kacey followed him.

The bed was doused in blood, there was blood splatter on the walls and curtains and a thick coppery smell hung in the air. Dermot lay sprawled out on the bed wearing nothing but boxers. His hands were tied to the headboard, his feet tied to the footboard. His face was distorted but it was hard to determine the cause. There were papers all over his body. Words all kinds of words appeared to be stuck inside a milky white substance that coated his body.

There was another scent in the room that immediately assaulted the nostrils of the two detectives. Kacey was the first to speak, "What is that odor?"

"I don't know. Smells, almost like… like glue," Drake said.

"Back out and let's call it in," Kacey said retracing her steps, being careful to not touch anything.

Sparlow was still bent forward over the toilet in the bathroom.

"Sparlow, you okay? We have to get out of here. Did you touch anything?"

Wiping his mouth with the back of his hand, he pointed at the toilet. "I flushed it and I might have grabbed the door frame or the walls," his voice trembled.

"Don't touch anything else and let's get outside."

Drake was already on his cell phone. After placing the initial call, he dialed another number.

"Chief, it's Drake."

Kacey stood close enough that she could hear the chief starting to chew on Drake.

"Chief, listen. It's Dermot. He's dead."

Kacey watched as Drake stood there for a moment waiting. Finally, she could hear the chief asking questions. Drake answered and gave the address then disconnected.

Kacey looked at him. "We need to call Connor and Spinelli."

Drake nodded his head and dialed a third number.

Within the hour Dermot's house was crawling with cops, forensics specialists, and reporters clamoring outside.

Doc had arrived, and Drake and Kacey had gone back inside. Sparlow was too shaken up and had to be taken back to the precinct by another officer.

Kacey stood over Dermot's body. With gloved hands she looked at the scene on the bed. Dermot's body was coated in some sort of adhesive material. The lab analysts had taken samples, and Doc was doing his usual sniff test.

"Smells like your run of the mill heavy duty construction adhesive."

Affixed to the body were all kinds of words cut from newspaper and magazines—words like *Bitch, Tease, Cock, Uptight.* Lab specialist snapped photos.

"What's wrong with his eyes?" Kacey asked.

"Glued shut. His mouth too," Doc answered.

The chief had been standing in the doorway watching. "Jesus Christ!"

"Chief, I'd like to talk with you," Connor requested.

The two stepped out of the bedroom and returned down the hall to the kitchen where they could talk freely.

"The press is looking for a statement. I'd like to speak with them. Maybe I can turn the heat down on this a little," Connor said.

"How so?"

"I'd like to let them know that we are involved and running every possible lead. It might buy us some time and keep them from trying to hang this on the department. They may turn their attention on us rather than your team. It won't buy us long, but it might buy us some time."

The chief stood rubbing his thick fingers over his jaw. "That is my man that is dead in there."

"I understand and my intent is to give you time to work this case. If we don't handle this right, it will get pulled."

Chief Dalton sighed heavily and nodded in agreement. "Keep it brief."

"You have my word," Connor replied before turning towards the front door.

***

"My name is Agent Connor. I'm with the FBI. Earlier today the body of one of our local police officers was found. The crime is being investigated as a homicide. At this time we are not prepared to release the name of the officer."

A reporter in the front shouted out, "What are you going to do to stop the killings in our city?"

"We have our best on this case. We will not rest until the suspect or suspects are found and brought to justice."

"Do you have any suspects?" Another reporter shouted from somewhere in the middle of the crowd.

"I cannot discuss the details of an ongoing investigation, but we are exploring many leads."

"Don't you think it is interesting that two of our local detectives seem to be directly associated with all of these crimes?"

"As I said, we are investigating every lead and will bring the killer to justice. We are following the evidence and will not stop until we have a conviction. Thank you."

Connor stepped away from the front lawn and disappeared back into the house.

Drake and Kacey watched the FBI agent from the depths of the home as Connor gave his statement. As Connor re-entered the house, Drake approached. "How long does that buy us?"

"I can't say for sure, but my guess is not long. They will no doubt have the name of the resident of this house in a matter of minutes, if they don't have it already

"Great," Kacey said as she paced the living room. Her eyes caught sight of something. She walked over to the coffee table and the newspapers that appeared to be neatly stacked. A single piece was sticking out from the stack.

With gloved hands Kacey carefully lifted the top paper. "Hey, Drake, check this out," she called out. "Get the CSI in here."

Drake snapped his fingers at one of the analysts that was fingerprinting the hallway. The analyst followed Drake over to where Kacey was standing.

Kacey looked up. "Do you have tweezers?"

The analyst pulled a pair of long needle-looking tweezers from his vest that was assorted with several different flapped pockets and handed them to Kacey.

"Evidence bag–large," Kacey said holding out her hand as she began to work the newspapers apart with the tweezers. She removed the top paper and slid it off, one after another until she had worked the pages down to the one she was trying to get to. She lifted the top page and folded it back, exposing the inside. There were words removed from the pages. Refolding the page, she lifted it and dropped the paper into the evidence bag.

"Collect all of those papers and try to find a straight edge blade, scissors, or whatever was used to remove the words."

Kacey handed the evidence bag and tweezers back to the analyst and headed back down the hall to where Dermot's body remained exposed on the bed.

Doc stood over the body still examining. "Doc, do you have a murder weapon?"

Doc looked up at Kacey. "He was cut a number of times. There were a lot of superficial wounds, at least fifteen, maybe more. The fatal wound was to the jugular."

Drake and Connor joined Kacey, and Spinelli now stepped inside the room too.

"Any hesitation marks?" Kacey continued.

"No, the cuts are all straight. Each appears to be purposeful, meant to inflict pain but not be fatal. Until this one," he pointed to Dermot's neck.

The senior analyst that was on site at Jessica Sperry's murder was collecting fibers from the bed. She looked at the people in the room. "We need to clear the room. There are too many people in here. We don't want to risk contamination."

"We understand. Just one more thing? Was a murder weapon recovered?"

"Nothing so far, but we aren't done collecting evidence."

"We need to know if a weapon is recovered."

"I'll let you know what we find," the analyst agreed.

The media shoved microphones in their faces as they pushed through the crowd of crazed reporters to their cars and quietly accepted the silence interrupted only by the roar of the engine. Drake and Kacey returned to the precinct followed directly by Connor and Spinelli.

Inside the building Chief Dalton was talking with Sparlow and looked up when they walked in. Dalton had left the scene a while before they had, and his face now showed signs of aging. This case was obviously consuming him. He put his big hand on Sparlow's shoulder then stood and walked over to the group.

"We need to conduct an official interview with him. I.A. is on the way over. I called them in. Standard for an officer-involved crime."

Connor nodded his head. "I can lead it if you'd like."

"I think that would be best." He looked from Drake then to Kacey, neither of which put up any resistance.

As they spoke, a tall black man walked up. He was dressed in a suit and held a briefcase in his left hand. "Chief, good to see you again. I'm sorry it's under these circumstances."

The chief shook his hand then turned to the rest of the team. "Detectives Drake and James and FBI Special Agents Connor and Spinelli. This is Tyrone Williams from Internal Affairs."

Everyone shook hands. Chief Dalton nodded towards Sparlow who was still seated at his desk. "Officer Sparlow was Dermot's partner for the past three months. If anyone knows why Dermot was targeted, I'd say he is our best bet. I've asked Agent Connor to conduct the interview. You're here as a precaution to ensure the process is air tight."

Walking over to Sparlow, the chief introduced Williams and asked if Sparlow wanted to have a union rep present. Sparlow declined the offer.

Connor and Williams led Sparlow into an interview room while the rest watched.

"Is he okay?" Kacey asked.

"I think so. He's pretty shook up. Practically a rookie, so tough for him to see his partner go down like that. We'll see if he toughs it out or decides the risk is too high."

Drake switched the conversation. "Chief, Kacey discovered something at the scene after you left. The killer used the newspapers from inside the house to cut out the words. Probably magazines too, the lab geeks are collecting everything. We also had them searching for a weapon. Seems he might have used something in the house."

"The mayor is all over me," the chief said almost to himself.

Drake nodded. Kacey didn't say anything for a few moments, then finally spoke, "Chief, could we talk to you for a moment?"

"Privately?" Drake added glancing at Spinelli.

The chief excused them from Spinelli and led them to his office. "This better be good."

"We need to share with you something Janet ran across earlier today."

The chief's thick eyebrows raised. "And what would that be?"

"Well, right before we went to check on Dermot we were going to come get you. Janet ran a random search on words that included fire, needle, pork chop, you know the single most detail about each crime," Drake stated

"And?" It was obvious the chief was losing patience with them.

"She got a hit on taunts that kids tend to use when they bully each other at school."

"I'm not following."

"So for example, '*Liar, Liar, Pants on Fire,* and *You are so ugly your mom had to tie a pork chop around your neck to get the dog to play with you'*."

Suddenly the chief's face started to show signs of understanding. "Have you shared this with Connor and Spinelli?"

"No, we literally just got the information when Sparlow came to us saying Dermot was still AWOL. We left to check on him and well..."

"Okay, we need to move fast."

"Chief? There are more taunts, as well, and the method used in Dermot's murder is on the list," Kacey gently stated.

Drake continued, "*'I'm rubber you're glue. Whatever you say bounces off of me and sticks to you'*."

"Christ!" The chief stood there rubbing his hand on his head. "Are there more?"

"Yes, I'm afraid there are."

"The minute Connor comes out of that room we need all four of you working that list. We need to mark off any that have already happened and then determine which ones are still pending. If we can figure out what he will do next, maybe we can figure out who the target is."

***

Sparlow exited the room and glanced over at Kacey then darted his eyes away from Drake. A patrol officer had gone into the interview room a few minutes earlier to speak quietly to Sparlow and the two of them left together.

Connor came out of the room and went towards the chief's office. Drake caught up with him. "Hey, we have a lead that the chief wants us to work on."

Connor stopped and looked at Drake. "Sure, let me give Chief Dalton an update real quick and then we can get started."

"Great," Drake said, but something in the way Connor looked at him told him there was more to the update than Connor let on.

Drake went into the investigation room where Kacey and Spinelli had already migrated to and looked at Kacey. "Should we get started and then bring Connor up to speed when he gets in here?"

"Yeah, why not."

Just as they were about to explain to Spinelli the information Janet had shared, Connor and Dalton entered the room.

"Drake, we need to speak with you."

Drake looked at them and then over to Kacey. "Sure."

Kacey and Spinelli watched as Drake left the room.

Spinelli probed, "Wonder what that is all about?"

Kacey shook her head even though she had a pretty good idea.

∗∗∗

Kacey was called out of the room and led to the interview room where Tyrone Williams and Connor had led Sparlow an hour earlier.

Walking into the room, Kacey saw Williams and the chief sitting at the table. Connor took a seat after offering her the seat opposite the three of them.

Williams turned on a recording device and identified himself, recited the date and time and who all was present in the room.

Kacey bit on the inside of her mouth, taking every bit of resolve to not unload on them about what the hell was going on.

"Do you know why you are in here?" Connor asked.

"No," Kacey answered, although in her mind she thought she might know why, but she knew enough about IA to not offer anything not specifically asked.

"What can you tell us about the altercation between Detective Drake and Dermot last night?"

"I wouldn't call it an altercation."

"No, what would you call it?"

"A disagreement."

"Did Detective Drake place his hands on Dermot and push him against the wall?"

"Yes, I guess he did."

"Can you tell us why?"

"Dermot was getting mouthy. Drake stopped him. That's all."

"What specifically was said?"

"I don't remember the exact words. Dermot was making crude comments. You know, being rude. Drake told him to shut up, and when he continued Drake shoved him into the wall."

"Who was Dermot being rude to?"

"Me., I guess."

"You guess?"

"Yeah. Me."

"Did you have to pull Drake off of Dermot?"

"No. I just got him out of the building to shake it off."

"Has it happened before?"

"Has what happened before?"

"Drake and Dermot getting into a...disagreement?"

"No."

"Are you sure?"

Kacey paused thinking about the time at the diner. Nothing really happened. Then she thought of the night Dermot came to her apartment. No one knew about that unless Dermot told someone.

"No, nothing like that has happened before."

"Where did Drake go after the disagreement with Dermot?"

"Home."

"Did you see him go home?"

Kacey paused again. "No. He told me he was going home."

"So, you don't really know if Drake went home?"

"I know he told me he was going home and that's good enough for me."

"Is there anything else we need to know?"

"No, that was it."

"Thank you, Detective James."

Williams turned off the tape recorder as Kacey stood to leave.

"Where's Drake?"

This time the chief answered. "He'll be taking some time off."

"Chief..." Kacey stopped herself, knowing she'd have to talk to him alone. She kicked the chair up against the table and stormed out of the room.

Heading directly to the women's room she entered and checked under each stall before pulling her cell phone out and clicking on Drake's name from her contact list.

After three rings he picked up. "What's up, Kacey?"

"Damn it, Drake. What the hell is going on?"

"You know the case is hot. The mayor is up the chief's ass, and well, I pushed our latest murder victim up against the wall on the very night he was murdered. Seems cut and dry to me."

"This is not funny, Drake. What are we going to do?"

"Well, you are going to work the case with Connor and Spinelli, and I apparently am going to take some time off."

"Bullshit."

"I'll call you later, Kacey. Take care and watch your back."

Kacey stared down at the cell phone that suddenly disconnected.

Chapter Thirty

The day had been long and stressful. Iz was finally home sitting on the couch stretched out with boots on the coffee table and sipping on a beer.

Picking up the remote control, Iz turned on the T.V. The ten o'clock news had just started. Iz leaned forward and took another swig of the beer as the screen filled with photos of a small house. Yellow crime scene tape draped the edges outlining the sidewalk, awkwardly blocking the world from the gruesome scene inside.

Iz took another sip of the beer, unblinking eyes fixed on the screen, and keenly listened to the report of how an officer had been murdered in his own home. Sliding forward, Iz watched as a FBI agent spoke to the reporters in a short public address, making promises of swift closure. In the background, just inside the opened front door, two detectives could be seen. A smile crept across Iz's face.

Look, Iz. Do you see that?
I sure do.
What should we do?
Nothing.
Nothing? We have to do something.
No. We wait.
What are we waiting for, Iz?
The perfect moment.
How will we know when the perfect moment is?
We'll just know.
Iz?

Yes?
Will we have to wait long?
No. We won't wait long at all.
Good. I don't like waiting.
I don't like waiting either.
Iz?
Yes?
I don't like waiting. It's harder now.
I know. I don't like it either. It won't wait long.
Promise?
I promise.

Chapter Thirty One

Kacey returned to the investigation room and briefed Spinelli on the childhood taunts theory. They spent the next hour matching up every aspect of the murders. After completing that task, they began researching other taunts including those that Janet had already provided. Ultimately, they had two lists. The first included the crimes already committed, and the second included the remaining well known taunts that could potentially be on the list of new crimes to come.

Victim	Taunt
F. Parker	Cross my heart and hope to die, stick a needle in my eye.
C. Jackson your	You're so ugly, your mother had to put a pork chop around
	neck to get the dog to play with you.
H. Sloan	Fatty fatty two by four, can't fit through the bathroom door.
T. Ward	Liar, liar pants on fire, hang 'em from the telephone wire.
J. Sperry	Take a picture. It will last longer.
C. Dermot	I'm rubber, you're glue! Whatever you say bounces off of me and sticks to you!

Taunt

- Step on a crack, break your mother's back.
- K-I-S-S-I-N-G. First comes love, then comes marriage, then comes baby in the baby carriage.
- Sticks and stones may break my bones but words will never hurt me.
- Roses are red, violets are blue. I'm pretty but what happened to you?

Connor entered the room. Kacey looked at Connor and felt her cheeks starting to flush.

"Detective James, can I speak to you?"

Kacey took a deep breath, pushed back from the table, and followed Connor out into the hall.

"Detective James, I know that was difficult earlier. I want to assure you that we will find the killer."

"It seems you've already decided who that is."

"Quite the contrary, we don't know who the killer is, but to protect the integrity of this investigation we had to remove Drake. For now. Once we clear him he can come back in. We need to work very hard to clear him."

"Well, while you were working hard to put him on administrative leave, I have been working hard to find the *right* killer." She applied a lot of emphasis on the word *right*.

"I'd like to see what you have."

Kacey nodded and led Connor back into the room where Spinelli sat plucking away at computer keys.

An hour later they had covered all of the findings and agreed to go home to get rest for the night. The next day would, no doubt, be a long day as they tried to identify who might be the next victim and which taunt might be next.

***

Kacey left the precinct and for the first time let her emotions loose, beating at the steering wheel of her car. It was past eight o'clock. She wanted to check on Drake but decided she should go home first just in case for some reason she was being tailed. A shower sounded good too.

Kacey allowed herself time to enjoy the shower after sitting down and taking a few moments to collect her thoughts. She dressed and exited the apartment back out into the night air. The weather finally had hints of spring. The breeze didn't have that official bite that had been so familiar lately. Breathing in the air, she contemplated what she might face when arriving at Drake's. Would he even answer his door?

Kacey pulled into a parking space outside of Drake's apartment. His truck was parked in a nearby slot, indicating he was at least at home.

Outside the door she paused for a moment and listened. No noise from inside. Rapping on the door, she waited. Still no noise fronm inside. She glanced at her watch. It was nearly eleven o'clock. Knocking again, she waited and listened intently.

She heard a rustling noise then the door popped open slightly. "Hey, Drake." She couldn't think of what else to say.

"Kacey, what are you doing here?"

"I needed to see you."

"It's not a good idea. You shouldn't be here."

"I don't much care what I should or shouldn't do. I needed to see you." Kacey paused and looked into Drake's eyes waiting. "So, are you going to let me in or what?"

Drake stared at her for what seemed like a long time before stepping back and allowing just enough room for her to slip inside.

Kacey wrapped her arms around his neck and kissed him as he shut the door. Drake resisted her advance.

Pulling back, he took her by the arms and backed her up where he could look into her eyes. Studying her face, he tried to smile. "Damn, you are beautiful, but you shouldn't be here. You will be linked to me and then the chief will put you on suspension too."

"I don't care about that right now. I don't understand your suspension anyway, but don't worry, we are all working to clear you one hundred percent so you can get back to work with us."

"It might not be that easy."

"We could just confess about our relationship and then tell them we were together."

"But we weren't together."

"They could never prove that," Kacey leaned into him again.

Drake continued to push her back, but couldn't resist her seductive advance any longer and pulled her into to him. They kissed deeply, their bodies pushing together. Kacey rubbed her firm breasts against his hard chest.

Drake led her away from the front door then lifted her onto the counter in between the small dining set and kitchen. He slid her across the tiled surface and pushed her legs apart pulling her thighs up around his hips. Kacey complied without hesitation, tightening her feet behind him and forcing him against her.

He strung kisses down her neck, dipping his tongue gently along her shirt line. She dug her hands into his hair, pulling his head deep into her breasts. His hands fumbled with the button and zipper on her jeans as she released her legs from their locked position behind him long enough to kick at her police issued boots. The shoes dropped to the floor with a thud at the same moment Drake began working the pants down her thighs and past her knees, causing them to drop in a pile on the floor.

Kacey dug her fingers into his pants, popping the button and fly loose and pulling his thick erection free and guiding him inside her and pushing hard against him.

Drake pulled her to him, thrusting into her. Their moans filled the room as their bodies contacted and worked together. Drake wrapped his tongue around hers as they sucked each other's breath. His mouth tasted of beer.

Kacey arched her back, driving him even further into her, placing her palms on the counter behind her, pushing up and down on him as they worked to drive each other over the edge. Kacey shuddered as they released in unison.

As their bodies relaxed, Drake pulled back and looked at Kacey. Her face was flushed and seemed to glow in the soft lighting that filtered into the room from the living room lamp. Her jet black hair hung to one side as she tilted her head and ran her tongue over her lips.

Drake kissed her neck then lifted her off the hard surface and carried her to the bedroom. She draped her arms around her neck. "Where are you taking me?"

"I think you know the answer to that. I want to feel your whole body next to mine," Drake said entering the bedroom and slowly laying her down against the pillows. He gently removed all of her clothes, admiring her long lean legs and flat stomach. Next, he removed his own clothes, kicking out of his boxers and boots.

Sliding onto the bed he raised his body over hers and leaned into her. Her body responded and again their bodies began a rhythmic dance, this time slower more tenderly. Their mouths explored each other and their hands intertwined. Their fingers laced together; their passion rising with each move. With a final thrust Drake released just as Kacey's body began to tremble under his, orgasm tearing through them both.

***

Kacey stirred in the bed. For a second time she'd stayed the whole night at his apartment. The night had been fantastic, and she'd fallen into a deep sleep in Drake's arms. As she tried to stretch her legs she found them still tangled with Drake and the sheets. He stirred next to her pulling her towards him.

Kacey glanced at the clock on the nightstand. It was already six thirty. She needed to get up and get going. It was going to be up to her to make sure Drake was cleared and brought back to work. She kissed his cheek and pushed back the hair on his forehead then slid out from under his legs.

Drake rolled over and watched as she stood next to the bed. "Where are you sneaking off to?"

"Well, it would seem that I need to go to work so I can clear your sexy ass."

Drake rolled onto his back and pushed his left arm under his head propping his head up on the pillow so he could see her better. "I have to admit, you are the sexiest partner a detective could ever have."

Kacey paused for a moment and gave him a look that said she knew he was sucking up to her.

"Seriously, you are truly amazing, Kacey James. You shouldn't have come here last night, and I should have been able to resist you."

"Well, you apparently couldn't. I'm just so damn irresistible." Kacey laughed. "I'm showering and then I've got to get into the precinct."

Drake nodded in agreement. "I'll make some coffee and rustle up some eggs or something."

"Spoil me, I won't complain." Kacey laughed and shook her perfectly shaped rear end at him before disappearing into the bathroom.

Drake rolled out of the bed and collected the pants he had dropped on the floor the night before. He slipped them on then padded down the hall in bare feet in search of what the refrigerator might offer for a quick breakfast.

With an egg scramble prepared, Drake called to Kacey before heading down the hall to inform her that the coffee and food were ready. As he neared the bathroom he could hear talking.

He smiled as he entered the bathroom. "Who are you talking to?" he asked seeing Kacey in front of the mirror.

"Oh, my hair is not cooperating with me so I was having a little talk with it." Kacey laughed, rubbing her hand over a strand that managed to poke out from the ponytail she'd wrapped the raven strands into.

Drake stepped behind her and circled his arm around her waist. "I happen to love that unruly strand." He ran his palm across the piece she'd been struggling with and tucked it behind her ear. "Leave it. You look amazing and breakfast is getting cold."

"Okay," she conceded smiling back at him in the mirror.

With fingers webbed together, Drake led Kacey down the hall to the small dinette set then gathered two cups of coffee and two plates. Offering Kacey a fork, he watched as she scooped a forkful of the fluffy dish into her mouth.

"What?" she asked looking up and catching him watching her.

"We don't know what is going to happen. I just want you to know that no matter what, I thank you for everything you do for me and for being a great partner."

"This is more than me being your partner."

"I know," Drake paused then continued. "Kacey, I know we've tried to move slowly. After what happened with Sophie we pulled away, both of us isolating ourselves. We moved away from each other and for the longest time blamed ourselves and maybe even each other for what happened to her."

"Drake, I never blamed you. Not for a minute."

Stopping her, "Hear me out."

Kacey laid her fork down and picked up her mug to stare at him over the cup.

"No matter what the pain, guilt, whatever it was, we pulled away. I have you back in my life again. I mean, you've been in my life, but you are really back in my life and I don't want to lose you, but I also don't want to bring you down with me if the chief needs a scapegoat to close this case."

"It's not going to end up like that."

"Kacey, I love you. I don't want you hurt."

Kacey stared at Drake.

"I know not the best time to drop that on you. I'm sorry, that wasn't fair, but you need to know how I feel."

"Drake, we are going to be fine. Trust me. Just give me a few days."

"It's just a matter of time before the press gets wind of the fact that I pushed Dermot against the wall. They will go crazy with that and tag it onto to the theory that somehow we are associated with all of these murders. I don't want you dragged into this. We'll need to stay away from each other until this is settled."

"I can't promise you that."

Kacey scooped the last bite of food from her plate into her mouth then stood and took her plate to the sink. Returning to the table she wrapped her arms around his neck. "Let's not do anything drastic. We are going to catch this guy and when we do you'll be cleared."

"You aren't going to listen to me are you?"

"Probably not, besides I may need you to help work this case."

"I'm suspended, Kacey. I can't work the case."

"Really?" Kacey kissed his cheek releasing her hug to sit on the couch to put her shoes on. After collecting her keys and coat, she kissed him one more time before leaving the apartment with him still sitting at the table. His eyes followed her as she went out the door.

Chapter Thirty Two

Kacey got to the precinct before seven thirty and was greeted in the investigation room by only Agent Spinelli. The slender woman looked up and offered a slight smile as Kacey entered the room.

"Good morning," Kacey said dropping her computer bag down on the table next to Spinelli.

"Good morning, Detective James." Spinelli eyed Kacey for a moment then continued, "How is Drake?"

Kacey paused and looked at Spinelli. Her face seemed genuinely interested in an answer. "I think he's fine." She left the answer vague, not wanting to add anything else, nor wanting to deny that they'd been together. She felt she had to be careful just in case someone was tailing her last night, although she had been careful and hadn't notice any cars following then or this morning.

Spinelli's eyes narrowed just a little. "That's good."

Kacey could tell the FBI agent knew more and just wasn't sharing, so she decided she better continue in order to not seem too guarded. "Look, I appreciate your concern, but there is no way on earth Drake is involved in these crimes in any way. Well, other than trying to find the killer, and frankly, him not being on the case is a mistake. We would get to the killer faster with him here where he should be. At this point, all I want to do is close this as fast as we can so we can get back to normal."

Spinelli's face relaxed and she smiled again. "Then let's do just that."

Kacey tried to watch Spinelli's body language from the corner of her eye and felt confident she'd put the agent back in the right frame of mind.

"Now that we have a list of possible methods in which our killer might act out, we need to immediately start thinking about a list of possible victims. I've been trying to pull a list together and I need you to try to figure out how every one of the victims are connected because everything ties to Fields, except Dermot. He doesn't follow the pattern." Spinelli was talking while occasionally pointing to the white board covered in photographs.

"What pattern would that be?" Connor asked entering the room.

"Oh, we were just talking about the link to Fields." Spinelli answered, turning her attention to the tall man as he entered the room.

"I disagree," Kacey stated in a matter of fact tone. "Candice Jackson didn't fit for a connection to Fields either. That being said, I still think that sick bastard is behind all of this somehow."

Connor looked at the white board. "I agree. Candice Jackson has no link to Robert Fields either."

"That we know of," Kacey stated holding eye contact with Connor.

"Have we tried to find a connection between Fields and Candice?" Connor asked.

"No. All we know about any connection is that she was here in the precinct, picked up for solicitation. She shouted some comments out at me as I passed."

"And Drake heard her?" Spinelli asked with some accusation in her voice.

"He was with me, yes."

Connor looked over at Spinelli with a grim look on his face.

Kacey could barely contain her frustration. "You know one thing we never looked at was whether or not Fields was being held here at the same time. He could have seen her." Kacey immediately reached for the files that were scattered out on the table, searching for a certain one. Finally, laying her hands on the one she was seeking, she flipped through the pages and found what she was looking for.

Reaching for her phone, she swiped the screen to search the contacts, and then punched the button. A moment later she spoke, "Janet. Hey, it's Kacey. I need you to look up something for me.

Can you to check a date in your system and tell me whether Robert Fields was here at the precinct."

Kacey hung up after waiting for a few minutes. She turned to Connor and Spinelli, "Fields was being held here the day Candice Jackson was here. It was the first day of his hearing for appeal."

"So it is possible he saw Candice Jackson. But how on earth would he have known her name or how to find her?"

"I don't know but *HE* was here at the same time. They could have been held in the hallway just long enough to exchange words."

"Who was the DA at the time? Maybe we can find out more information."

"Matt Wilson has been the DA for the past four years. He worked Fields's appeal."

"I'm going to go on over and talk with him. You two stay here and try to find more of a connection."

"Actually, I was planning on going over to see Doc. He should have the full results on Jessica and at least a preliminary on Dermot. We need to know if there is anything else he has found."

"Okay, we can accomplish the most this way. Spinelli you see if there is any other connection or paths that may have crossed with any of the victims and Robert Fields."

"Actually, there's another possible angle I'd like to dig into. If we assume for a moment that Drake isn't our guy, then someone else within the police department could be involved. Is there anyone that either you or Drake had issues with in the past? Co-workers, the DA, ADA, anyone from within the system?" Spinelli asked surprising Kacey.

Kacey thought for a moment. "Nothing comes to mind off the top, but I'll think about it."

"I'll dig around a little."

"Thanks," Kacey said before grabbing her phone and coat.

Once outside Kacey picked up her phone and called Janet again as she walked to her car. "Hey, sorry to keep pressing you, but Drake needs our help."

Janet paused briefly then said, "I heard. What can I do?"

"Can you dig into Drake's past partners?"

"Sure, but what's up?"

"I don't know. Call it a hunch."

"What specifically am I looking for?"

"Anything, connections, write-ups. Honestly, Janet, I don't know, but anything that might be cause for revenge. Or anything really unusual."

"Got it."

"Janet, thank you."

The line disconnected and Kacey put the car in reverse, pulling out of the parking space pointing the vehicle towards Doc and any information he might have.

Before Kacey could get out of the parking lot her cell phone rang again. Seeing Janet's name on the screen she picked up. "Hey, Janet. What'd we forget?"

"Sorry, Kacey, I was going to tell Drake but, well, you know. Anyway, he asked me to look into something for him and it's interesting. Sparlow is on the visitor's log for Fields about three months after he was sentenced and sent to the mental hospital."

"That puts it, what, about eighteen months ago?"

"That's right. Sparlow was in the Academy, and there's something else. Sparlow's step-father was Drake's ex-partner. He retired after a battle with the bottle. Looks like Sparlow is second generation."

Kacey thought for a few moments, and then thanked Janet and hung up the call. Using the Bluetooth in her car she used the voice recognition to connect with Drake. There wasn't any answer, and she hoped he was out and about. Deciding it was not a good idea to leave a full message, she simply said she was calling to check on him and asked for him to call her.

Continuing to the morgue, Kacey considered what she had just been told. Sparlow could be linked to Fields and all the others. She definitely had to wonder why he'd gone to visit Fields in the first place.

After pulling into the parking lot of the morgue Kacey hesitated briefly, gathering her resolve, before exiting the car to go inside the dreary building. Instantly, images of Sophie came slamming back into her head. That poor young girl laying on the steel table with the Y shaped cut across her chest peeking out from under the sheet Doc so carefully placed over her small body.

She recalled more images of Fields violating the young girl, torturing her for hours while police stood by outside waiting for the certain release of the little girl. *No, not the police. You, Kacey. You waited outside and release did come, just not the way they had hoped it would.* Sophie was released from her pain through death, with Fields slobbering and grinning through his jagged teeth and two-day old stubble.

Shaking off the past, Kacey started to walk inside when her cell rang. Looking at the screen she saw Drake's name on the face and immediately picked up. "Drake, hey, I'm glad you called me back."

"What's up, Kacey? I could tell by your message you really wanted me to call you."

"I did. Listen, Janet called me. Ready for this? Sparlow is related to your ex-partner. Turns out that he is his step-father and he went to see Fields eighteen months ago. Sparlow's on the visitor's log."

"Really," Drake said letting out a heavy sigh. "Bobby Barrett got himself into some trouble and retired. I knew he had a step-son, but I never really met him."

"Did Barrett blame you for his ... problems?"

"I don't think so. I was interviewed. Didn't say much at the time, but afterwards I told him straight up he needed to retire or I would speak up."

"Is it possible Sparlow blames you for his stepdad's downfall?"

"I guess," Drake shook his head. "I don't really know."

"It's odd that he never mentioned his step-dad to you, right?"

"It does seem strange."

"Okay, well, we need to follow up on that. Right now I'm at the morgue trying to see what Doc might have. After that I may run out to see Fields again, see what he has to say about Sparlow's visit back then."

"Kacey, it's not safe for you to go out there, especially by yourself."

"They'll have one of the interns right outside the door."

"Kacey, take one of the agents with you."

"It'll be fine, Drake. It may be a dead end, but if not, we need this to clear you and close the case."

"Kacey, be careful. I don't want anything to happen to you. I love you, Kacey."

"I'll be fine and will let you know what I find."

Before Drake could say another word the line went dead.

Chapter Thirty Three

Drake had a bad feeling. Kacey should not be going out to talk to Fields alone. If Fields was involved somehow with Sparlow and together they had collaborated in the killing of all of these people, then Fields might do anything if confronted right now.

With his mind racing between what to do and the ultimate consequences if the chief found out he had crossed the line of the suspension, he picked up his keys and cell phone. He pulled on his boots and coat, collected his back up weapon from inside the closet next to the front door, and walked out into the cool air after checking the weapon for ammo, even though he knew it was loaded. It was always loaded.

Settling his large frame behind the wheel of his truck, he fired up the engine and backed out of the space as he glanced in his mirrors. Confident no one had followed him, he began making his way to the highway that led north out of town and towards the hospital.

His mind whirled as he drove. He had never met Barrett's son, had he? No, he was certain he hadn't, even though he had been to Barrett's house many number of times. Was it weird that Sparlow had never mentioned that his step-dad was his ex-partner?

Deciding that he had already taken enough risks, he picked up his cell phone. One more risk wasn't going to matter. He called Janet.

"Janet, it's Drake. Listen, you shouldn't be talking to me. I need to say that before anything else, but I need your help. I need Sparlow's number."

"Drake, how are you?"

"I'm good, Janet, really. I just need to talk to Sparlow."

"Drake, you know I'd do anything for you, but are you sure this is a good idea?"

"I'm sure. I have to find out some things."

"Okay, hold on."

Two minutes later Drake had Sparlow's number punched in his phone and was waiting for an answer. After three rings Sparlow picked up. He sounded like he had been sleeping.

"Sparlow, it's Drake."

"Drake? Weren't you placed on suspension?"

Drake ignored the question. "Why didn't you ever tell me that you are Bobby Barrett's step-son?"

Drake could almost hear the shock through the line. "Ummm, because I was embarrassed."

"For what?"

"My good ol' step-dad was a drunk, and you know, I was kinda hoping you'd never figure out that we were related."

"Yeah, well, we did figure it out and we figured out a couple of other things too."

"What's that?"

"Why did you go pay a visit to Robert Fields?"

"Fields?" Sparlow seems surprised again. "Oh, man that was a long time ago. I interviewed him for an assignment at the Academy."

"Why Fields?"

"Seriously? It was the hottest case this place has ever seen. I wasn't the best student in the Academy so I figured if I delivered on the interview it would lift my grade. And guess what, it did. I graduated and now I'm a cop."

"Why haven't you mentioned it to anyone?"

"That shit is in my police academy records for God's sake. I didn't think it mattered."

"Didn't matter? Seriously, you're an idiot, Sparlow. Kacey is on her way out to the hospital to talk to that sick bastard by herself!" Drake hung up the call.

Gripping the steering wheel, he glanced in his mirrors again and drove faster.

***

Drake drove the truck into the hospital parking lot and scanned looking for Kacey's car or one of the police cruisers. At first he didn't see anything, but as he was about to exit the vehicle his eyes spotted the familiar sedan. She was already there. He checked his gun one more time and then reached into the glove box and removed a long, slender knife. The blade glinted in the sunlight that shone through the window.

Pausing for a second, he considered what his next steps should be. After deciding, he slid his cell phone from his front pocket and scanned recent calls to pick the number he wanted.

After two rings the line connected. "It's Drake. I'm at the mental hospital. Yeah, where Fields is. You might want to get out here." Without saying another word he disconnected the call and stepped out of the vehicle.

As Drake walked through the glass front doors and stepped onto the marbled floor, his eyes skimmed the lobby. The familiar medicinal smell assaulted his nostrils. The woman at the reception desk looked up, recognition covered her face, followed by a confused smile.

Drake smiled back trying to put the woman at ease. "Hi, I'm trying to catch up with my partner. I believe she already has gone in to see Robert Fields." He purposely leaned in on the counter overlooking the desk trying to appear more casual than he felt. He hoped she didn't ask to see his badge–the one he currently didn't have.

Her confusion turned to a brighter smile. "She sure is. I'll walk you back."

"I know the way, if it's not against policy," Drake offered, hoping she'd let him navigate the long hall by himself.

"Not at all. The orderly should be nearby and your partner can let you in. Fields is restrained, been acting up lately."

"Really? How long has that been going on?"

She seemed to think about the question for a moment before answering. "It's been escalating, but probably since Dr. Ward's…passing." A sad uncomfortable look cast over her eyes as she thought of the words to use.

"That's good to know. Thank you," Drake said before turning towards the hallway that led to Robert Fields's solitary isolation.

Drake's boots echoed through the stark hallways, causing one of the residents to wail and another to chatter on about something completely unintelligible. Ignoring the sounds, he focused on the door at the end of the hall.

As he approached Drake could hear two distinct voices. One was Kacey's and the other sounded like a male, but not the typical rant of Robert Fields. He immediately wondered who was in there with her.

He glanced around the bend in the hall to see if the orderly was present, and finding no one near, he speculated the orderly was inside the room with Kacey. Slipping his hand inside his coat, his fingers slid across the knife. The same hand then dropped to his waist and palmed his gun.

As he got closer the voices were louder, but he still couldn't make a connection to the male's voice, although it sounded vaguely familiar. He hoped Kacey had considered his warning and had brought someone with her.

Arriving at the door, Drake grabbed the chrome door knob and gave it a twist but, as expected, found it locked. As he peered through the small window that sat high in the door he could barely make out the back of Kacey against the wall closest to the door.

Rapping his knuckles on the door he called out, "Kacey, open the door. It's Drake. The orderly is not here to let me in."

There was a long pause and scuffling and muffled voices as Drake waited. "Kacey, is everything okay? Let me in."

The door knob twisted in Drake's hand as he continued his attempt to open the door. The door cracked open, allowing him entrance, and closed behind him.

The hair on Drake's neck stood on end as he took in the scene in front of him. Kacey stepped away from the door and towards the bed where the battered body of Robert Fields lay awkwardly dangling off the edge with his wrists attached by straps to the bed rail.

Kacey held tightly gripped in her hand a police baton. On the end, a large rock was affixed with a rope, making it oddly into a sort of mace from the ancient Roman times.

Drake's eyes traveled up from the baton to her face as he struggled with what to say. "Kacey, Jesus, what happened?"

"Don't tell him anything, Iz. You can't trust him any more than you can trust any of the others."

"He's good. I can trust him. He's my partner."

"No! You can't trust anyone. You know this."

Drake stared in astonishment. "Kacey, who are you talking to?"

Kacey's turned to face Drake, but her eyes were glazed over and unrecognizable. The typically controlled, powerful woman that Drake spent his days and many of his nights with was lost behind a tough menacing smile.

"Iz isn't here right now. You'll have to deal with me."

Drake's mind raced. Uncertain what to do he asked, "Okay, who are you?" His mind tried to make sense of the male voice projecting out of the mouth of the woman he loved.

"I'm Tommy. Don't act like you don't know about me." The voice was angry, and Kacey jutted her shoulders back, her body language defensive and boyishly immature.

"Tommy?" Drake asked confusion filling him.

"I know my Izzy has told you about me."

"Izzy?" Drake continued, trying to understand what was happening.

"Yeah, my s...i...s...s...y," Kacey dragged out the word in a long and deliberate manner.

Drake suddenly started to understand. "Tommy, you're Kacey's brother. I'm sorry I didn't recognize you," Drake said making an attempt to bring Kacey's defenses down.

"That's right. I knew my Izzy told you all about me."

Drake suddenly remembered the morning he had heard voices in his bathroom, Kacey had been getting ready. When he had walked in she had said she was talking to herself and blamed it on being frustrated with her hair. His stomach tightened and he quickly decided to try and reason with Kacey's dead brother Tommy.

"She did tell me about you. In fact, she told me how close you two have always been. I've always wanted to meet you."

"She did?"

"Yes. She told me stories of you as kids playing together." Drake's approach seemed to be working.

"Oh." Kacey's grip seemed to be relaxing on the baton.

"Can I talk to Kacey?" Drake asked careful to not push too hard.

"No."

"Why not?" Drake asked then continued, "I really need to tell her something important."

"Yeah? What's that?" Kacey's body language remained defiant and slightly masculine.

"Well, I want to tell her that I miss her. You see, we are good friends and really close too."

"No! You just want to take her away from me!" Kacey's hand gripped the baton again.

"That's not true, Tommy. I want to help Kacey. I love her and I am sure you and me can be good friends too." Drake grasped at words that he hoped would allow him to get closer. He took a step forward.

"You just say you love her. You don't. You're a liar and a user just like everyone else."

"No, Tommy. I do want to help her. And, I want to help you too. I know people have gotten hurt lately and I can help but I have to understand why."

Kacey's face twisted in a laugh. "Oh really, Izzy never told you the way people treated us, always making fun of us because our clothes were old, because our father was a drunk."

"No, she never told me those things. But, I can help. I can make them stop."

"No you can't. They do what they want. Even YOU. Saying you love her. You just want her for sex!

"That';s not true Tommy. I really do love her and I could love you too." Drake continued trying to reach the woman he

262

loved still not believing Kacey had done all these things. Staring at her now she was so different, almost unrecognizable.

"No one can ever love us. No one ever has. You're a liar just like everyone else we've ever known!"

Kacey's hand swiftly moved and a loud crack snapped as the baton swung through the air and landed squarely on the left side of Drake's head. His body spun, and he slowly dropped to the floor as blood spilled around him.

You did it Iz. You took care of him too. You're so smart, Iz. So smart. Sticks and stones will break your bones but words will never hurt me! He can't hurt you now, Izzy.

Kacey's eyes began to clear. She looked around the room. Robert Fields lay dead on the bed with his legs swung to one side and Drake lay on the floor. Kacey could hear footsteps approaching in the hallway.

She looked down at the baton in her hand.

Hide it.

She swiftly slid it into Drake's right hand, making sure it made contact with the entire base as it pushed against his palm. She squeezed his fingers around it making sure his prints were on it. And let the baton drop to the floor still in his grasp.

Iz, they're coming, I hear people coming.

Shhh, hush now, Tommy. They'll hear you.

Okay. I'll be quiet now, but don't leave me.

Kacey swung the door open and called out, "Security!"

The footsteps picked up pace, and Kacey saw Spinelli and Connor running towards her. Sparlow was behind them in the hallway a few paces back and an orderly came running from the other direction.

"What happened?" Connor asked seeing blood on the front of Kasey. "Are you okay?"

"I came here to talk to Fields. Drake showed up. Fields started calling him names and bringing up all the things he had done to Sophie. Drake went nuts and started beating the hell out of Fields with that baton." She pointed to the weapon laying on the floor.

"I tried to stop him, and he took a swing at me. We wrestled a little bit and I got a grip on it and kicked it from his hand. I clocked him pretty good."

Connor immediately knelt down next to Drake, placing his index and middle finger on the vein in Drake's throat. He shook his head. "He's dead."

Kacey sucked in a deep breath and began to sob.

Sparlow asked, "You mean Drake is our killer?"

Kacey nodded her head.

Connor and Spinelli looked around the room. On the floor by the bed with Fields's body was a black duffle bag with Drake's name and badge number embroidered on one side.

Connor stepped closer to the bag and, using a pen from his pocket, slid the bag open to reveal the contents. In his view was a Polaroid camera, a knife, sticky note pads, duct tape, and a few other items. He stood and turned back to the others. "It's a kill kit."

Sparlow stood in the door frame. "He never said he was coming here, but he sounded crazy on the phone when he called me. He said you were coming out here," nodding to Kacey. "So I thought I should tell these guys. Then when Connor got the call from Drake saying he was coming here I thought maybe something had happened to you, but I never thought..." His words trailed off as he looked down at Drake laying on the floor.

Spinelli called for an ambulance. The hall outside the room quickly filled with orderlies and nurses. Odd sounds rang out from the other rooms. It was as if the residents could smell death through the ventilation system.

Connor pulled Kacey by the elbow from the room where she stood staring down at Drake's lifeless body, a halo of blood surrounding his head.

"We have to take your statement. I know this is tough, but we need to do this while everything is fresh."

Kacey looked up at Connor and nodded. "Just get me out of here."

Connor could see the obvious pain in her eyes. He looked at Spinelli. "You stay here and ensure the scene stays secure. Make sure the items are properly collected. No mistakes here."

Spinelli nodded.

"I'm going to take Detective James back to the precinct."

He turned once more to Kacey. Assessing her and the spattered blood on her clothes, he asked, "Are you hurt? Do you need medical attention?"

"I'm fine. I've got a change of clothes at the precinct. You'll need to collect these for the CSI."

Connor nodded in understanding. He saw Sparlow standing against the wall. "Can you provide a ride for Spinelli back to the precinct when they're done here?"

Sparlow nodded in agreement, "Yes, sir."

Connor led Kacey down the hall where the other residents spouted unintelligible words, noises and grunts, and clattered against the walls or doors. One walked out into view and was immediately ushered back inside by an orderly that stood guarding the hall.

As Connor pulled the door open to escort Kacey through into the daylight, Doc approached them coming up the walkway. He glanced at Connor but then his eyes shifted to Kacey. Kacey looked up to meet his gaze briefly then looked away back towards the ground where her eyes had remained as they walked through the stark building.

Just loud enough for Doc to hear, she stated in a matter of fact tone, "Fields is dead." After a slight pause she continued, "So is Drake."

"Damn, Kacey...I..." Doc stopped. He reached out and lightly touched her shoulder. "Anything you need, let me know."

Her eyes flittered up to meet his again. "Take care of him."

"I will. You have my word."

Kacey slid past Doc and headed to her car. Connor stopped her. "I'll drive."

Kacey reached into her pocket and handed him the keys, then automatically went to the passenger side to enter the vehicle.

The ride back to the precinct was silent. Kacey stared out the window or at the floorboard. Connor periodically glanced her way. He felt her pain, as he had lost a partner once in a drug trafficking sting that had gone horribly wrong. His throat tightened as he remembered that day.

Arriving back at the precinct, they were immediately greeted at the door by other officers. Word had obviously gotten out quickly. Some nodded out of respect, others averted their eyes, unsure how to face Kacey as they walked through the hallway. The chief met them about half way down the hall.

"James. You okay?"

Kacey nodded. Her shoulder pushed back slightly as her typical tough edge took over, forcing the tears away that she feared would flow at any moment.

"Your union rep is here and IA is two minutes out and a CSI is here to collect your clothes."

"Thanks, Chief."

She was escorted to the locker room and asked to strip down while a crime investigator collected her clothes and samples of the blood that was on her skin. Her union rep stood by during the entire process, just around the corner allowing her privacy through the process.

After being allowed to shower, she changed clothes and exited the locker room. Her dark hair, still wet, hung around her shoulders trailing down her back and leaving water spots on the back of her shirt. The chief waited in the hall.

Before her hair could even dry, Kacey found herself in Interview Room #2 recanting the events that had happened. She explained how she had gone to interview Fields one more time on a hunch and how Drake had shown up. She admitted to calling him prior to going out to the hospital. She explained that Drake had knocked on the door and she'd let him in. The orderly had left the area, though she was not sure for how long. She explained that Fields had started in on Drake about Sophie, and Drake exploded. He retrieved the baton rigged with the rock on the end from inside his duty bag and he had gone crazy bludgeoning Fields to death. She said that when she saw the baton with the rock on it at first she didn't understand, but then Drake was saying things to Fields about how he was a bully, and about how he had bullied Sophie then murdered her in cold blood and how the words couldn't hurt him. She said Drake said that sticks and stones now that had power. After that comment Drake launched onto Fields.

266

As he was beating Fields, she explained, she then suddenly understood that Drake was their killer and Fields was the next victim. Drake was acting out the sticks and stones taunt from their list. She said that she'd tried to stop him, which had led to a struggle. He'd pushed her into the wall pretty hard, causing her to hit her head. But ultimately, she had gotten the baton from him and swung at him, making contact with his head. She hadn't meant to hurt him. She just wanted him to stop, but it was as if he was someone else. He hadn't responded to anything she said. Everything had happened so fast.

It was nearly three hours later that Kacey walked out of the room. She gave her statement several times for the FBI, IA, and for the chief. Her union rep sat in on each series of interviews.

Chief Dalton walked out with her. "A patrol car is going to drive you home. You'll be on paid leave until you are cleared. Should only be a couple of days."

Instinctively, Kacey handed over her badge and gun. "I'm okay, Chief. I'd like to drive myself if that's okay."

His brow furrowed as he stared into her eyes. Finally, he nodded. "You're sure?"

"I am."

Watching her walk away, the chief stood with his hands on his hips casting a broad shadow on the marble floor. Connor walked up behind him.

"You think she's okay?"

"She's tough. She'll be alright."

"We're going to have to issue a statement to the press soon," Connor said, appraising Chief Dalton.

"It's still my case. It's my detective. I'll do it."

"I understand."

Chapter Thirty Four

Kacey ignored the awkward glances as she walked through the building and pushed her way out into the open air. The sun had set already and the night air was crisp. A chill ran down her spine as she made her way to her car.

Pressing the button on her key she heard the locks disengage, so she quickly opened the door and slid behind the wheel. Her hands grasped the steering wheel as tears poured from her eyes.

Iz, why are you crying?

"Shut up!"

Glancing around Kacey was suddenly aware she shouted. She started the car and backed out of the space, exiting the parking lot and turning the car towards her apartment.

Iz, you did good. I'm proud of you. Don't be sad. You know it never would have worked. HE couldn't be trusted.

He loved me.

Words, Iz. Those are just words. He would have never accepted us.

You don't know that!

I know it and so do you. You saw the look on his face when I tried to talk to him. You did good, Iz. It was a perfect plan.

Drake wasn't part of the plan. You were jealous.

It wouldn't work. You know that. And Fields, that was beautiful. That was my favorite. Killing that piece of shit!

Drake wasn't part of the plan. He shouldn't have been there.

Really, Izzy? Then why did you tell him? You knew he would come and you knew what we'd do. It was the perfect plan. We are safe again. We can do whatever we want. We can leave here, start over.

Start over? And go where?

Anywhere, we're free now.

Kacey's mind raced as she pulled into the parking space in front of her apartment. Glancing around, she became aware that she barely remembered driving there at all.

Chapter Thirty Five

The day was slightly overcast, and there was a slight mist as Kacey stood next to the casket, barely listening to the words shared by the pastor. Fellow officers, Chief Dalton, Spinelli, Connor, and Doc were all dressed for the occasion. The service seemed to last forever, and Kacey's body jolted with each of the shots fired during the traditional gun salute at officer funerals.

The American flag that draped the casket was removed and properly folded, and finally, the casket containing the body of her partner and lover was slowly lowered into the ground as small clods of dirt were tossed on.

One by one the people who had come to show respect had wandered off until only a few remained. Kacey turned to leave and was stopped by Chief Dalton.

"How are you holding up, James?"

Kacey shrugged. "Okay, I guess."

"I got the report from IA yesterday. You have been conditionally cleared to return to duty. The evidence supports your account. The bag had several other items in it that were used at the other crime scenes. It's hard to believe. I just didn't realize he was falling apart like that."

Kacey stared off at the hearse in the distance. She watched as a tall man in black suit with perfectly quaffed and overly hair sprayed hair that was rapidly losing the battle with the wind, flapping wildly atop his head, opened the door and got in the car. It slowly pulled away. The shiny, black object glinted through the mist of rain that continued to fall, causing her hair to dampen.

"We all should have known," she said shrugging.

Chief Dalton paused considering what she said.

"Well, you can come by and get your badge and gun. No hurry for you to return to work. Take as much time as you need," he said holding up his palms in a display of "no pressure".

Kacey nodded but continued to watch the cars pulling away one by one as they filed out of the cemetery.

"Oh, and you'll need to meet with the department shrink. Five visits. Procedure, you know." Dalton patted Kacey on the shoulder in an awkward show of concern, then turned and walked away.

Connor and Spinelli stood back allowing the chief to talk to Kacey. They stepped forward and Connor spoke first.

"Can we give you a ride? Maybe go grab a bite to eat?"

Kacey glanced back at the pile of dirt next to where the casket had been lowered into the ground. The row of chairs that sat under the small canopy were now empty, and even the few family members that Drake had never spoken of, and Kacey had never previously met, had slowly left the area.

"No, I have my car. I'm fine, really. I think I might just go for a drive."

"Are you sure you're okay?" Spinelli asked.

"Yes. I'm sure." Kacey's eyes scanned across the cemetery, landing on a strange looking angel that stood haphazardly, one of the wings broken and laying in pieces around the base on the ground.

"Detective James, it's been a pleasure working with you on this case. We'll be leaving in the morning. I wish things had turned out differently," Connor said with a rare extension of compassion in his voice.

Kacey glanced back at him. "Thank you for helping with the case."

"You should take some time off before returning to work. Go see some family," Spinelli stated.

Kacey looked up and met her eyes. "Yes, that's a good idea. I think I'll spend some time with my brother."

Connor extended his hand. Kacey's eyes dropped to the offer and robotically responded, and then did the same with

Spinelli. Beads of rain shook from the sleeve of Spinelli's black trench-style jacket and fell to the ground.

With a final nod, the two agents turned and walked away. Kacey watched as they carefully navigated their way through the headstones and entered one of the few remaining cars parked along the cemetery lane.

With a final glance back at the pile of dirt, Kacey turned away, but instead of walking to her own car she walked over to the broken angel and stood and stared up at the figure for a long while. The rain picked up and soon she stood wet and cold, seemingly transfixed on the figure.

Iz, you okay?

There was no response.

Iz, I'm cold. Can we go now?

Kacey seemed to suddenly hear the voice and looked around.

Iz, I'm cold. Can we go?

Yes.

What are we going to do now?

I don't know.

But, we have to decide.

Not now. We don't have to decide right now.

When then?

I don't know. Now please stop and let me think. I'll figure it out.

I'm sorry, Iz.

Chapter Thirty Six

Three days passed since the funeral. Kacey sat outside the precinct looking at the long building and the line of patrol cars through the windshield of her car. Two officers came out and got in a cruiser near where she was parked. She knew who they were but couldn't think of their names right now. She could hear the bantering and teasing they were exchanging. Something about too much cholesterol and coffee was going to kill them.

She almost laughed. *No, cholesterol and coffee aren't going to kill you. Things much graver kill you.*

Pulling on the door handle, she stepped out into the sunshine. The weather the past few days was much warmer, and she welcomed the feeling on her face.

She closed the door and began the walk across the parking lot and up the steps to the front doors. As soon as she was inside a few glances turned her way from the room adjacent the lobby. It was interesting how she could feel the stares more than see them. Instinct told her there were whispers that followed the eyes. She ignored them and made her way down the familiar corridor, and then stopped and rapped on a door.

After waiting a few moments, she heard footsteps and the door opened. Chief Dalton seemed surprised but then waved her into the room.

"James, it's good to see you." He went behind the desk after closing the door.

"Thanks, Chief."

Reaching into his desk drawer, he pulled out her badge and gun and laid them on the desk in front of her. "I'm guessing you are ready to get these back."

"Actually, Chief, I'm here to let you know I've decided to take an extended leave."

His bushy eyebrows shot up, and he let out a slight grunt. "I wasn't expecting that."

"I know, I'm sorry, but with Drake gone it just isn't the same for me here. I think I need more time. I'm planning on doing a little traveling. Clear my head and then see what's next."

"I see."

"I wanted to let you know myself, didn't just want to leave without talking to you first."

"You're a good detective, James, and what happened to Drake isn't your fault."

"I appreciate it, but it really is my fault."

"Any idea where you'll go?"

"Not really. Maybe California or Florida. I'm not really sure."

"I won't say I'm not disappointed, but I do understand."

"Thanks, Chief." Kacey turned to leave the room but stopped when he called out to her.

"James, stay in touch and let us know if you want to come back."

"I will, Chief. Thanks."

Kacey left the room with the chief watching as she walked away and closed the door behind her. The same eyes stared at her as she returned through the long corridor as they had when she'd entered. There seemed to be less whispering, but she knew it was still there.

Relieved to be outside, she sucked in a mouthful of fresh air as she made her way to her car. Back inside the vehicle, she pulled away making a few turns and entered the highway.

Where are we going to go, Iz?

Far from here and someplace we can get a new identity.

You're so smart, Iz. Always smart.

Kacey smiled and rolled the window down slightly allowing the fresh breeze to fill the car, her black hair blowing to one side.

Epilogue

Connor and Spinelli returned to the Quantico headquarters and were already assigned a new case, which had them flying with two of their fellow agents to South Dakota to investigate a serial rapist.

They barely had time to even repack before leaving, so they agreed to split up the work on the plane. Connor briefed on the new files while Spinelli typed up the closing case notes on Detective Colton Drake.

Spinelli sat with her computer on the small pop-up table in front of her. She had been working on the file for at least an hour and was finalizing the last of the notes. Reaching for her briefcase, she pulled out the rest of the case files so she could get the final details. The top file had Kacey James on the label across the top. Curiously, she flipped the file open.

A photo of James was on the inside flap. It showed her high cheek bones and dark hair. Glancing at the other flap, her eyes scanned the page that contained all the stats on James: age, birth date, graduation date from the police academy, the only girl born to parents Thomas and Denise James, one sibling. Biological father deceased. Mother remarried Kevin Wallace. Kacey was nine and sibling - brother Thomas (Tommy) was seven.

Her eyes followed the page a little further. Mother (Denise 39) and sibling (Thomas 11) deceased, both killed in an auto accident, Survived, Stepfather (Kevin 43) and child (Kacey 13). She read it again, then a third time.

Her mind returned to the cemetery and the last conversation she'd had with Kacey.

"You should take some time off before returning to work. Go see some family."

"Yes, that's a good idea. I think I'll spend some time with my brother."

Spinelli read the report again…

… one sibling…sibling (Thomas 11) deceased.

Spinelli remembered there'd been something strange in Kacey's eyes that day at the cemetery. She'd mistaken it for grief, but it was more sinister than that. Grabbing for the lab reports of the evidence taken from the scene at the mental hospital, her fingers grasped the folder. Flipping through several pages then finding the one she was looking for, her eyes scanned the page.

The black duffle bag had two sets of prints, both Kacey's and Drake's. No one had questioned Kacey's prints on the bag. Kacey and Drake were partners and likely had carried each other's duty bags on more than one occasion. Spinelli's throat tightened, instinct told her to look deeper.

Searching further through the file folder, she scanned several pages finally finding what she was looking for. Identified as evidence #15 from the contents within the black duffle bag was a small paper with directions written on it.

The directions had been identified as specific to a barn nearby where the body of Dr. Timothy Ward had been burned. The *Liar, liar, pants on fire* crime scene. Upon the discovery of the directions, the barn had been inspected and inside a tractor with a bucket loader, fencing wire and a gas can had been recovered. None of the items had any prints and no other evidence from the barn could specifically link Colton Drake to the murder of Dr. Timothy Ward, but the lease on the property had been paid for via mail in cash and the contract was in the name of Colton Drake. The property owner admitted to never having met the tenant in person, but he had described talking on the phone with someone that he believed was a male, although he couldn't completely validate that Colton Drake had rented the property.

Spinelli scanned more pages looking for a specific document. She stared at the leasing contract for the property and searched for the signature at the bottom of the page which clearly showed Colton Drake's name. The handwriting on both documents was unique with sharply arched letters that had a subtle drag at the end of each word. Next, Spinelli searched through other documents until she found one of the post crime scene reports that had been submitted to Chief Dalton.

Comparing the written directions, the signature on the contract and the signature on the report, her throat restricted further. She stared at all three pages realizing the handwriting was unmistakably written by the same person. But there was one problem, the signature at the bottom of the page on the crime report submitted by the detectives to Chief Dalton as part of process, was signed by Detective Kacey James.

Flipping through the file Spinelli found another report this time showing Colton Drake's signature. The signature though slightly similar was flatter and the drag was at the front of the words rather than at the end. This signature was definitely different. Colton Drake had not written the directions to the barn nor had he signed the lease on the property.

Shoving the files to the side she unbuckled the lap belt that held her in her seat. She stood and walked towards the back of the small plane carrying the three documents with her and handed them to Agent Connor.

"We have a problem. Colton Drake isn't our killer."

The End

About the Author

Valerie Knupp lives on seven acres outside the Tulsa area near Inola, Oklahoma. She loves to travel and is an avid reader of anything with a grisly plot. When not doing one of these things, she enjoys spending time around the house with her partner and two adopted children. This is her 4th.

If you find any errors while reading this book or any of the Jack Tyler Series books that I've also written, I would love the feedback. It is my goal to make your reading a pleasure and I always love hearing from my readers. Feel free to leave a review on Amazon.com or you can leave feedback as well as keep up with what is going on with future books by visiting my website at:

www.thrillersbyknupp.com

Acknowledgements

Hollie Zunun, my editor, you are the very best!!! Without you I am not sure I would have ever gotten any books written. I also can't thank you enough for the constant input, criticism and challenge you give in every paragraph. You make my thrillers more thrilling!

Shout out to Mom for giving me honest feedback all the way through.

Chris Snidow for the final touches after Hollie and I have exhausted every chance to get it right! Your keen eye is very much appreciated!

Of course my family and friends for all of your support and for being there for me, and being patient with me when my need to write takes time away from us.

My fans that follow me and push me to write more! You're the best!

Cover Photo

Thank you to my dear, long-time, school friend Gaylene Hostetler-Logue for letting me manipulate the beautiful photo you took into something much more ominous! I hope you like it! Love you Scabe!

Special Acknowledgement

While on a flight from Atlanta I was disposing of my cup and napkin and accidently threw away my flash drive that had about half of this book on it. I realized it pretty quickly, and as the airline attendant came back by, I told her I thought the drive was in the trash. The plane was about to land. I went back to the back of the plane and two of the attendants quickly went through the trash. Then the one that had agreed to help me, said "I think I traded bags with the girl up in the front of the plane."

She picked up the phone and called up front. In her desire to hurry and help me she accidently called the cockpit and got the pilot. Hanging up she dialed again this time asking the attendant up front to check the trash. She told me to go back and take my seat and she'd let me know but that I could no longer stand up since the plane was landing. My heart sank. I was certain my entire writing thus far was lost. I returned to my seat and just as the plane was about to land I could see the attendant heading my way. She had a smile on her face. When she reached my seat she silently handed me the flash drive, the smile never leaving her face.

I couldn't believe it. The drive was wet and I was worried it wouldn't work but after drying it out, I was thrilled to find my data was fine.

As I exited the plane I requested the attendants name to learn it was, Linda Martin.

Thank you, Linda Martin and American Airlines. You saved the day!!!!

www.ingramcontent.com/pod-product-compliance
Lightning Source LLC
Chambersburg PA
CBHW071303170626
46809CB00001B/332